POWER SHIFT

SHIFTER LORDS

— 3 —

S.E. BABIN

OLIVERHEBERBOOKS

CHAPTER

One

The Shifter Lord and I were at war. Not literal war—think psychological warfare mixed with a hefty dose of passive aggression. Like most great wars, it started innocently enough.

A few months ago, Caelan sent Simone over with a request to hire me to make twelve table centerpieces for an event at the Keep.

Fair enough. I rarely turned down good money, even though I had a 'no travel to the Keep' clause in all my contracts now. Caelan either had to pick up any arrangements he ordered from the shop, or I sent Moira or Ash to deliver them, and occasionally a trusted courier.

It had worked well for the last three months, even though everyone knew Caelan was trying to get me to break and talk to him. No one needed that many centerpieces in ninety days, and now that I knew Caelan had rarely planned events at the Keep until after I came into his life, I realized this was a poorly veiled attempt to wiggle his way back in.

That was not going to happen.

Simone's warning rang in my ears once more, the same way it

had for the last several months. The Shifter Lords had been quiet, too quiet, lately, and I'd been on edge since the moment I'd stepped out of Caelan's home after the debacle of his wedding.

He'd reached out to me multiple times since then, and I'd rebuffed him every time.

I would have softened toward him eventually, I think. And then I found out he'd nominated Ben for the open Shifter Lord position, replacing Halvard, effectively forcing the Healer to move to a new territory, far away from here.

Not that we were dating. We weren't. Ben and I had started the engine. It sputtered a few times, and then the vehicle died before ever moving forward. I hoped to find a good mechanic and get it working again, but thanks to Caelan, that engine was now across the country.

Convenient for Caelan. Bad for me and Ben. Just the way the Shifter Lord wanted things.

So now, the Lord could rot in hell for all I cared.

I'd keep taking his money, but I'd die before I let him into my life again.

I wasn't thrilled when Simone showed up, but she wasn't the one I was angry at. Her request is what pissed me off.

Twelve table centerpieces was a normal order—if I were making them for anyone other than a Shifter Lord. What pissed me off was *why* he wanted them.

The event's name was a nod to my burgeoning power, and Caelan's request for themed centerpieces felt oddly *specific*.

He requested three centerpieces per table, four tables in total. I muttered a running commentary on the tiny size of Caelan's assets while pressing fresh blooms into wet floral foam.

Moira breezed into the shop, holding two cups, one full of tea and the other blessed java.

"Lir gave you an extra shot of espresso on the house," she said as she set the coffee down. "He said he saw you biking aggressively on the way home last night and thought maybe you could use a little boost of love."

Brewtide Beans was Joy Springs' local merfolk-owned coffee shop. Their offerings ranged from the unusual to the mundane, and so far, I hadn't had a single thing from there I disliked.

"Thank the gods," I muttered, setting down my floral shears and picking up the cup.

Moira picked up the contract Simone had brought over. I hadn't read it all the way through yet, but the price we agreed on was insane, even for me.

"Blooming Wild: Celebrating the Magical Diversity and Rare Gifts of Joy Springs through the Lens of Local Flora." Moira's nose wrinkled. "Gross." She flipped through the contract, pale brow wrinkling as she skimmed the contents. A low whistle pierced the air.

"Holy shit," she murmured, her gaze flying to mine. "This price is highway robbery." A slow grin curved her lips. "Always knew you had it in you, girl." Moira wiggled her hips. "Vegas, here I come."

I shuddered. "Vegas? That's where you'd go?" The thought of being pressed against all those strangers made my throat tighten.

"Hell yeah." Moira tapped a bright nail on the worktable. "All those lights and the noise, and those handsome men with deep pockets. The free booze." Her nostrils flared. "Vegas makes me feel alive."

I shook my head. "I think I may go visit Rowan soon. It'd be nice to visit home again and explore his Keep."

Moira wiggled her eyebrows. "Plus, he is super-hot."

"Yes, but all the Lords are hot. And I'm not in the market for a Lord or a shifter or anything with a penis."

"Ooh. What about the innie?"

I laughed. "No innies, either. No situation where I have to worry about how my breath smells in the morning or how my hair looks. I want peace in the valley for a while."

Moira leaned over and sniffed one of the blooms. "Peace is overrated. You know what isn't?"

I gave her the side-eye. "What?"

"Hot, dirty, uncomplicated sex." She flicked my nose and darted away before I could slap her hand away.

"You know I don't do casual." That had stopped on a clear, starry night in a field in Scotland.

Moira's face softened. "One man can do a lot of damage, but one day I hope to see you shine again. Take the time you need, Evie. Even if it's years from now."

I shrugged. "Maybe one day."

"One day is a good start," my friend said. She gently stroked one of the blooms. "All of these flowers seem oddly themed."

"Yeah," I grumbled. "Because the Shifter Lord is a dick."

Moira snorted a laugh. "Let me guess. You have plans for these arrangements?"

I could feel the crazy shining on my face. "Who, me? I would never."

The vampire grinned. "There you are friend. I was wondering if you'd retired your sassy pants."

"My sassy pants have been lost in the laundry for a while."

"Laundry is the worst chore, but isn't it nice when you get to wear your fresh, clean sassy pants again?"

I tossed an extra leaf at her. "Why are you so weird?"

She snatched the golden leaf from the air and fanned herself with it. "You like weird, Evie Quinn."

"Not necessarily," I grumbled. "But I do like you."

"Aww," Moira cooed. "BFFs forever."

"Go do something useful, will you? I have to finish putting this together so I can drop it at the courier."

Moira waved the contract at me. "Umm. You may want to look over this paperwork."

My hands stilled. "What did he do?"

Moira winced. "He didn't do anything, but I think he knows how much all of us like vacations."

I snatched the paper from her fingers and skimmed.

Moira helpfully pointed out the passage in question.

I swore like a sailor and closed my eyes, slowly counting to ten in my head.

"It's a lot of money," Moira said quietly.

"He always does this," I snarled. "And I always fall into his stupid trap because we're a small business, and we all need money to retire, eventually."

Moira's eyes crinkled at the edges. "Honey." She laid a hand on my arm. "We're all immortal. The only one who might not have a retirement fund or an assload of money in the bank is Tess. She's the only one of us who's young."

My shoulders slumped as Moira brought me in for a tight hug. "You worry far too much about everyone else and never about yourself." A hand stroked down my hair. "We love you far more than we love the money."

"Money really does buy happiness, though," I mumbled against her shoulder.

She laughed. "Yes, but not at the risk of your health." Moira gently pushed me away and held me by both arms. "But I still think you should take it."

I stared. "That speech that just rolled off your tongue was all a lie, then?"

Moira sniffed and leaned against the bottom cabinets. "No. We don't need the money. But that isn't the reason you should take it."

I put down my shears and crossed my arms. "Oh? This should be good. Why should I take his offer?"

Her eyes darkened. "You should go and show them who Evie Quinn is. No more hiding. No more staying in your shop and keeping your head down. The Chimera threat is hanging over Joy Springs, and we are the only ones who know."

"Moira." A hysterical laugh bubbled from me. "I can't show anyone that I'm a Chimera. The Lords will string me up and feed me to the wolves."

"You don't have to show them the Chimera to show them who

you are." She sighed. "My best friend is powerful beyond all reason, and she hides herself behind her pretty flower arrangements. You are not only a Chimera, and you are not only a Floromancer. You are a frigging demi-god, Evie, the daughter of a powerful goddess. And you're all the other things combined. If you don't think you can kick the shit out of a Shifter Lord..." Moira laughed. "Then you haven't been paying attention."

My heart warmed even as fear flooded my veins. "I've been avoiding this my entire life."

Her smile was sad. "Maybe it's time to stop running."

I mulled it over. "Caelan *is* paying an obscene amount of money for me to attend."

Moira's eyes glittered. "Every contract with him is negotiable. Ask him for another dress." She shrugged. "Shit. Ask him for the damn moon. I'm sure he'd figure out a way to lasso it."

"You think it's the right step? Going into the Keep and showing everyone who I am?"

"I don't think you need to plan on razing the place down, but if the opportunity presents itself or someone tries to dominate you..." Her voice trailed off. "Then I think you should kick some ass and take some names."

The door opened. Ash poked his head in and grinned. "Seconded! We've been waiting for this moment for years."

The dryad was tall and lean, his skin naturally golden brown due to his nature. His hair was a gorgeous mix of light and dark brown, and his eyes were a deep mossy green that changed to emerald when his magic rose. Tess trailed behind him, the banshee dressed in brighter colors than I'd ever seen.

She wore a soft pink dress and an emerald-green cardigan, her pale hair pulled into a messy bun. Bangles clinked on her wrist as she lifted her hand in a wave. "Thirded." Her smile was soft and tentative. Tess was soft-spoken and quiet, but she was smart as a whip and powerful, though she kept the most powerful tool in her arsenal tightly leashed.

None of us had ever heard Tess's wail or the mournful cry that signified a looming death. The cry wouldn't harm us, but her scream might end us all if she failed to control her power.

"Guess I'm outvoted," I said lightly.

Tess reached for me, taking both my hands in her pale, cool ones. She so rarely touched anyone that the gesture took me by surprise. "None of us is immortal," she began. "Immortality is a myth. We can be killed at any moment of the day. Eternal life is a gift and not one to be squandered."

Where was she going with this? I stayed silent and waited.

"If you walk through the world hiding yourself, eternal life becomes a chore, Evangeline. We love you. We love working with you and being your friend. But all of us see the sadness in your eyes."

I blinked my tears away. "Tess—"

Her eyes glowed pale silver. "You're worried about us. Don't be. We'll be fine." She smiled, a bright, unexpected gesture that made my lower lip wobble. "You might be the most powerful, but none of us are helpless."

"I know you're not helpless—" I protested.

Tess interrupted me. "And yet you still hold yourself back because you want to keep us safe."

I closed my mouth and stared at her.

"Aww," Moira said softly. "Our baby has grown up."

Ash placed his hand on Tess's shoulder. "She's right, Evie. Stop rolling over." He dropped a kiss atop the banshee's head. "Hiding yourself only gives them power. They're working behind the scenes to control you. Don't let them."

I put my hands on my hips and stared at them suspiciously. "Is this an intervention?"

Three pairs of innocent eyes avoided looking at each other.

"Guys…" My voice held a note of warning.

"Normally, we would never consider an intervention, especially not for you, but things with the Shifter Lord have gotten out of hand. And with Finn back in the picture, we think you should have more of a presence."

I gave her a flat look. "Presence? What exactly does that mean?"

Ash rolled his eyes. "She means stop hiding at home and the shop and maybe get out into the community and do some things for yourself. You haven't even gotten takeout since the wedding!"

"Are you depressed?" Tess asked.

"What? No!" An exasperated breath escaped me. They didn't know about Gianna and the discovery in my backyard. Plausible deniability is what I kept telling myself. I'd destroyed any trace of Caelan's ex-fiancée in the unique way only a Floromancer could.

The poor woman was officially part of the Joy Springs ecosystem, not a single recognizable or identifiable piece of her left because I'd turned her to mulch, and I was now the brand-new owner of a large, unusually healthy Japanese maple planted in the spot where someone had buried her. To make it less suspicious, I planted a small grove in a circle and dug out a fire pit in the middle. A little morbid for some since I liked to take my tea out in my new cozy space, but from the universe we came and to the universe we returned.

Eventually.

Many things bothered me about Gianna's death, but the main one I hadn't come to terms with was my belief that I'd never met the real woman. She'd been dead for at least two weeks before we found her, but it's possible she'd been gone for longer. Had all my dealings been with Gianna, or had I been speaking with another Chimera the entire time?

And if I had, who was it?

And why had Finn told me I was the only one left? Was he as much in the dark as I was?

Impossible.

"I'm not depressed. I'm cautious. That's all. I wanted things to die down before I resumed normal life."

Ash, who had a strange knack for unearthing secrets I wanted to keep buried, gave me a long look, but he didn't pry.

Not in front of everyone.

He'd catch me when I was alone and twist my arm until I spilled the beans.

Or try to, at least.

Keeping my friends safe would mean this is one secret that would have to stay buried.

CHAPTER

Two

Ash and Tess busied themselves with finishing up Hattie's autumn arrangement, a gorgeous mix of fall-colored blooms in a pretty handmade wicker basket I'd sourced from a witch down the street while I finished up Caelan's arrangements.

I cursed myself for not looking over that contract earlier, assuming Simone, Caelan's Omega, had taken my restrictions to heart before bringing it to the shop.

But blaming her wasn't right. She was beholden to the Shifter Lord, and he was infamous for pushing boundaries to get what he wanted.

For hours now, I'd mulled over my friends' words, and as much as I desired to push back and deny everything, they were right. Hiding became a way of life for me, and I'd diminished myself. Not only when I arrived in Joy Springs, but years prior, right around the time my marriage had fallen apart.

For so long, I'd prevented myself from doing the one thing my body craved.

Bloom.

I'd used my magic to coax other things to bloom and had held myself back from doing the same. First, because my world had fallen apart after I fled Seattle. Or so I'd thought. Only after Scotland had I truly diminished myself, became someone small and meek and *afraid*.

Disgust at myself filled me, and I shook my head, even as I tried to shake those thoughts off. But they stubbornly refused to go.

Look at me, they whispered.

Look what you've become.

The bloom in my hand turned to ash, a gentle wind blowing its remains across my worktable.

"Shit," I whispered. "I'm sorry."

And that was the other side of the coin, the one I'd been hiding. Moira and the others knew my magic had been malfunctioning and encouraged me to allow my Chimera to fully merge with my body. Even Cernunnos, who may or may not be my father, said I'd die if I kept the beast at bay any longer.

I'd done it and found a new power I couldn't have imagined. But...as with all wonderful things concerning magic, there were some side effects. A few, like the amount of meat I ate daily, were harmless, except for the pain my new appetite caused my pocketbook. Others, like the ferocious boost in Floromancy power and how much more upper body strength I had, were a little more concerning.

I could probably lift a car if I wanted to now. Not that I'd ever had the urge, but I could probably rage out properly if ever given the motivation.

Which is why I should stay away from the Shifter Lord. The male could push all my buttons in all the wrong ways, and I'd done some stupid things over it.

Then again, the amount of money he was offering for me to show up at this stupid gala was nothing to sneeze at. I could fund Tess's retirement account, give everyone a healthy bonus, and expand my property quite a bit if I wanted to. All I had to do was show my face, set the arrangements up, smile and wave, and haul ass home. That's all the contract said, in not quite those words, but close enough.

Show up half an hour early. Stay for dinner. Remove the arrangements once the event was over, and I was free to leave, no earlier than twenty minutes after the set closing time. If I played my cards right, I'd be out of there by ten thirty.

I pulled the contract back over and read through the clause again.

My contract has a no-delivery clause, I texted Caelan.

He responded almost immediately.

I'm aware. Exceptions are common in contracts.

Not mine.

A beat of silence before three dots appeared again.

An addendum, then.

I thought about it.

Alright. Here are my terms. Non-negotiable.

Everything in business is negotiable.

Keep pushing me, and I'll flood your land with poison ivy and man-eating vines.

I could almost see his manic grin.

Very well. I reserve the right to decline.

First, I doubled the amount of money in the contract to an eye-popping amount.

Done. What else?

I almost swallowed my tongue. "Dammit. I should have tripled it."

Every time you try to speak to me, you'll pay a day's worth of triple-time wages.

That's unreasonable.

I never claimed to be a reasonable person.

I'll think about it.

I'm not done.

Evie.

Every time you try to touch me, the contract fee increases by 25%.

Evie. Goddammit. I am not a monster.

You will send me a dress to wear.

With pleasure.

And matching jewelry.

Amethyst?

Ass.

Yes. and Aquamarine. Make sure the dress matches the stones.

Done.

I hated myself for loving the dresses he sent and his jewelry.

And you will find another florist to do business with in the future.

Absolutely not.

Remember how non-negotiable this is?

No.

Yes.

This is beyond unreasonable and borderline foolish.

Anger spiraled through my veins.

My shop did just fine before you came into my life. I don't want people coming in here because of morbid curiosity. I want them here because of my talent.

We both know that's not the only reason people come in. But you're also smart enough to know that my patronizing a business often brings a boost to the shop owner's bottom line. Having a Shifter Lord plug a business can turn the place into gold.

I didn't care about any of that.

Then I will send the arrangements by courier this evening, Lord. I hope you have an enjoyable event.

Goddammit, Evie!

I turned my phone to silent and placed the screen face down.

Moira brought me a steaming cup of coffee. "You look like you could use this." She jerked her head toward my phone. "Were you texting Caelan?"

"Yup. We could not come to a mutual agreement on the contract addendum."

Moira pressed her lips together, her eyes sparkling. "Oh?" she breathed after a beat of silence. "Mutual, huh?"

"I didn't say it was mutually beneficial," I said primly.

Moira snickered. "What was the dealbreaker?"

"Finding another florist for the future."

Moira blinked. "Oh." She leaned against the register desk and studied me. "Are you sure that's what you want him to do?"

"I can't disagree with anything you said earlier."

"I sense a 'but' coming."

"But Caelan is famous for sailing through whatever personal boundary I've put up. I want peace, Moira. And he brings me stress."

Her lips turned down. A beat of silence, then a thoughtful nod. "Okay. That's both true and fair. Caelan has brought a ton of chaos to your life since he walked in here." She reached over and touched my hand. "But don't count the Shifter Lord out yet. It's fair to ask him to patronize another business, but it doesn't mean you have to cut him out of your life completely. I know you like the guy."

"Ugh."

Moira laughed. "You do."

"When he's not being a controlling dick, sure." The words were harsh but true. Caelan was used to being in control, and he made things difficult when he didn't get his way. But when he was relaxed and calm, he was sexy and charming and…

Moira snorted. "You do," she repeated. "No use lying to a born liar."

"It doesn't matter. We've had this conversation a dozen times. I can't pursue anything with Caelan or anyone of prominence." My lips twisted. "Maybe no one at all."

Her eyes softened. "Evie. That's not true."

"How can I trust anyone not to give me away? I'd risk my own life and all of yours if I trusted the wrong person."

Moira nodded. "I get it. I really do. But you took a chance on me. On Ash and Tess. And we're worth it, aren't we?"

My heart softened. Trusting them hadn't been easy, but it was the best thing I'd ever done. We'd built a life here. A good one. "You know you are."

"Good." She refilled my mug. "There are other people out there worthy of your trust. Don't forget that."

I sipped my coffee. "Why are you being so sage? You're a regular vampire Gandhi today."

Moira grinned. "My best friend hasn't been up to the task lately, so I thought I'd step into her shoes for a bit while she gets her groove back." With a light shoulder nudge, Moira tipped her mug at me and winked.

I waved her away. "Can you call the courier and have her pick these up at six?"

She gave me a searching look. "Are you sure?"

"Yep. I have a few more things to do to these, but I'll be done by then. You all can head out early this evening if you want."

"I want!" Ash shouted.

Tess followed.

Moira slid behind the counter. "I'll head out right when the shop closes, so you don't get interrupted too much."

"No hot dates on the schedule?" I slid in a fiery orange bloom next to the Moulin Rouge sunflower. Next to it, a few deep orange dahlias.

"Nah. No one has tickled my fancy for quite a while."

I gave her a sly glance. "Not even Soren?"

Moira's eyes tightened, the gesture there and gone in less than a heartbeat.

My hands stilled. "Moira? Everything okay?"

She flicked a hand. "Totally fine. Soren left for his territory a long time ago. We barely spent any time together, and after seeing the chaos Caelan caused, I'm not sure I want to entangle myself with a Lord."

Moira was lying. "Oh. Not even for a brief tete-a-tete?"

"I don't do those much anymore," Moira said as she plopped down onto the stool. "Maybe I'm finally feeling my age."

"Heaven forbid," I said with a gasp. "The sky must be falling."

She snorted and opened her mouth to retort when the bell jingled.

In breezed a frazzled Simone. She wore casual clothes today—a pair of slim, straight-legged jeans, topped with a cream-colored cable knit sweater, and brown leather loafers.

"You look decidedly non-wolfish today," I said by way of greeting.

The Omega was the picture of quiet luxury, looking like she stepped out of any Ivy League university. Her blonde hair was caught up in a small claw clip, strands of hair arranged artfully around her face with careless elegance.

But that was the extent of her normalness.

Simone had death in her eyes and those pretty baby blues were locked on their target.

Me.

I took a step back and held up my hands. "Whatever this is, I want no part of it."

"You," she hissed. "Can you play nice just *once*?"

"Um." I turned wide eyes to Moira, who turned her head and coughed.

"It's my day off," she growled. "I have a lunch date in twenty minutes, and I got interrupted to come deal with *you*!"

Caelan. "Simone, this is not my fault."

"I don't care whose fault it is! You know what I want?"

"Um," I said again.

"I want hot tomato soup from that great cafe around the corner." Her nostrils flared. "And bread, for fuck's sake. Delicious, crusty, buttered bread. The real butter. Not that shit humans disguise as butter and pretend to like. And coffee. A cup of glorious, freshly ground dark roast. And maybe cake. Coconut. Or chocolate. I don't even give a shit. Just cake. Any cake."

I blinked at her, nonplussed. "Can't you get that at the Keep?"

All that did was piss her off. "No. Can you believe that shit? Ever since that bitch Gianna showed up, the entire menu changed, and now all we get is meat and veggies. Maybe a piece of fruit."

"It's been months," Moira said. "He hasn't changed it yet?"

Simone's hand jerked downward in a harsh slicing motion.

"No. And he won't let me! He keeps saying he'll get to it." She reached across my worktable and grabbed me by the shirt collar, jerking me halfway across the table "Has a man ever gotten to *anything* in a timely manner?"

"Err. No?" I squeaked. Not once had I seen the Omega with a hair out of place. She was always calm, cool, and completely collected. Not this well-dressed harridan in my face.

Blue eyes locked onto my soul. "I beg of you, Evie. Bend on this. Just this once. So I can get carbs and sugar and good coffee." Her voice was a desperate, shrill whisper.

"What part?"

Simone's eyes closed. "You know what part." She let go of me. "You aren't going to, are you?" Her nostrils flared as she tilted her head up to stare at my ceiling. I could almost hear her counting in her head. "Why must you antagonize me so?"

Moira barked a laugh.

Simone sent her a withering glare. "And you are a born instigator. Why can't either of you bend?"

"It's a matter of principle," Moira said simply. "Your Shifter Lord will bend on everything except for Evie. He'll throw money at her, give her whatever earthly desire she might want, but when it comes to setting boundaries, Caelan stomps all over them like a bully on the beach when they see a sandcastle."

Simone's shoulders slumped. She neither agreed nor disagreed. "What can I say or do to get you to show up tonight?"

Moira slid a look my way and jerked her head toward the kitchen.

"Give us a second, would you?" I asked.

Simone sighed. "Whatever gets me out of here and gets my face in a bowl of soup."

Moira took my arm and led me toward the kitchen doors. Once we were inside, she leaned in.

"Simone looks like she needs to be committed. Maybe we should give her something."

"I won't cave on this one."

"What about one order max on a quarterly basis?"

"Four per year?" I frowned. "Feels like too much."

"Start at the absolute least you'll accept. He'll bargain you down. Can you deal with three?"

I grimaced.

"Two?"

Reasonable as long as my intrusive thoughts didn't run away from me and make me worry about those visits for the entire year. "Seems doable. Once every six months. No Keep weddings, nothing I have to attend."

"He'll bargain for that, too."

"You really think I should bend?"

"For Simone. Not Caelan. The girl needs bread."

We laughed. "Alright. Let's do it for the bread."

Simone paced back and forth, stopping abruptly when she saw us. "Well?"

"One order per year. No Keep weddings. No events where my presence is required. The previously agreed rates and everything else we discussed prior to your visit stand."

Simone's lips thinned, but she held a finger up. "Hold that thought."

With admirable speed, the Omega's fingers flew over her cell as she typed a message out, presumably to Caelan.

"Four per year. He agreed to no weddings but wants to reserve the option to have your presence at certain events." Her eyes glittered with the thrill of a deal, but I was about to disappoint her.

"Two. No weddings. Attendance at one event only, no more than half an hour of my time billed at quadruple the rate."

Simone's eyes flickered with disappointment. "Evie. Caelan isn't bad."

"No one said he was," Moira blurted before I could open my mouth.

"Then why are you treating him like he is?" Her fingers flew over the phone keyboard as she typed the message.

"Again, this goes back to personal boundaries and how your

Shifter Lord likes to pretend he's the Lord of the Dance when he gets close to one."

Moira barked a laugh.

Simone sucked in a breath a second later, slowly shaking her head as she lifted her gaze. "The Lord has agreed to your terms."

Moira blinked in surprise. "Holy shit," she murmured.

Simone held up her finger. "Caveat."

Of course there was. I waited.

"This event does not count toward that number."

I opened my mouth to argue, but Moira shoved me so hard I almost fell over. "Agreed!" she blurted.

Simone's face fell in relief. "Thank the gods," she muttered. The Omega took a moment to rummage through her bag, pulling out a familiar document a few moments later.

"You carry contracts for lunch dates?" I asked.

"Only when there's a pain in the ass Floromancer my Shifter Lord loves to bargain with," she muttered. Simone snapped the pen's plunge, flipped to the second page and scribbled something down, muttering under her breath.

When she finished, she shoved the pen and paper at me. "Everything's there. Read over everything, initial in the right blocks, and please sign on the damn line."

Moira chuckled. "You really want that soup."

"I'd stab someone in the jugular for that soup," she huffed.

Much to Simone's annoyance, I read over the entire contract again, not trusting that Caelan hadn't changed something, and double-checked Simone's harried scribbles. After I confirmed everything, I took a deep breath, initialed the proper areas, and signed the contract.

Once again, I was a subcontractor for the Shifter Lord. But after this, I'd only have to deal with him twice a year. It was a win all the way around.

I'd barely picked up the pen from the paper when Simone snatched it away, shoved it into her bag, and breezed toward the door. "Nice doing business with you!" she called out as the bell jingled.

"If wolves could have a heart attack, she'd be the first one to go," Moira observed.

"Could you imagine working for Caelan?" I shuddered. "Twenty-four hours a day?"

Moira shook her head. "That's why I'm so glad I work for an undemanding Floromancer who keeps me supplied with tea and coffee."

Two hours later, right when everyone was gone, and I was walking over to lock the shop, a courier pushed the door open and poked her head in.

"Evie Quinn?" she asked, double checking the name on the box.

My heart sped up. The size was familiar. How in the world…

"That's me."

I signed for the box and the courier left in a hurry, plunging the shop into silence.

You already had this made, I accused Caelan via text.

Unveiling the mysteries behind my methods takes the magic away, came the response.

I smiled despite my annoyance.

Have you opened it?

No. I'm finishing up the arrangements and have to load them in the van. It will have to be a surprise until I'm ready to get dressed because I'm running low on time.

Hold that thought.

I frowned, but when he didn't send anything else, I tucked my phone into my pocket and put the final touches on the last spell. All twelve arrangements sat snug in their boxes, their blooms and leaves waving in the breezeless room. A smile touched my lips as I stroked the petal of a deep yellow calendula. Caelan might be an ass sometimes, but he never forced me into a color palette or a design I hadn't made. He always let me run with things as I saw fit.

With that disturbing thought in my head, I picked up the first box and went to prop open the door. Three massive men stood on the curb, right by my van.

Nerves flooded me, but I opened the door with my foot. "Can I help you?" I called.

The first one, a tall blond wolf with a fuzzy five o'clock shadow on his face, stepped forward. "Miss Quinn?"

I had a bad feeling about this. "Yes?"

"We're from the Keep. The Lord sent us to help you load."

"Am I allowed to refuse?" I said grumpily.

Sympathy touched his smile. "No ma'am. Just direct us where you want us and we'll take care of everything. We've been instructed to take the van straight to the Keep and unload it into the ballroom."

"You're not on my insurance."

A dark-haired shifter stepped up then. "Ma'am, I'm the safest driver out of everyone. If something happens, the Shifter Lord will replace your van."

"And then some," the blond said.

Good grief. After an aggrieved sigh, I jerked my head. "Here," I said as I handed him the box. "The van is open. Don't jostle any of the boxes and load them in the slots. You'll see what I'm talking about when you open the back. They can't be allowed to move around much. Each arrangement is spelled, and I can't risk it going off before the event."

The dark-haired shifter blanched. "Spelled?"

"Yes," I said slowly. "I am a Floromancer. That's what we do."

The blond shifter elbowed him. "We understand. May I have your phone number so I can text you once we arrive safely at the Keep?"

Cute and thoughtful. "What's your name?"

"Jericho, ma'am." He jerked a thumb at the dark one. "That's Mike, and the other one is Henry."

"Nice to meet you. I'm Evie."

Jericho's eyes sparkled. "Yes, ma'am. We know who you are."

The amusement in his voice didn't bode well for what he'd heard of me. "Everything is on my worktable. Be careful with the surface and avoid bumping into anything. Some of the plants are temperamental."

Jericho laughed in delight while the dark-haired one blinked. Henry had lighter brown hair and amber eyes, and not much of any kind of facial expression at all. I held the door open. "Straight back. You'll see the table."

In less than five minutes, every box and accessory was loaded, and Jericho held the keys. "I'll treat it like my own, ma'am."

I held up my index finger. "No. You're far too young. Treat it like your mother's."

Jericho grinned. "Like my mother's, then. I promise."

When the van pulled away and a tanned hand waved out the window, I shook my head and went back inside to get my purse and the dress.

Before I pulled away from the curb, I sent Caelan a begrudging thank-you text.

Are you ill?

Funny.

I'll see you in two hours, Evie.

My heart did a weird skip thump. I put my phone back into my purse and drove away.

It would be fine, right?

Who was I kidding? I was a walking disaster every time I stepped into the Keep.

CHAPTER

Three

Once I was back at the house, I texted Moira, asking her if she wanted to come with me.

Within seconds, she'd texted back saying she was in, but she'd have to dig up something to wear.

Like that was a problem. The woman had a closet with one of those rotating rods in it because she had so many clothes, she lost track of them all.

We agreed to meet in an hour, and I hurried to the bathroom to get ready, leaving the dress box unopened on the bed. Caelan's wolves had texted a few minutes ago letting me know everything arrived safely and all the arrangements were unloaded and still in their boxes.

Twenty minutes later, clean, shaved, plucked, moisturized and made up, I hovered over the box with trepidation, wondering what he'd done this time. Moments later, I held up a tea-length deep blue dress, every inch of it embroidered with flowers.

I sucked in a shocked gasp. Running my fingers down the intricate blooms, tears filled my eyes at the natural magic pulsing from the threads. Not every flower had a seed in it this time, but seventy-five percent held some form of life nestled within. But as stunning as that was, there were other things in the box. I pulled out three additional wrapped items, two in small boxes and one in an oblong shape.

Curious, I opened the larger one first, only to see a pair of matching shoes. In my size. Because of course Caelan would have gone through my closet at some point to note it.

"Weirdo," I said on a sigh.

Moving on to the first box, I opened it to reveal a stunning amethyst necklace, the gems rose cut and sparkling, encased in meticulous silver scrollwork of leaves and blooms. The earrings were a mix of aquamarine and amethyst, smaller and set in silver, and a delicate bracelet with a focal stone of carved aquamarine in the shape of a helichrysum flower.

My throat closed for a moment, and I wondered what would have happened if I'd met Caelan under different circumstances when I'd just been me, a simple Floromancer with a complicated family history, instead of the Evie now, a woman with the same nutso family, but with a curse in her blood that could ruin everything.

Shaking those thoughts away, I carefully set the jewelry down and stepped into the dress, unsurprised when it fit like a glove. I fastened the jewelry next and ignored the shoes until the last moment.

I left my hair down, quickly running over the ends with a curling iron before shaking the curls out to loosen them. A couple spritzes of perfume and a mad dash to the closet to find a small purse that would work, and I was rushing to the door, hopping as I shoved my feet into those surprisingly comfortable heels.

Moira had just pulled into the driveway and was sliding out of the vehicle when she spotted me. She wolf-whistled and gestured me over. "I'll drive tonight. Take a load off."

Without arguing, I got into the vehicle, and we were off.

"That's a fantastic dress," Moira observed. "Is it heavy with all that embroidery?"

"Not at all. That tailor is magnificent."

"With all the money that poor Lord is paying you, maybe you can retain him on an indefinite basis."

"True," I said with a laugh. We'd walk out of Caelan's keep with a massive paycheck this evening.

"Now that you've had time to think about it, you'd still go to Vegas?"

"Absolutely. But if Vegas was out, I'd go to Ibiza."

"Gracious. Don't they have a ton of drugs there?"

Moira laughed. "There are drugs everywhere if you know the right questions to ask."

I blinked. "Do you know the right questions?"

Moira stayed silent.

I gasped. "Moira! Are you a closet party girl?"

"I'm a vacation party girl. Big difference. I'm content with my life here, but if I get the chance to let my hair down far away from here, I'll take it."

Her words made me sad. "You can, you know. Any time you want. Just say the word."

Moira clicked her tongue. "You sap. I know I can. I'm not that girl all the time, nor do I want to be. Plus, I don't have anyone to go with me right now. We've only been in Joy Springs for a few years, and we all know how paranoid magical people can be about trusting others." She pointedly did not look at me.

"I'm aware," I said dryly. "Maybe I'll go with you one day."

She looked at me with horror. "Absolutely not. You're far too pretty to be set loose in a party situation. There could be an international incident."

"Moira!" I snickered. "You're such an ass sometimes."

She reached over and patted my knee. "Let's go somewhere tamer. How about Burning Man?"

The look I gave her sent her into a spiral of giggles. "How about somewhere with good food and good shopping?"

"I like both of those things far more than I should," Moira admitted.

"But not snobby shopping. Cool shopping. Like artisan stuff. Things we won't find anywhere else."

Moira and I pondered as we drove, arriving at Caelan's a short time later. As the gates opened without us having to use the call box, Moira snapped her fingers. "New Orleans. How about it?"

I'd never been there, though everyone knew the place was steeped in old magic. "Hmm. Invite Tess and Ash or just you and me?"

Moira's eyes glittered. "We invite them both. I can't wait to see what Tess does when someone throws beads and screams at her to show some skin."

"Maybe we should avoid Bourbon," I murmured. The street was infamous even to humans, who congregated there on week-ends for debauchery and sin. I'd like to see it once, but a place like that wasn't high on my bucket list. I slid a look at the vampire and had to laugh at her dejected look. "Fine. One night on Bourbon, as long as we spend most of our time in the Art and Garden districts."

"Done." She came to a stop and handed the keys to a hand-some, young shifter. He grinned in appreciation as she slid from the car, showing a long swath of pale, lean thigh when her dress rode up. "It's vintage," she said. "Try not to drool too much when you drive it away."

The shifter blinked as he looked at the keys and realized he was about to drive a Honda away.

Moira blew him a kiss and took me by the arm. "You ready?" she murmured softly.

"How bad could it be?"

We both laughed as we walked up the steps to the Keep's mansion.

"My gods," Moira murmured as we stopped not too far into the entrance of the Keep.

Blood rushed to my face, and my back broke into a cold sweat.

My fists clenched at my sides. "What in the absolute hell?" I whispered.

"Oh, Caelan," the vampire said, her voice thick with amusement. "What have you done?"

A banner hung above the interior hall emblazoned with floral typography announcing the name of the event. All fine. All normal.

But below it, in slightly smaller letters, but no less aggressive, were the words that struck horror in my soul.

Honoring Evie Quinn

"I am going to cut off his legs and shove a rod up his ass all the way through his mouth. Then I'm going to cook him like I'm the chef at a Louisiana pig roast."

Moira choked. "Vivid," she wheezed.

"Then I'm going to fillet him into tiny pieces and feed him to all the carnivorous plants in his yard that will start growing in the next five minutes."

Cool fingers gripped my hand. "Try to calm down. We have to set up the event first. Then you can retaliate to your heart's content. But maybe try to think this through." Moira leaned closer. "I've seen at least two of the other Lords. Remember. The best revenge is one they never see coming."

I sucked in a strangled breath of air and let my eyes flutter shut while I counted to five. "You're right."

"As much as I'd love to see you skewer him over this fucked up paranormal debutante ball Caelan has planned, I think you should take some time. Plant some seeds on the way out. Be in it for the long game."

I squared my shoulders and nodded. "I like the long game."

Moira squeezed my fingers. "I know you do. There you go." She fished through her purse and handed me a tube of lipstick. "You've chewed all yours off. Put your lips back on, add a smile, and pretend you do not give a shit about this."

I swiped on my favorite color, the one Moira always carried

because she knew I'd forget mine, smoothed my skirt down, and slapped on a smile.

"Maybe tone down the crazy a few more notches," she whispered. "You look like you've just been released from the asylum."

I snorted and tried again.

"There you go." Moira released my hand and tucked a stray strand of hair behind my ear. "Just the perfect amount of crazy. Now, let's go in and set this bullshit up. We can plot while we work."

I shot her a grateful look. "I love you."

"Right back atcha. One day, I hope you'll have my back when someone drives me to consider committing justifiable homicide."

"Are you kidding? I'll be in jail right beside you."

"That's my girl."

CHAPTER

Four

To Simone's credit, she wore a look of sympathy when she spotted us and grabbed me by the arm. "I swear to you, I did not know."

"I won't stay here a second longer than the contract requires," I said under my breath.

Simone let out a frustrated breath. "I'm sorry, Evie. Caelan is… unreasonable around you."

Moira barked out a laugh. "The dude is straight-up psychotic."

Simone shot her a dark look. "He is not *psychotic*."

"Your Shifter Lord is certifiable sometimes." I shoved an arrangement into Simone's hand. "Far left table, if you don't mind."

Simone sputtered but hurried the flowers over to the table. When she returned, a hesitant look crossed her face. "Um, Evie. I know the banner is a little unhinged, but I hope we can agree that there's no need to respond, right?"

My hands stilled in the act of activating one of the altered spells on the blooms. "You want me to let it go?"

Her expression cleared. "Yes! That would be wonderful!"

Moira burst out laughing. "Simone, meet Evie. She's never found a grudge she didn't cling to."

"The banner is one thing," I said, ignoring Moira. "But this entire event appears to be about me. Even if I didn't respond to the first, there's no way I can let the second go."

Simone's jaw tightened. "If I ask you nicely?"

"I'd say I appreciate your input, but I've decided to go another way."

Her fingers tightened around her clipboard. "Can you at least wait until everyone is gone?"

I smiled at her and returned to my work.

"Fuck," Simone muttered as she clacked away on her too-high heels.

"Someone's getting fucked tonight, and it ain't Evie," Moira sang after her.

The Omega lifted her hand and gave the vampire the middle finger.

"I'll think about it!" Moira shouted.

Yep. Tonight was going to be *awesome*.

It wasn't long after the setup was finished that Moira sidled over to me. "What did you do?" she whispered.

I chewed on my lip. "If I said nothing, would you believe me?"

"Nope." She wiggled her index finger at one of the arrangements. "Your hands were different when you messed with them."

"My hands?"

"Yes. You moved them a different way when you worked with them the first time. So what did you do?"

I stared at her for a long beat. "You notice what I do with my hands?"

"Not always. But I pay attention when the Shifter Lord is involved because it usually means trouble."

Wasn't that the truth. "I might have altered their function. A little."

One of her dark eyebrows rose. "Oh?"

"Dependent upon what happens tonight."

Moira's lips twitched. "And what will those lovely little arrangements do if the circumstances are right?"

A slow grin slid over my face. "I'd hate to ruin the surprise."

Moira's wicked chuckle made me laugh. "Being nice is overrated and not your style. I'll remember that next time I urge you to use caution."

"Oh no. This is not the only thing I'm planning."

She snorted. "Good to know. I'll keep a close watch on the centerpieces tonight."

A few minutes later, noise picked up in the foyer, the sound of Caelan's guests arriving. Thankful he hadn't made an appearance beforehand, I double-checked all the arrangements, then activated the first spell. Every bloom began to sway back and forth, all the greenery furling and unfurling. The small round mirrors the centerpieces sat on began to rotate slowly, the lights hovering above the arrangement bouncing off the mirror, casting the entire table in a colorful prism of gorgeous light.

"Whoa," Moira said. "Stunning."

"Thank you." I was pretty happy with how everything turned out. I'd made each arrangement in autumn colors, deep reds and burgundies, russet orange and mustard yellow blooms, and deep, glimmering bronzes and browns. Whoever had decorated the room had done the same. Deep brown tablecloths topped the tables, and bronze candlesticks dotted the middle of the table every few feet.

Someone had turned the lights down low, casting a warm ambiance over the ample space. I'd say one thing about Simone. The woman knew how to decorate.

I wandered over to the Omega. "Where are Moira and I seated?"

"Head table."

I stiffened. "Simone."

"Couldn't be helped," she snapped. "You know how he is."

"And you know how I am," I said softly.

"Please behave tonight, Evie. I beg of you."

"It depends on how your Shifter Lord behaves."

She gave me side eye. "He's your Lord, too."

"A mere technicality based on locale."

Her aggrieved sigh made my lips twitch.

"Are we still meeting for drinks on Tuesday?" she asked.

"Yes. You still drinking those martinis?"

"Yes. You still have that good liqueur?"

"I do."

Simone sniffed. "Fine. Seven?"

"Bring a snack."

Her lips pulled into a smile. "You know one day someone's going to get hurt with this, don't you?"

"Sure do. You know it will probably be Caelan?"

Simone snorted. "Go have a seat, weirdo. And please try to act civilized tonight."

"I make no promises."

She shook her head and closed her eyes, dragging in a long breath. "Okay. Turn it on, Simone."

A second later, she wore a dazzling smile and strolled to the door to greet the Shifter Lord's guests.

"I wish I could turn it on like that," Moira murmured.

"She has years of experience working for a Lord. Everyone here is gifted at hiding their emotions." I took her by the arm. "We're seated at the head table."

Moira grimaced. "Seriously?"

"Oh yes. I'm the guest of honor, remember?"

Moira let me lead her over. "How could I forget you're the very special sparkle princess tonight?"

"Never say that to me again."

Moira bent into a dramatic bow as she pulled my chair out. "My liege," she said in a terrible English accent.

I swatted her hand away and took my seat. "Idiot."

"Mmm. You love me."

I eyed her as magic pooled in the palm of my hand. The centerpiece for the head table was the prettiest one, and since Caelan was sitting here, there was less chance of someone over-hearing what was about to happen. Stifling my grin, I finished the alterations and snuffed my power before Simone could notice.

"Unfortunately, I do. Also, you look super-hot tonight. Where are you finding all these amazing dresses?"

She wore a sleek black sheath dress topped with a sparkling belt. Her hair was scooped into a slick bob, and she wore minimal jewelry, just a pair of juicy red rubies dangling from her earlobes and a delicate ruby bracelet. Her feet were encased in heels the same color as her earrings. Moira rarely wore much makeup. She didn't need it.

I'd never met an ugly vampire, and Moira was no exception. She reminded me a little of a fairytale princess. With her shiny, long black hair, dark eyes, and pale, creamy skin, Moira looked like a runway model. She was long and leanly muscled and had the type of elegant style I could never match.

"This old thing," she said lightly.

"The only old thing here is you."

"True." A server came over and filled our glasses, then breezed away like he was never there. "There's a great little boutique right at the edge of the downtown strip of shops. The proprietor is a stitching witch." Moira's face lit up with a smile. "I've never seen such talent. She could be in New York or Milan or working for one of the larger fashion houses, but she's here. There's a story there, Evie. I can feel it."

Moira was rarely wrong about people. She'd been wrong once, a long time ago in her youth, and it changed her on a fundamental level. After that, she'd developed an almost uncanny sense when it came to others. "Maybe we should pop by her shop again so I can check it out."

"Yeah?"

"Of course. It's about time I get back into the world, isn't it?"

Moira patted my knee. "It's a trip down the road. You'll be fine. And who knows? Maybe we'll make a new friend."

A punch of power boomed through the room. Soren walked in first, a handsome, smooth-talking Shifter Lord who ruled over the Deep Southern territories. Moira sucked in a soft breath when she saw him. Their gazes clashed and held for a long moment before Soren sauntered toward our table and took his seat. "Moira," he drawled.

"Lord," Moira said, inclining her head.

"Evie," Soren acknowledged. "It must be an honor for you to have a Lord host a gala for you in his home."

Moira snorted softly.

"I don't like surprise parties, Lord."

Soren's eyes narrowed. "You didn't know?"

I was saved from answering him by the crack of power heralding Caelan's arrival. His magic, usually tightly leashed to his body, rolled around him, snaps of lightning around his skin. A show of power for the other Lords and guests, telling them they were in his domain, and he ruled over all.

My breath caught as he walked inside. I hadn't seen him close up in months. He was just as handsome as he always was, but there was an edge to him that hadn't been there before. A sharpness in his eyes, a hint of violence as his gaze swept the room.

The stormy gray of his eyes snared me in their net. Everything inside me tightened. Caelan's face was blank, but emotion burned in his eyes.

If only things were different, maybe I could have loved him.

The thought took me by surprise, considering I wanted to punch him in his stupid face about eighty percent of the time.

His hair was shorter than normal, artfully arranged, and still a little messy. His jaw was clenched tight. Something must have happened just before he walked in. Caelan was a master at managing his emotions in public, but while his face was blank, anger beat from his tense form.

He made a beeline over to the table. I sat, frozen, hoping he would choose a seat by Soren or Moira, but my luck had run out. Caelan chose the seat right next to me. Even before he sat down, his power crackled against my skin, a testament to his power.

"Evie," he murmured. "It's nice to see you again."

I studied him for a long moment. "One day I'm going to stab you in the kidney, and you'll never see it coming."

His low, wicked chuckle rolled down my spine. "Nice to see you haven't changed a bit."

Now that the Lords were seated, the other guests entered the ballroom, Simone directing people to their seats with her trademark efficiency.

"Why are you doing this?" I hissed under my breath.

"Because our local Floromancer has chosen to ignore every request for a meeting I'd sent her over the last few months."

"So you throw a ball in my honor without telling me? What kind of fucked up shit is that?"

"Evie," Moira said quietly.

"The kind of fucked up that gets your attention," Caelan said. He made a gesture that had two servers hurrying over. "Red, please. Evie?"

"Red as well."

They refilled mine and filled a different glass for Caelan, a deep royal blue goblet.

"Fancy," I said, unable to keep the shitty note from my voice.

He laughed under his breath. "You're so easy to antagonize, Evangeline."

"Stop calling me that." One visit with my mother, and Caelan assumed he knew everything about me.

"It's a beautiful name. Why don't you want to use it?"

"Because it's none of your business." I flicked a hand at the rest of his adoring audience. "Can we get on with this so I can get out of here?"

"I'm wounded you find my presence so appalling. Many women consider me handsome and alluring. They fall all over themselves—"

"Please stop," I begged.

"And crawl into my bed," he continued. "Short women, tall women, pale women, tanned women…"

Soren snorted with disgust.

Caelan shot him a look tinged with violence. "And yet, one simple Floromancer continues to elude me."

"I am not a quest, you asshat."

"Aren't you?"

I facepalmed myself. "Caelan, can you please use your *alluring handsomeness* to get this show on the road?"

He wiggled his eyebrows. "We still have five minutes before the gala is set to begin. Five more minutes for you to drink your fill of me."

"For the gods' sake," I muttered. "If you want adoration, get it from your harem."

"He's bullshitting you, Evie," Soren said from a few seats down. "The old bastard hasn't wet his whistle with a woman in months."

Caelan's eyes flicked to Soren, the gold flecks in his irises glowing. "Soren," he rumbled.

"Please, Caelan, I can see you're besotted with the poor girl and have been since the second you met her. Can we all stop pretending?" Soren leaned back in his chair with a huff.

Caelan's brow furrowed, a thoughtful look in his eyes as he studied the other Lord.

I clicked my tongue. "No harem, then? How sad for you."

"Evie could have a harem if she wanted one," Moira said helpfully.

Soren burst out laughing.

"Moira. A harem would be about as appealing as public speaking. No thank you." I squirmed in my seat and discreetly checked my phone. Two minutes until whatever this was began.

"Just saying. You could, you know. All those men coming into your shop don't give a damn about flowers. They've just heard about the pretty dark-haired witch who owns the place."

Caelan's chest rumbled.

Moira grinned. "You might have your alluring handsomeness, Lord, but most of your appeal comes from the power you hold over this town. Evie's comes because she's drop dead gorgeous, talented, and puts up with zero bullshit." She winked at Caelan. "As evidenced by the pretty, pretty wild garden right outside these windows."

"That Jacaranda is impressive as hell," Soren murmured.

"Right?" Moira said. "Can you imagine how much she'll save on her own wedding flowers once she finally picks the lucky man who gets to walk her down the aisle?"

Caelan abruptly rose and strode over to the podium set up with a mic and a small glass of water.

Soren shook his head. "Antagonizing him isn't wise," he said softly.

"Oh, but it's so much fun," Moira responded.

"This is already awful enough," I whispered. "Can you stop picking at him? I don't want him to drag this thing on longer than necessary."

Soren chuckled.

"And why are you here, Lord?" I demanded. "We both know you don't give a shit about flowers."

Soren brushed an imaginary speck from his lapel. "I have my reasons."

"None of them to do with flowers," I muttered.

His gaze flicked to Moira before returning to me. "I go where I'm invited. Doing so allows me to take the pulse of a town."

"You were just here a few months ago," Moira said archly.

Their eyes held. "Much can change in a few months."

I rolled my eyes and returned my attention to Caelan. He cut a powerful figure in his charcoal gray suit and slate blue tie. But I felt a sense of fierce satisfaction when I noticed he wasn't wearing a boutonniere. The last time he'd worn one, I'd turned it into ash on the table and sent him one I'd made.

Afterward, I realized I'd gone a bit crazy and acted possessive, which in hindsight wasn't a good idea. But at the time, I couldn't help myself.

I toed the bag at my feet and wondered if I should give him the one I'd brought tonight.

Caelan's voice rumbled through the room as he spoke. All side conversations ceased as everyone focused on the Shifter Lord.

But as he spoke, anger grew inside me like a cancer. He had done this to get me here and disguised it as a charitable event. Any donations given during the night would be sent to a local hospital and used to sponsor events for sick children.

If I punched him in the kidney, it would have to be private because I didn't want the world to think I hated sick kids.

Just Caelan's manipulation tactics.

And I always fell for the damn things.

After he sang my praises for a little while and spoke about medical research, Caelan wished everyone a good night and made sure they knew who to give their checks to before retaking his seat.

"You must be feeling quite smug," I whispered.

"The bastard is always smug," Soren said.

Servers peeled from the walls and rushed the tables. Drinks were refilled and first course salads were served.

"Will you activate the arrangements?" Caelan asked.

I reached down and pulled a small carton out. "This is for you."

Caelan's lips parted as he took the carton and opened the top, revealing a boutonniere with deep burgundy ribbons and a creamy dahlia in the middle. Pretty, but nothing spectacular until you saw what was around those dahlias.

"Evie," he murmured, reaching out to stroke one of the dozen traps of the flytrap plant I'd bordered the dahlia with.

That trap reached out quick as a snake and latched onto Caelan's finger.

The Shifter Lord hissed in pain before a huff of laughter escaped him. "Is this one poisonous?"

"Paralyzing you in front of the community seemed like a bad idea," I said sweetly. "Plus I didn't have time to add the poison."

Moira muttered a prayer under her breath. Soren's eyes widened when several of the other traps began to sway in search of blood.

"I so love your violent gifts, Evangeline." Caelan wiped the beaded drop of blood from his fingertip onto his napkin and carefully fastened the boutonniere to his lapel.

"Are you sure you want to wear that?" Soren asked.

"Of course, I do. This event is for Evie, and this is but a small display of her wild power."

"Maybe don't touch it again," Soren said, his brow furrowed as he leaned over to study the carnivorous boutonniere.

"I plan to introduce this one to Seymour when the party is over," Caelan said. "How long will this one last?"

My heart warmed. Maybe I should stop giving Caelan things. All he was doing was endearing himself to me every time I tried to get a negative reaction from him. "The flytrap can be gently extricated from the boutonniere and planted, but the others will only last for a few more days. There's no preservation spell included."

"Good to know." A strange smile curved his lips. "Is it programmed to bite only me?"

"Anyone in the Keep is in danger if they come too close."

His laugh made something uncurl deep inside, and I realized I'd rarely managed to piss him off. The automaton stunt did it, but he wasn't as angry as I expected. Then he'd kept the garden and Seymour and somehow formed a bond with the bloodthirsty little flytrap.

He kept surprising me. Surprises were like finding a raisin in an oatmeal cookie when you could have sworn it was supposed to be chocolate.

"Another little demon then," he said, scratching the underside of one of the traps and snatching his finger out of the way before the plant could bite him.

The bastard laughed again.

Shit. I was in trouble.

I whispered the activation words for the table's centerpieces and picked my wine glass up. Nudging Moira, I motioned for her to do the same. A thorned vine whipped out and knocked Caelan's glass over.

The Lord swore and jumped from his seat before any wine could spill on his suit.

But the vine wasn't done. His salad plate crashed to the floor a second later, earning me an annoyed look.

"I don't like vegetables anyway," he said mildly as servants rushed over to clean up the mess.

I apologized to them because I'd forgotten someone else would have to clean the mess up and deactivated that particular spell. Once his chair was clean, Caelan sat back down. "Are you twelve?" he asked mildly.

I wiggled my finger. One of the vines whipped out and popped him on the side of the thumb. Caelan hissed.

"Goddammit, Evie."

Soren cackled.

The other Shifter Lord had never done anything to me, but they all wanted me to either marry one of them or be bound to a contract to diminish my power, so I sent the other centerpiece thumping closer to him. It sent up several thorned vines and waved them menacingly but didn't attack.

Soren swore and shoved his chair back.

At the other tables, the centerpieces were busy putting on a light and blooming show, showers of food and environment safe glitter going off repeatedly like tiny bombs. All we could hear were the oohs and ahs of the other guests.

"You are a menace," Soren growled.

I batted my eyes at him. "Aww. Does that mean you don't want to be the one to marry me, Lord Soren?"

Moira hid her smile behind her wine glass. Soren stilled.

Caelan snorted. "Told you she'd find out."

"Can it, Caelan." Soren eyed the centerpiece warily. "Is it safe to sit?"

"Try it and find out," I said sweetly.

"Don't be a baby," Caelan chided. "This one isn't poisonous, either."

"Maybe it's slow acting," Moira said and grinned.

Moira was a menace, too.

The dinner went on and on, and people approached our table before the main course, an exorbitant number of women making up the majority of visitors.

All of them gave me a once-over and dismissed me immediately.

Honestly? It was kind of nice. Never had I felt less pressure to be something I was not. And let's face it. No one here gave a shit about charity. They were here at the Shifter Lord's behest to get face time and because Caelan was single once more.

Once the umpteenth female visitor left after simpering for an appropriate amount of time, I squirmed in my seat. I had to pee, and I wanted to leave. Not necessarily in that order.

"Jealous, flower girl?"

The heat of my scoff took even me by surprise. "Hardly. If this is the field you're playing, you should have married Gianna."

Caelan barked a laugh. "She did have more bite than everyone so far."

Soren finally took his seat, though he didn't scoot his chair all the way in.

"Relax, Lord. She'll play nice if you do."

He sent me an incredulous look. "She? You know it's a girl?"

"Of course. You don't think a male plant is this angry, do you?"

Moira smiled into her wine. "Gods. I love hanging out with you, Evie. Especially when it has to do with the Lords."

"Your friend should take care with the way she treats her betters," Soren said.

Everyone froze. A punch of power rocked the room, blazing against my skin like the sun. Caelan's eyes went pure gold.

"Oh shit," Moira breathed. "You done stepped in it now."

I rarely touched Caelan of my own volition, but this time I lay a gentle hand across his thigh, where none of the curious guests—most of whom were looking our way—could see. "Caelan. I'll handle this."

A warm, calloused hand came over mine, Caelan's magic soaking into my skin. His muscles weren't as tense as they were a moment before, but his eyes still blazed gold.

I kept my voice low and steady, even though fury blazed through my blood. "I know why you want me to bow to the Lord's will."

Soren's eyes blazed, Moira an uncomfortable barrier between us.

I let a sardonic smile curve my lips. "You and your other Lords are afraid of what I might do. I am a threat to your power base. Little old me with my man-eating vines." I coaxed those vines closer to Soren. They grew along the table and curled around his dinner plate.

Soren snorted, but I didn't miss the hard swallow of his throat. "You're awful full of yourself for a Floromancer."

The disgust in his voice sent my hackles up. Floromancy was a relatively rare magic, and most people dismissed it. And they were right to, for the most part. The vast majority of people with my type of magic were content to act as landscapers and gardeners, or they ran shops like mine in smaller towns where their powers were easier to hide.

Caelan's low chuckle was a caress down my spine.

"Keep telling yourself that I am only a Floromancer, Lord Soren. I hope it helps you sleep at night."

I turned away from him just as the servers approached with the main course and tried to slide my hand from Caelan's thigh. He gripped it tightly, keeping it pressed there.

And heaven help me, I let him.

. . .

Just as the dinner was winding down, and I was gathering my bag, a woman with cool blonde hair and bright green eyes approached the table. Caelan stiffened, almost imperceptibly. Since my hand was still locked on his thigh, I felt the play of muscle.

"Lord," the woman said, her voice low and cultured. Her eyes swept over the table and snagged on me, a slight curl of distaste on her lip.

"Hello, Nadia."

She tilted her head. "I wonder if you have a moment where I might speak with you in private."

Caelan's brow furrowed. "You may speak freely at this table."

"Caelan," Soren warned.

"They are both aware of many of the goings-on at my Keep, Lord Soren."

Nadia flicked her gaze at me once more, her eyes lingering longer this time.

"I'm aware your engagement to my cousin is broken, but we have not seen her since that night."

I froze, careful to keep my expression blank. We were swimming in dangerous waters now. Carefully extricating my hand from under Caelan's, I pushed my plate away and started to rise. "This seems like a private family matter."

"Stay, Evie. I'd like to speak to you afterward."

The look in Caelan's eyes made me pause. I gave him a short nod and turned to Moira who was watching me carefully.

"Gianna packed a small bag and fled the Keep not long after the Bonding ceremony. I'm sorry, but I haven't seen her since. I can send out a few scouts to retrace her whereabouts if it will help."

Nadia inclined her head. "That would be most appreciated, Lord. As you can imagine, my uncle is fraught with worry. We all are."

Caelan studied her. "It's been months, Nadia. Why has no one contacted the Keep?"

"Her father received a letter from Gianna a few weeks after her departure from the Keep, or so we thought it was, claiming she needed some time to regroup before she came home. We've been unable to trace her cell phone, and all her accounts have no spending activity."

Caelan's jaw tightened. "Please leave your contact information with my Omega, Simone. I'll send scouts out tonight and contact you as soon as I hear anything."

"You are most gracious, Lord," Nadia said. She inclined her head once more and turned to go.

"I'm happy to send Riker out," Soren said quietly. "It's unusual for someone like Gianna to stay away that long."

"We'd appreciate having Riker with us. Allow me to brief Simone before you contact him. I know it will take him at least a day to get here."

"Of course." Soren rose and carefully folded his napkins. "Ladies," he said to us, though his eyes lingered on Moira. "I can't say it's been a pleasure, but events with you two are always... interesting."

Moira gave him a little wave. "See you around, Lord."

His lips twitched. "I hope you do."

As soon as he was out of earshot, Moira slumped in her chair. "Gods. No one should have the right to be that hot."

"He knows it. Minus twenty points."

Moira laughed. "Yeah. Most of those pretty boys do." She tossed her napkin on top of her plate. "Your Lord is giving me get-the-hell-out-of-here eyes, so I'll be waiting in the foyer for you. Don't take too long. I'm tired and want to kick these heels off."

Caelan's eyes glittered. "Find someone and ask her to show you to the library. You can kick your heels off there. It's empty right now."

Moira's face lit up. "You are a god among men, Lord Caelan,

and my sore little piggies thank you." She winked at me and rose, hurrying over to find the Omega.

"There's a fix to this," Caelan murmured as the rest of the guests filed out. A few beelined straight for him, but when they saw his still glowing eyes, they thought better of it and made an abrupt turn toward the door.

"Me building a fortress and warding it against Lords?" I grumbled.

His teeth flashed. "It wouldn't keep me out."

"You'd be surprised."

"Mmm. Maybe I would. But no, that's not the answer."

I sighed. "Fine. I'm tired and against my better judgment, I'll bite. Tell me the fix, oh wise one."

His golden gaze flicked to my lips. "I adore your smart mouth."

"Focus, Caelan."

He grinned. "You said my name."

"Don't make me regret it. Now spit it out."

"So feisty, Evangeline."

"And stop calling me that," I snapped.

The smile fell from his face. "You could marry me."

The bottom dropped out of my world. I stared at him for a long moment, my thoughts stretching like taffy. "I—um. That's—um."

"Your only true choice if you don't want the lords to hamstring your power."

My jaw tightened. "Once again, I think the Lords are underestimating both my tenacity and willingness to fuck their world up."

Caelan's eyes still glowed a deep, burnished gold. His emotions were high, and his magic was reacting, making my own react to him. The embroidery on my dress shifted, several flowers blooming against the expensive satin.

"Your dress is flowering," Caelan said in a rumbled voice.

"I can't marry you," I breathed. "That would be insanity."

The room had emptied out and someone had closed the doors, leaving me and the Lord alone. Caelan reached a calloused finger out and tilted my chin up. "Am I so terrible, Evie? Hideous to look at? Do I have a terrible personality? No sense of humor. Do you not like the way I dress? The way I speak? What is it about me that so offends you?"

My heart crashed against my ribs. "You don't love me."

A flash of teeth. A flicker of silver in that gold. "Says who?" he whispered, moving so close I felt the heat of his words against my lips.

"Says…everyone. Me. I say you don't." I was rambling. His words had taken me by surprise. Was he serious? Or baiting me? He was always baiting me, so why would this be any different?

He tucked my hair behind my ear. "Does it matter, flower girl?"

I blinked. "Uh. Yes. It does. Why wouldn't it?"

His eyes widened a hair. "You're a romantic. Such a wild and ferocious heart hiding such a soft, squishy middle."

"You should never use the words *soft, squishy middle* when speaking to a woman."

"Mmm. Noted. You're changing the subject, Evangeline."

"I swear to the gods. Stop calling me that." I wanted to pull away but couldn't make myself. His fingers lingered on my jaw, the touch heating my skin.

"You don't like your name?"

"My mother calls me that."

"And you don't like your mother." A non-judgmental tone, more curious than anything.

"My mother is a goddess."

Those five words told Caelan all he needed to know. He nodded. "I do not have many dealings with the gods, but they are known to have fickle hearts. What about your father?"

He might be the king of the fae, but Cernunnos, like all the gods, was being a cagey asshat right now and refused to answer the paternity question. Cernunnos claimed now wasn't the right time to answer but had conveniently forgotten to mention *when* that time might be.

"My mother never said much about him." I shook away the spell that Caelan was casting over me and pulled away from his touch. "It's time for me to go. I've already spent too much time here."

"Is it so bad to spend time with me?" Caelan dropped his hand.

"You are a Lord. Your future lies before you like a map on a table. The world is your oyster, Caelan. Any woman, any land, anything you want, you could walk in and take it."

His eyes slowly faded from their burnished gold to the gold-flecked stormy gray I was familiar with.

"I am a small-town florist with a hair-trigger temper when it comes to you."

His lips twitched.

"We are not meant for each other. I'm a curiosity to you, nothing more."

"How wrong you are, Evie Quinn." Caelan sighed and pushed his chair back. "You are much more than you claim to be and so much more than I ever imagined."

Unsure how to respond, I hiked my purse up and leaned close. Calling up a whisper of magic in my palm, I touched it to his boutonniere, closed my eyes, and poured my power into the flytrap.

When I opened them, Caelan's intense stare took my breath away. He stared at me like he knew my inner heart. But that was impossible. No one did. "What did you do?"

I stroked a finger over one of the traps and smiled. "*Now* it's poisonous."

With a wink, I turned and headed out of the ballroom, Caelan's shout of laughter echoing behind me.

CHAPTER

Five

CAELAN

L ove. The missing piece was love. Not missing on my part. But how was I to tell Evie I loved her when I wasn't sure what love was? For a Lord, love meant power. Loyalty. Dominance.

Not the kind of soft, tender thing I knew Evie craved.

I swore under my breath and rubbed a hand through my hair. Every time she walked away, I itched to run after her, capture her, and force her to stay.

That couldn't be love. This intense feeling of need, of *want*. I wanted her to stay and wanted her to wake up next to me every single day. I wanted her face to be the first thing I saw each morning and the last thing I saw before I closed my eyes each night.

"Fuck." I sank onto the couch in my study and buried my face in my hands.

A sharp knock on the door before Soren poked his head in.

"What?" I snapped.

The bastard laughed and stepped inside, closing the door behind him. He'd taken his suit jacket and tie off and untucked his shirt, lending a rumpled, befuddled air about him.

Soren collapsed into the chair opposite me. "Those two women are harridans."

A surprised laugh burst from me. "That they are."

"Evie seems worse."

I took no umbrage. Soren didn't sound angry or hateful, more like he was making a hedging observation. "She has reason to be more volatile than Moira. The Lords are sniffing at her door. Anyone would lash out."

"But she doesn't," he observed. "Only when you poke at her."

Seymour, my carnivorous bespelled and bloodthirsty Red Dragon flytrap, thumped down from the windowsill and made his way over to the couch.

Soren sucked in a breath as he watched Seymour make his way over. "Goddamn. Evie is everywhere in this Keep, Caelan. Don't your people wonder about her?"

I grinned and rubbed the top of Seymour's main trap. "Let them wonder."

Soren made a noise deep in his throat. "You've changed."

I looked up. "So have you." Soren and I had never had an antagonistic relationship, but we'd never been friends. Nor had we always seen eye to eye. But Soren was a good leader in his territory, and he'd never made a move against me. Maybe things could change in the future between us.

He scrubbed a hand over his jaw and closed his eyes, letting out a heavy breath. "Yeah. I'm tired, Caelan. When does it stop being so difficult?"

Seymour thumped his pot again, sailing from the arm of the couch right into my lap. I caught him before he could do himself harm and settled him onto my lap.

Soren choked. "That thing is poisonous, isn't it?"

"If it bites you, yes."

Soren huffed a laugh. "I never thought the day would come when I'd see you cuddle a carnivorous plant."

"Cats and dogs..." I murmured.

"Living together," Soren added.

"Complete anarchy."

Soren crossed an ankle over his knee and cleared his throat. "Other Lords will make their move soon."

I stilled. "Are you one of them?"

Soren's dark chuckle echoed through the room. "I'm afraid I have my eye on another unattainable woman."

"The vampire, Soren?" I'd seen the way he looked at her during the planning dinner when Gianna was here. "I took you for a purist."

"The heart wants what the heart wants." Soren looked around the room. "You got any whiskey?"

"By the back wall."

Soren groaned as he rose. A moment later he was back with two glasses, amber liquid swirling in their depths. He handed me one and settled onto the loveseat, stretching out his length on the couch.

"I've begun to wonder about the other Lords before us. Do you know if there are written histories?"

"Perhaps to see if other Lords have taken non-shifter brides?"

Soren gave me a dark look. "She doesn't want me anyhow, so the point is probably moot."

"Oh? What happened?"

Soren looked away, his gaze focused on a spot outside the window. "I fucked up."

"I already assumed so. Most problems are fixable."

A sharp shake of his head. "Not this one. She is polite but cold and refuses to return my texts or phone calls."

"Have you tried breaking into her house or destroying her shop?" I asked dryly.

A crack of laughter. "I'm afraid I'm much less physically destructive than you are. If I were more like you, perhaps Moira would still look at me like she once did."

"Is there another woman?" The Lords were not without constant company. Some took advantage of it and had revolving doors of female companionship in and out of their Keeps. I'd never wanted for a woman, but my tastes had always been much more discerning than some of the other Lords. And Soren was known to have a different woman on his arm every week.

When he didn't answer, I knew. "Ouch."

"I don't know why," Soren murmured. "Every woman pales in comparison to her, but I thought this was part of being Lord."

"The revolving door of women?" I probed before shaking my head. "The good people we have in our territories would much rather have a Lord who cares for and protects them. Women serve only to inflate our egos, and many of them are traps, designed to weaken our resolve and soften our reign, so another Lord can swoop in and steal our territory."

Soren snorted. "Paranoid much?"

I stared at him. "Have you learned nothing from the past year? The other Lords refuse to sanction a relationship between Evie and me because they are afraid of us holding too much power."

Soren drained his glass, rose, and brought the decanter back with him, stopping to fill my glass again before his own. "I'm surprised Rowan isn't here."

Soren looked far too tired and beat down to betray me, and the male had changed, so I took a chance and told the truth. "Donovan is sniffing around his territory looking for weaknesses. Leaving might be detrimental."

"Fucking asshole," the other Lord snarled. "Wonder where I'm at on Donovan's list."

"He'll go for Ben next. Him approving Ben's ascension was a move to take our attention off his recent antics. Give it a few months and he'll start sniffing around."

"You believe Ben will prove successful?"

"I have no doubts." Ben would more than prove worthy and he deserved his own territory, but my reasons for sending him were less my unshakable confidence in his abilities and more of a personal nature. Evie liked Ben, and I suspected he more than liked her.

A huge dick move on my part, but I didn't regret the decision.

"If you marry the Floromancer, your hold on this region would be unshakeable." Soren put his glass on the side table and rose.

I studied him with curiosity, never having seen this side of him. "You'd support the union?"

Soren flashed a grin as he headed toward the door. "I'm not interested in getting my head torn off, so you'd get a yes vote from me."

I tipped my glass to him. "Good to know."

Soren gave a little salute and headed out the door.

I picked Seymour up and headed down to the gardens at the back of the property, stopping at the stone bench I'd placed a few months back. Once I sat, the pot hopped off my lap and thumped away, no doubt in search of delicious bugs or maybe a dinosaur. Who the hell knew with Seymour.

Every time I sat out here, I felt like Evie sat right next to me. Her power had soaked into the land, mingling with mine, claiming a piece of the Keep even without her physical presence. My shifters adored this part of the Keep, and I'd stumbled on young lovers hidden among the flowers more than once. A heady fragrance floated through the air, the deep scent of moonflowers and night blooming tobacco tantalizing my nose. I let out a heavy breath and basked in Evie's flowers.

Everything weighed on me these days. Evie's constant rejection and the ever-growing danger of the Lords' attention on her, as well as the Chimera threat that had gone suspiciously quiet.

An overwhelming sense of doom had settled over me, and I knew the writing was on the wall. If I didn't press Evie to accept my advances, she'd find herself in a much worse situation.

As soon as the thought occurred, I laughed at myself. Evie would allow no one to push her around or force her to do something she did not want to do. Not even me.

I'd have to go about this in a different way. My normal mode of running headfirst at an issue was not going to help me with Evie. Nor would it help me with the Chimera threat. A Chimera could appear as anyone, even my own people, and there was little

I could do to prevent someone from infiltrating my Keep, other than paying rapt attention. None of the Lords realized Halvar was overtaken until it was far too late.

And with the Chimera's rapt attention on Evie, I couldn't afford to relax around anyone. My magic strained against the leash I'd kept it on. If anyone had the slightest hint of a changing scent, I'd know immediately. Scent was a shifter's most powerful weapon, and the only reason I hadn't noticed the Halvard deception was because I'd never met the Lord alone. We'd always been in a room with several others, where a change in scent wouldn't always be noticed when several others intermingled.

I drained the rest of the whiskey and set the glass on the bench. "Seymour."

The dull thump of his pot made me grin. Of all the gifts I'd received during my years as a Lord, this was my favorite.

Even if Evie had enchanted it to constantly bite me.

I rose when I spotted Seymour thumping his way back over, scooping him up on my way back into the Keep.

Those problems would hold for another day.

Figuring a way to win Evie's heart would take a lot longer.

CHAPTER
Six

"Of all the heavy-handed, oafish things to do," I muttered under my breath, clipping off the woody stem ends before sticking them into wet floral foam. "Arrogant wolf."

Moira snickered from her spot by the register. "Still fuming over the Lord's proposal?"

"Moira! Shhh." She was the only one who knew about Caelan's insane semi-proposal last night.

"Proposal?" Ash exclaimed from the succulent area; hands paused over his work. "Caelan *proposed* to you?" His eyes were comically wide. "Is there going to be a wedding?" He clapped his hands together. "This is wonderful news!"

"Ash."

"Can you imagine the floral display we can do?" Ash grabbed a pen and a clipboard. "Dahlias." He scribbled something on the clipboard. "Everywhere. A riot of color."

"Ash!" I barked.

The pen stilled. "What? I'm assuming you want to get married sooner rather than later. We should start planning now."

"There is no wedding. No marriage. No nothing. Caelan is

being presumptive." I thumped my shears on the table. "He thinks a quickie wedding will solve all our problems. Insanity."

Tess appeared through the wall, a trick she'd been using more and more lately. When I first saw her do it, I damn near jumped out of my skin.

"A betrothal!" she said in her whispery voice. "How romantic!" Tess floated over. "And tragic, too."

"Tragic?" Moira asked. "Weddings are anything but sad."

"Tragic because Caelan will find out where Gianna lies."

I went motionless, my heart caught in my throat.

"Excuse me?" Did she know? How could she know? I'd told no one and scattered Gianna's ashes to the wind.

Tess hovered by Ash. "I felt her spirit leave her body."

A tense silence fell in the shop. "Gianna is dead?" Moira blurted.

The clipboard slipped from Ash's hands, the crack of sound like a bullet in the quiet shop.

"Her body lies on Evie's property. I sensed her spirit the last time I was there." Tess floated toward the coffee pot like she hadn't just dropped a bomb.

"Evie?" Moira's face was white with concern. "Did you know?"

The shop hadn't opened yet, thank the gods, but we only had a few minutes before I had to unlock the doors.

My pause went on too long.

"Holy shit." Ash stared at me in horror. "Did you—" he swallowed. "Did you kill her?"

"What? No! Of course I didn't kill her. Geez."

"Then why is her body on your land?" Moira said quietly, no judgment on her face, but a concerned curiosity.

I glanced at the clock and wished I could speed it forward, so I didn't have to have this conversation. "Cernunnos told me. Otherwise I never would have known she was there.

Moira and Ash swore in unison, the vampire coming out from

behind the register to stand right in front of me. "What did you do?"

I couldn't bear the look in her eyes. Dropping my gaze, I whispered, "Sent her back to the earth. No one will ever know she was there."

"Except for me," Tess said as she added an ungodly amount of sugar to her coffee.

I clenched my jaw. "Except for the meddling banshee," I grumbled.

"Does Caelan know?" Moira asked.

A bark of laughter escaped me. "You want me to tell a Shifter Lord that I found his fiancée's *dead* body in my yard?"

"He's going to find out," Ash said. "Whoever put her there means to bring trouble to your door."

"They'll never find her. I made sure of it." The grim assurance in my voice didn't dim the worried light in Moira's eyes.

"I'm the only banshee in this town," Tess said as she floated back over. "No one else knows where she lies."

"And no one can know," I said quietly. "A secret like this might get us all killed."

"Which is why you didn't tell us," Moira said archly, a strong note of disapproval in her voice.

Ash turned away, shoving both hands through his hair. "Who would have done something like that?"

"Evie is the one who had motive," Moira said.

At my squawk of indignation, the vampire rolled her eyes. "Relax. No one here thinks you killed her, but it's true. Anyone with two working eyeballs would have seen the sparks flying between you and Caelan, and you were not exactly inconspicuous when he escorted you out and you two teenagers slipped away into a hidden alcove."

I blinked. "Um."

"Yep. I heard about it later. You fools thought you were so sneaky."

Heat colored my cheeks. "In my defense, I was walking to the door and was yanked into said alcove."

"Mm hm." Moira clicked her tongue. "Regardless, you were the spurned wannabe lover of a Shifter Lord and thought if you got Gianna out of the way, he'd return to you."

I gaped at her like a fish. "That's insane!"

"But it fits," Ash said. He settled heavily against the wall and sighed. "We owe Cernunnos a debt of gratitude. If he hadn't pointed Gianna's body out, Evie's property might be crawling with cops."

"And our lovely little Evie would be in the clinker," Moira finished.

The thought of a magical prison made me shudder. "I don't look good in orange."

"You really don't," Tess agreed and floated away.

Ash chuckled. "You always know where you stand with her, don't you?"

"Is that a banshee trait or just a Tess trait?" I wondered aloud.

"I'm not sure I want to meet another banshee," Moira said. "Two women moaning about death all the time is too much."

Ash snorted. "Flowers are a way of life for Evie. Death is Tess's. She can't help herself. For Tess, death is as natural as the sun rising in the east."

Guilt flooded me. "Ash is right. I never think about how annoying it must be to hear me talk about flowers all the time, and I didn't give Tess the same courtesy."

Moira grunted. "True, though my caveat is corpses are way different than dahlias, but I get your point."

Tess's voice came through the wall. "You know I can hear you."

"Sorry, Tess!"

"It's fine." Her voice trailed off before adding, "But maybe we could buy fewer lilies? They remind me of a funeral home."

Ash burst out laughing.

"I—yes," I said with a huff of amusement. "Fewer lilies and more patience on all our parts. Deal?"

"Deal."

"I think we should redirect this conversation toward ways of getting Caelan back for his presumptuousness," Moira said.

I held up a hand. "Absolutely not. Antagonizing him only seems to excite Caelan. I'd like him to focus on other things. We'll deal with the Lords when they show their hand."

Tess floated back in with her coffee mug. I wish I knew how it didn't fly out of her hand when she went incorporeal.

"Another flytrap?" Ash suggested.

"Already did one in his boutonniere." I rolled my eyes. "He loved it."

"Maybe instead of being violent, you could go romantic and befuddle him," Moira said.

"Nope. I'm happy with the way things are. It's fall. He gets two events per year. Hopefully, he'll write the rest of the year off and start things up next year."

"I wouldn't hold my breath," Ash said.

"Especially since one of the Keep vehicles just pulled up." Tess pointed to the window as a dark SUV pulled into the front parking spot.

All of us spun toward the door at the same time.

My shoulders fell in relief as Simone stepped out. But that relief was short-lived when the driver's side door opened, and Caelan stepped out.

"Here we go," Moira murmured.

"Hush. Let's plan on a normal visit," I hissed as I reached toward one of the vines and had it reach over to unlock the door.

All three of my friends started laughing.

CHAPTER
Seven

Caelan was a river when he walked, everyone parting around him without a conscious thought. Tourists crowded the walkways early today. Joy Springs was popular all throughout the year, but autumn brought more visitors than normal. The town was a popular hotspot for fall color, relatively rare in Texas.

He held the door open for Simone, the Omega breezing inside holding her ever-trusty clipboard. She smiled when she saw me, but the gesture didn't reach her eyes. Whatever they were here for, it wasn't an event.

Caelan came in after her, and the store felt two sizes too small. All the plants became alert, sensing a threat in their midst. I sent out a calming pulse of magic. The Shifter Lord might be a lot of things, but he wasn't destructive without cause, and he had a soft spot for plants.

His eyes locked on me, heat swirling in the stormy depths of his eyes. I swallowed hard, squashing the internal thrill I felt at his possessive behavior.

"Good morning. How can I help you today?" I offered a polite smile.

Simone laughed. "It's way too early to act so weird, Evie." She set her clipboard down on the register desk and fumbled through her purse for a pen. "We're here to schedule you again."

Moira coughed to cover a laugh.

"The Shifter Lord is becoming a regular social butterfly," I observed dryly. "If this is short notice, different rates will apply."

Simone rolled her eyes. "Caelan will pay whatever is required."

"Caelan also owes us a check from the last event," Moira said.

"I wired it to your business account this morning." Simone's attention rested on the Lord. "Caelan? Care to tell Evie what you want since you were reticent to discuss it with me?"

Her acerbic tone did enough to tell me how annoyed she was with the Lord.

But Caelan's gaze rested on my worktable, where an unfinished boutonniere sat. I'd started messing with a new design earlier that morning before remembering I had to finish up Hattie's arrangement.

This one was missing any sentient plants, but I'd embedded poisonous belladonna and a perfect, purple berry into the design. He stepped forward and leaned over the table to study it.

"If this one bites, I might think you're subtly wooing me," Caelan mused, reaching out a finger to touch it.

I slapped his hand away. Simone sucked in a breath. "Poisonous," I snapped. "Extremely deadly. Don't touch and don't get too close."

Caelan straightened, a furrow on his brow. "Why would you create something like that?"

I shrugged. "I'm immune and can deactivate the toxins in plants." A grin touched my lips. "If I want to."

Simone rolled her eyes and tapped her clipboard with her pen.

"Deadly and beautiful," Caelan said. "Just like a Floromancer I know."

Moira lay her hand over her heart and pretended to swoon.

Simone gagged behind Caelan's back. "Can we get back to the

scheduling? You have a busy schedule today, and I'm sure Evie has things she needs to get back to."

Caelan's thinly veiled look of annoyance made me wince, but he pulled a small piece of paper from his shirt pocket. "We have a small working dinner planned. Two seasonal centerpieces, but we'd like them similar to the first ones you created."

"Automatons?" I asked, intrigued despite my desire to be left alone.

Caelan nodded. "Something historical and seasonally appropriate. We'll leave it up to you."

Simone's pen stalled. "Are you sure? Have you forgotten about last time?" Her eyes flicked to me.

Caelan grinned. "How could I forget that glorious display of power?"

"I need a vacation," Simone muttered to herself, but loud enough for everyone to hear. "Can you please keep it less offensive to the shifters this time?"

"I make no promises," I said solemnly.

The Omega grumbled something and turned to leave. "Let me grab my notes. There are a couple of things I'm forgetting. We need to get on your schedule for next summer and next Christmas."

"And one more event this year," Caelan interjected, one dark eyebrow rising as if daring me to argue.

Contracts. He would use them against me, wouldn't he?

Simone left her purse and clipboard on the desk and hurried outside.

Tess had disappeared when Caelan walked in as she normally did. She did the same thing when my mother came around, and I thought it was because my mother was technically her queen, but I wondered if her disappearances had anything to do with her powers and how much violence swirled around Caelan and my mother.

Something to ask her later if I remembered.

"We're booked for several events during December. If you

need us, it's going to depend on the size and what exactly you need as to whether we can accommodate you."

Caelan stepped closer, heat pouring off his body like a furnace.

Moira cleared her throat. "I'm going to the back to get… something."

"I'll help!" Ash hurried after Moira, leaving me alone with the Lord.

Caelan shifted to lean against the desk. "You promised two events per year."

"I did. If you'll notice the wording of the contract, it does depend on my availability. Since we only came to an agreement a day ago and my calendar has been booked for months…"

"I see," Caelan murmured. "How about you open your calendar and let me see your availability?"

My heart thudded against my ribs at his proximity. "Sorry," I breathed. "Our calendar is internal and used for other things other than shop business."

A ripple of stunning magic flooded the street, trickling in through the shop wards. I sucked in a breath and stilled as power bloomed in the sky, culminating in the form of a tall, leanly built figure. Tall, powerful, dark-haired and dark-eyed, the male stood on the other side of the road, the same way he had when he first appeared to me several months ago.

He wore brown armor this time instead of black, but the same crimson runes glowed on the leather and his skins. His eyes, threaded with violet power simmering in their depths.

Caelan sensed the threat in the air and spun, shifting in a heartbeat. He landed on the ground in front of me in wolf form, a snarl already forming in his throat.

One of Neit's dark eyebrows rose as his gaze found the wolf before me.

Caelan lowered his head, his magic cracking through the air. I tried to step around him, but the Lord wouldn't allow it.

"I know him," I said softly, though being acquaintances with a god didn't matter if they really wanted to kill you.

Caelan's soft snarl made me freeze.

"Fine," I huffed. "You overprotective oaf."

A smile touched Neit's full lips before he tilted his head and raised a hand. Some would think it a friendly acknowledgment, but it was impossible to miss the threat of bloodshed in the air.

Neit disappeared in a swirl of golden magic, leaving behind nothing but a kiss of power in the air.

Simone burst through the door holding a small bag. She thrust it at Caelan right as a burst of magic popped and the Lord stood before me bare-chested and …

Holy shit.

I launched my gaze to the ceiling and turned away much to Caelan's wicked amusement.

"Cat got your tongue, Evie?" he said in a delicious drawl.

"For the love of the gods, please put some pants on."

"Mm. And if I don't?"

Simone snorted. "If you don't, there's bound to be a riot. You've attracted an audience."

Caelan swore under his breath. The sound of rustling fabric reached me and moments later, Simone told me the coast was clear.

I turned to see a crowd of gawking passersby holding their hands cupped to the window, all trying to get a gander at the Shifter Lord's backside. An audible groan of disappointment went up as Caelan tied the drawstring on the joggers Simone had brought from the vehicle, his normal clothing in a pile on my floor.

"It must be hard being so popular," I mused.

Caelan wiggled his eyebrows. "I never shift in public."

"They're less concerned by the shifting, Lord. Don't be surprised if your bare ass goes viral," said Simone.

Caelan's eyes flickered with annoyance. "That's why I have you and a team of lawyers."

Simone's look of ill-concealed annoyance made me press my

lips together to keep from laughing. "Or you could maybe not get naked in public."

Caelan studied her for a long moment. "You didn't see him."

"Who?" Simone's eyes narrowed. "All I saw was a flash of light and your goodies on display." She shook her head. "If the Lord continues to patronize your business, maybe we can pay for window tinting?"

"Nope. The bay window brings all the tourists to my yard. Our seasonal displays drive as many customers here as our online ads do. The Shifter Lord is going to have to learn to control himself better."

Caelan blinked. "There was a god on the other side of the street."

Simone's eyebrows went up. "A what?"

"A god." He scrubbed a hand over his jaw. "And Evie seems far less disturbed by the sight than she should be."

Caelan's power rumbled through the shop like an unleashed storm. "Care to share why that is?"

The way he was staring at me sent a chill down my spine. His look was reminiscent of a fox stalking a rabbit, and I didn't like it. There was only one fox in this messed up arrangement and it was me.

"No idea why he popped in, but I try not to get too disturbed by a god's presence considering who my mother is." I didn't want or need his protection. Allowing it meant giving away a piece of myself and letting Caelan get one step closer to unearthing secrets that needed to stay buried if I was to stay alive.

Simone stared. "Wait." She looked between me and Caelan. "My Lord is keeping secrets. Pray tell, who is your mother?"

"Cliona," Caelan growled. "A fact I discovered by accident."

Simone nodded slowly. "Right. Of course it is. How silly of me to assume anything about you two is *normal*."

"Why was he so interested in you?" Caelan demanded.

Tess floated in, saving me from answering. She stayed far away from Caelan. "Death comes," she intoned, her eyes glowing an unearthly silver. "The bell peals its final toll. One will fall. All will suffer."

Ash, who'd just stepped out from the back, sucked in a breath and did an about face. Tess popped out of existence a second later.

Silence fell for an uncomfortable moment.

"Right," Simone said. "Should we be concerned about that announcement?"

Tess had never done that before. Hopefully Ash was with her.

"Business as usual," I said with a forced smile. "Being in close proximity with a banshee can get weird at times."

But Caelan's eyes lingered on the spot where Tess had appeared. "One day I'm going to figure you out, Evie Quinn. And hope we all live through the process."

Let's hope the hell he didn't figure anything out.

Keeping my secrets kept us all alive.

Our gazes locked, Caelan's stare probing in the deepest corners of my soul.

Simone cleared her throat, breaking the spell between us. "Let's get on Evie's schedule and get out of here before you miss your next meeting."

She tapped her clipboard twice, and we were off to the races.

CHAPTER

Eight

CAELAN

S imone didn't say a word until we were halfway home. I braced myself for the litany of curses coming my way, but when she finally spoke, her tone was calm but worried.

"I didn't see the god." For Simone to admit something like that took a lot of steel. She prided herself on noticing everything. "There was a small blip where it felt like time skipped a beat, but I put it down to Joy Springs nonsense. Who was it?"

It frustrated me to no end, but I couldn't place him. "No idea. He was dressed like a warrior and had glowing runes on his skin and armor."

Simone frowned and shook her head after a moment. "I've never had dealings with the gods, but I can ask around."

Many things bothered me about the sighting, but one thing made my blood boil. The flicker of fear I felt when the god appeared hadn't come from me. It came from Evie. Even though her words belied her emotions, I'd smelled her bone-deep fear in the air when she spotted him across the street. She knew him, and I wanted to know why.

"I'll ask Rowan." Maybe Soren, too. "He's more in tune with the wild parts of the world and may have sensed something."

We drove in silence for a while. Just as we were about to turn onto the main road to take us to the Keep, I glanced up and spotted the same god sitting on top of a roof, those same runes glowing crimson under the morning sun, watching our vehicle as we drove past.

As soon as he spotted me watching, he lifted his hand in a mocking salute, grinned, and disappeared, divine magic shimmering in the air.

A trickle of unease ran through my veins.

"Did you see him?" I asked quietly.

Simone's hands tightened on the steering wheel. "Dammit. No. Why is he only appearing to you?"

I held my tongue. There could be only one reason.

Evie.

SOREN WAS WAITING in my office, his feet kicked up on the coffee table, while Seymour waved his traps at him from a few feet away.

Relief flashed in his eyes when I walked in. "That thing is an abomination," he said. "Why do you keep it around?"

Seymour took umbrage and snapped at Soren's boots, cracking a piece of the rubber sole off. He happily munched on it as Soren looked on in horror.

"Because he's a good deterrent against guests," I muttered.

Soren's bark of laughter made me snort. "There's more of Evie inside that thing than I expected."

"She can be quite prickly," I admitted as I took a seat on the couch. "To what do I owe the pleasure of this visit?"

Simone came inside at that moment, spotted Soren, rolled her eyes and sat on the opposite side of the couch. "Do I need to take notes?"

Soren leaned forward, his eyes glittering. "Do you ever put that pen down?"

Simone leaned into his space. "Only when I use it to stab someone in the eye."

Soren grinned. "How much does Caelan pay you?"

"Enough to make your bank account shrivel up and die," Simone said sweetly.

"Try to steal her and I'll let Seymour eat you." It was true. I paid Simone an exorbitant amount of money, directly equivalent to the amount of bullshit she had to deal with. Being a Shifter Lord meant Simone was up to her eyeballs in bullshit, and the less I had to deal with, the more I happily shelled out to her.

The woman was worth every wince from my accountant when he direct deposited her monthly paycheck.

Soren sat back. "Do you have a sister as equally competent? A niece or friend?"

"I have no friends," Simone said deadpan.

The Lord rolled his eyes. "Fine. This discussion isn't over, though."

Simone flicked her fingers. "I'm not leaving. A pretty face and pretty words will never be enough to win my loyalty."

"So you think I'm pretty then?" Soren said, his lips twitching.

"For the love of the gods, can we get on with it?" I wanted to sit in peace for a while and unravel everything that happened this morning, and I couldn't do so with these two knuckleheads verbally sparring in my presence.

"Chimera energy is popping up all over your territory."

I straightened. "Where?"

"I went for a run in the woods behind your property and sensed a disturbance at the town edge. After that, I stopped at a coffee shop, Mer-owned, I think, and sensed it again. We should reach out to the other Lords and see if they've sensed the same."

"We don't want to cause a panic. If Donovan smells blood in the water, he'll complicate shit."

"True. Rowan then?"

I nodded. "Rowan first. We'll discuss telling the others once we know if Rowan's territory remains stable."

"That's not all." Soren's expression sobered. "There are whispers about your Floromancer. I've not heard anything directly, but my Second has caught wind of her name mixed up with rumors of magical anomalies in your territory."

Had to be the gods. I nodded, keeping my face blank. "We all know Evie herself is an anomaly with the strength of her Floromancy. I'll send Garrett out and see if he can substantiate any of the rumors."

"She's a weakness, Caelan." Soren's voice was solemn, his voice lacking the usual teasing note.

"One man's weakness is another man's strength," I responded, not bothering to deny the observation.

"Are you sure she's yours?"

"She's obstinate and refuses to have much to do with me, so right now she's merely my on-retainer florist."

Soren laughed and rose. "When you want to formalize things with her, call me first and I'll try to soften up the others."

I watched him. "Why are you being so agreeable?"

The other Lord's eyes flickered. "Evie is Moira's best friend."

A surprised laugh burst from me. "Right. On the surface it's a good idea, but I suspect Moira is as hard-headed as Evie in different ways."

"I think you're right, but I can throw everything at the wall, can't I?" He thumped the wall once and disappeared down the hall.

Evie and I were barreling toward something. Whether it was good or bad remained to be seen.

CHAPTER
Nine

Things were calm at the shop the next morning. Ash and Tess had their heads together coming up with ideas for next week's seasonal arrangement. We didn't do those every week, but our business boomed during the holidays and people who normally didn't bother decorating started coming in asking for table arrangements and holiday centerpieces. With Caelan's wire transfer sitting in the bank account and all the extra business coming up, I was thinking about doing something special for the others in the form of a trip or a large bonus.

Moira was making tea for both of us, and I was putting the finishing touches on Hattie's bouquet, this time with a joint pain spell. As my spells went, this one was mild, but my favorite customer should get some relief in her hips once we delivered the newest bouquet.

We'd opened the doors twenty minutes ago and hadn't had any customers yet, but it was Friday morning, and things tended to be a little slow those mornings. Once lunch time came around, we'd get slammed with people looking for flowers and plants for the weekend.

Moira handed me a cup of tea, the scent of bergamot and

lavender rising from the steaming mug. I inhaled and smiled my thanks. "New blend?"

The scent was a touch different from her normal brand.

"Lir added a touch of lemon balm. I'm dubious about it, but he gave me a deluxe sample to try." She stared down into her mug. "He said he made it special for us and that he hoped it would calm us a little bit."

Moira snickered. "I didn't have the heart to ask him why he thought we might need calming for fear he might actually answer."

I snorted. "Everyone's heard about naked Caelan by now."

The vampire whistled low. "You could bounce a quarter off dat ass."

"Moira!"

She rolled her eyes. "If you weren't so prim and modest, you could have looked your fill." A sip of her tea, then, "I know I did."

Ash chuckled from the corner.

"I don't want to see anyone naked," I mumbled. "Especially not in my shop."

"And that is the reason why you are still single," Moira said. "You don't have to date them to see them naked."

"Hush." I waved her words away and sipped the tea. "This is surprisingly good."

Moira frowned at her cup. "It is, but I don't want to tell Lir. He's too full of himself already."

Like most merfolk, Lir was tall, handsome, tan, and he knew it. I didn't think he was a bad guy, but he could be insufferable, especially every time he launched a new blend.

"Maybe that's his magic. We shouldn't deny him his successes just because he's annoying."

Moira shot me a look. "Spoken like a true kind-hearted person." She made a disgusted noise. "Let me finish the cup and I'll decide then."

Grinning, I reached for a coaster before setting my cup on top of the worktable. With Hattie's bouquet finished, I needed to pot the pothos I'd propagated. Since it was so easy for me to do, we'd all decided to start selling more plants. There was no cost for the plants because they were all cuttings of my pothos, and we'd reached out to a local potter to source cute pots at a wholesale discount. The cost of dirt was negligible, and I didn't need to buy fertilizer because all the nutrients they needed were in my magic.

Ten bucks a pop could net them an adorable, handmade little pot, and a healthy pothos for their home. We were netting a healthy profit and were thinking about adding more plants to the list. I had plenty I could propagate, but some would be more difficult to take care of because of their finicky nature.

For now, we were content enough with these. I listened to Ash and the others chatting with half an ear while I worked. Soon enough, I had twenty potted cuttings, and once I boosted their growth a touch, they were ready to be put on the shelves for sale.

Moira reached for them just as the bell above the door rang.

Power swept over the shop, making us all freeze. This wasn't Caelan's wild power, nor was it my mother's colder power.

Neit stood in the doorway, his crimson runes glowing as his eyes swept the shop.

"Evie," he greeted in his deep voice.

I stared for a beat. "You're going to scare the customers if you keep standing in the doorway like you're going to murder us all."

Neit blinked. "How have you not been killed yet?" he muttered to himself.

"I keep people on their toes, and all you ancient fuckers like being surprised. Don't deny it."

Everyone froze. Moira sucked in a breath. "*Evie.*"

But Neit burst out laughing. "True, daughter of Cliona. Time does seem to freeze when you're as old as me."

"Would you like a cup of tea?" I asked.

Neit nodded and stepped all the way into the store.

"There's a seating area to your right. You're welcome to have a seat." I made his tea and brought it over, tamping down my smile at the absurd sight of him on the couch in his armor.

His large hands wrapped around the china cup and saucer.

"Yesterday, you looked like you either wanted to kill me or talk. Which one are you here for today?"

He sipped his tea. "Only to chat."

Neit's magic made the shop feel like a pressure cooker. My chest was tight and my Floromancy struggled to stay contained, but even worse was the crimson magic flowing through my veins. The god was a threat, and he was in my territory. The overwhelming urge to get him out made my skin itch.

"Alright then. Normally chats come with a purchase, but I'll bite. What do you want?"

He studied me for a long moment, his dark eyes missing nothing. "Why do you diminish yourself so, demi-god?"

I'd been asked this question a few times, and it annoyed me every single time. "I'm happy with the way I am." The answer was the best I could give him. Not quite a truth, but not a lie either. I was happy with myself, even if the Chimera magic flooding my veins kept trying to take more and more from me every day.

"Few are happy with who they are," Neit answered. "Gods amass power. It keeps them from ennui. Humans amass things." His eyes roamed over my shelving snagging on the knick-knacks and masses of plants scattered around. "You amass flora. But that's too easy. What do you want?"

"I want to go home each day knowing I've helped someone."

Neit snorted.

Annoyance filled me. "Are you one of the gods who seek to bloat themselves with power?"

Neit waved a hand. "I am not like the others. My power came to me early and remains mine. As long as there is war, I never have to refill my well."

"That's a little sad, don't you think?" For your lifeforce to be directly connected with the worst thing on the planet seemed a horrible way to exist.

"War is as inevitable as the changing seasons," Neit said simply. "It is nothing I can control. I do not seek it out, but neither do I run."

"Could you stop them if you wanted to?"

A flash of teeth belied his amusement at my frank question. "Why would I when conflict is the source of my power?"

I stared at the crimson runes covering his skin and his armor. "Even if you're bloated with magic?"

He chuckled. "Such a frank and direct child you are. I bet it makes your mother crazy."

"My mother doesn't need any help there," I muttered.

Neit laughed. "True. Cliona has always been one of my greatest opponents. Unpredictability is rare and interesting, don't you think?"

"Depends on who it is and if it's me and I'm winning. Then unpredictability is great." I watched him sip his tea, surprised by how carefully he held the cup. "Are you here only to discuss my mother?"

"No. I'm here to tell you of the Chimeras." His eyes flashed violet, a blip of magic there and gone. "Though I suspect you already know."

My blood froze. "I'm not sure why you think I'd know anything about a Chimera."

Neit leaned forward, so close we could have kissed, and whispered. "One of my underestimated and little-known talents is sniffing out bloodlines, Evangeline. And yours is very curious indeed."

I swallowed hard and leaned away from him. "Is this why you're in Joy Springs?"

"I am here for more than one reason. Cliona is here, and I will locate her soon enough. The Chimera threat cannot be allowed to grow, but I am not allowed to interfere. Not yet." He smiled. "For that, you should be grateful."

Ash tensed. Moira's eyes flashed with anger. Tess narrowed her eyes and studied the god for a moment before she floated closer.

Neit's eyes flicked over her, dismissing her after a quick glance. "You've lost someone recently. Someone you loved."

Neit went deathly still. "Be careful, young banshee." His voice shook with anger.

But Tess spoke again. "She is beautiful. Would you like to see her?"

Neit's hand jerked, tea spilling over the edge of his cup. His tanned face went white with grief.

"Tess," I warned.

The banshee didn't wait for Neit to answer. Her eyes went an unholy silver, and her hair blew across her face in a phantom wind. "Be seen," she commanded, her voice echoing with the sound of a thousand lives overlapping.

A woman appeared beside Neit.

I sucked in a shocked gasp and froze.

"Tess," Ash said with horror.

Neit's attention snapped to the spectral figure, his handsome face falling. The woman appeared to be in her early thirties, the slight hand of time written in the faint crow lines of her eyes. She was dark-haired and green-eyed, dressed in a modern, mid-length sundress. Her coloring was faded, like watching a sun-washed moving picture.

Her hand trembled as it rose to cup Neit's cheek.

I quietly rose and jerked my head toward Moira and Ash. This was not for us to witness.

Tess's neck craned back, and her hands were palm up, spread away from her body in a T shape. Silver light washed over the shop as the temperature plummeted at least twenty degrees.

Ash's face tight with worry, he hurried to the door and turned the lock so no one would interrupt. On silent feet, we went into the small break room and shut the door.

"Holy shit," Moira whispered, her eyes wide. "Did we know she could do that?"

I rubbed my hands over my arms, trying to wash away the feeling of horror touching me. To hold the power over life and death must be extraordinarily difficult. "No," I whispered back. "I hope this doesn't get us all killed."

"It's a gift and a curse," Ash murmured. "Neit's face told us all we needed to know. What Tess has done is a violation but also a precious gift Neit will never forget. Whether he will thank her remains to be seen."

No one else said a word for several minutes. As soon as the temperature began to rise, I poked my head out the door. Neit still sat on the couch, his face wet with tears.

Tess was nowhere to be found.

Heart pounding, I stepped back into the main area of the shop and resumed my place on the couch. The silence was tense but fragile, and I hesitated to break it, but I was worried about Tess.

There was no evidence of violence in the room, but Neit could have dusted her in an instant if he wanted to.

"Who was that?" Neit croaked, lifting a hand to dash away the moisture in his eyes.

"Um. Tess. She's the shop assistant."

His voice cracked with a harsh laugh. "She is much more than an assistant, daughter of Cliona. Do you know who her mother is?"

"No idea. She never speaks of her." I waited a beat. "Is Tess… okay?"

"She's fine. How could she not be? Do you know how much power beats through her veins?"

I guess I never thought about it. "She's just Tess," I said lamely. "Banshee and our friend."

Neit gave me an undecipherable look. "Do not let your mother take her. She will use that young banshee as a weapon."

"What do you know that I don't?" I asked, my stomach roiling.

"That much power is unnatural," Neit said as he rose. He let out a shaky breath. "I came here to give you a warning and am leaving here with the greatest gift I've ever received."

Neit shook his head. "You and your people unnerve me."

A surprised laugh escaped me. "Excuse me? We're just trying to run a flower shop."

His expression was unreadable. "For the gift your Tess has given me, I will tell you this. Your mother searches for something she suspects you have. Never let her find whatever she seeks. She is plotting. I do not know what she plans, but Cliona only has her best interests at heart. You might be blood, but she will sacrifice you at the altar of her goals if you let her."

Before I could ask any questions, Neit disappeared in a shower of divine magic.

Ash and Moira came out of the kitchen a moment later.

"Where's Tess?" Ash demanded, his face pale with worry.

"Neit said she's fine." I leaned back against the couch and closed my eyes, wishing I could rewind this day.

"Oh and we're trusting the gods now?" Ash snapped. "Tess! TESS!"

The banshee popped back into the shop in a cold gust of wind.

"Thank the gods," Ash breathed, reaching for Tess to pull her into a tight hug. Moira ruffled the banshee's pale hair, but all the energy had gone out of my sails, and all I could muster was a faint smile and a wave.

"Maybe give us a warning next time?" I said quietly.

"Death waits for no one, Evie," Tess said as she brushed a kiss over Ash's cheek and floated back over to the register.

"Right," I said under my breath. "Of course."

Moira plopped down beside me and grabbed my cup. "Want some more tea?"

"Only if it's ninety-five percent whiskey."

More Chimera meant even more danger, though I half hoped Finn would put his focus on the other one instead of me. I'd seriously wounded Finn last time he came around, though I wasn't foolish enough to believe he was dead. I think I'd know the moment he passed from this world. He was part of me, and the threat of his power had hung over me like a scythe for almost a decade now.

Resting easy would never be an option while Finn was still alive.

CHAPTER

Ten

After changing into joggers and a long-sleeve shirt and sliding my feet into some slip-on tennis shoes, I grabbed a bottle of water and went out to the greenhouse to siphon some of my magic and try to shake off the day's weirdness.

But as I got closer, an odd energy pierced the air. Stopping just before the door, I sent a silent thread of magic into the greenhouse. Every plant inside had shrunk in on itself, wary of the intrusive energy.

Every hair on my arms stood up. Someone or something was inside. I sent my power seeking, searching until it landed on something new.

The magic felt somewhat familiar, but I'd never sensed it before. Anger rose within me. My greenhouse was the one place I felt safe in, the place I knew I could come and relax. I dropped the thread of power and reached for the door, careful not to make myself a target.

When I opened it and nothing happened, I went up the steps and peered around the door's edge, tightly leashing my power to my body, a ploy to make who or what was inside underestimate me.

A red-haired woman stood by the Dutchman's pipe vines, one finger lifted to stroke the edge of its strange flowers. She didn't acknowledge me when I walked in, and I could only see her face in profile. A sharp, straight nose, high cheekbones, and crimson lips made her look like she walked off a movie set, but when she turned, I realized she was much more than that.

The woman was drop dead gorgeous. Her hair was in perfect coiled curls, her makeup flawless. Her eyes were dark, almost obsidian. She wore a rust-colored shirt, green corduroy pants and a pair of leather loafers. No rings adorned her well-manicured hands, but she wore a gold chain around her throat.

A lion charm dangled from the end.

She smiled the smile of a toothpaste model, friendly and open. "Evie Quinn. I was beginning to think you were a figment of Finn's imagination."

I stilled, struck by the knowledge of why her magic seemed familiar.

"You must be the other Chimera."

The woman clapped politely. "He said you were beautiful but failed to tell me you were intelligent, too. No wonder he's so fixated on you."

"I take it he's not dead?" My plants came alive at my presence, their pots creaking and groaning as they strained to find me.

The woman's eyes flickered as she noticed, a hint of unease on her face there and gone so fast I thought I imagined it.

"You should know killing a Chimera is extraordinarily difficult." She ran her fingers over the other flowers, and I felt the greenhouse's unease like a living thing inside my body. "We are quite resilient, and with our ability to turn into anything, we can become a tiny atom and burrow deep until we heal."

"If that's true, why did your kind go extinct?"

"You may call me Rhona."

I didn't plan on calling her anything.

"Extinct is the wrong word as you well know. Though my

kind was decimated, all it takes is one scratch and one bite and our numbers are replenished."

"Finn lied to me then."

"You care what Finn thinks?" Rhona asked, disappointment brimming in her dark eyes.

"No, but it would have been nice to know if there were others like me."

"Others who were not him?" Her deep chuckle resonated around us. "Finn does have some sadistic tendencies which are not ideal for keeping our species a secret."

I couldn't stop my disgusted snort. "He's vile."

"And yet, he is my child." Rhona clicked her tongue. "Not of my womb," she said when she saw my expression. "Of my bite. Unfortunately, his personality was formed long before he became what he is."

"He thought you were dead?"

"Finn thought everyone was dead, which is why he made his ill-advised decision to come here." A flicker of distaste on her face. "This is a small place, a nothing town."

Hope flared within me. "Then you plan to leave?"

Rhona laughed. "At first, until I saw the delicious Lord who claims this territory." She ran blood red nails across the wood planting shelves. "If I were to align myself with him, I'd never need to scrounge for power again."

Realization struck me. "You were the one posing as Gianna."

Rhona lifted a shoulder in a careless shrug. "Not at first. Not until I saw her goal. She was easy enough to manipulate. People like her usually are."

"And placing her body on my property?"

Rhona smiled. "Insurance, but you are a clever girl, aren't you? Not a single trace of DNA on your land. How'd you do it?"

Finn hadn't told her how strong my Floromancy was. Confusion simmered in my mind. Why wouldn't he tell Rhona something that important?

I kept my heart rate steady. "Fire destroys many things. I

brought new dirt in and replaced it with the dirt I dug out and sent away."

Rhona's eyes narrowed. "Seems awfully strategic for someone who's supposedly not a killer. Finn mentioned you were gentle."

I almost laughed. That might be a word to describe the old me, before the world had so handily stepped in to fuck me over, but no one who knew me now would ever describe me that way. Not even Finn.

What was he playing at?

"I watch a lot of true crime documentaries."

Rhona moved around the greenhouse, occasionally reaching out to touch a plant, and I moved with her, ensuring I never put my back to the woman. "Why are you here?"

"Curiosity, mainly. Finn's unhealthy obsession warranted a look from me." Genuine amusement brimmed in her eyes. "But all I see is a woman with a strong green thumb. When he said you were a hybrid, I was interested in seeing what would happen with the Chimera blood when it merged with a hedgewitch."

If she'd bothered to do even a little digging around, she would realize I was not a normal Floromancer and *definitely* not a hedgewitch.

"I barely sense any of our power inside of you. A pity really. I came in at the tail end of the bonding ceremony planning, and thought you might be a strong Floromancer, but growing plants and making them move means nothing to someone like me. I could bring the world to heel if I wanted to."

"Floromancy is a gentle art." I shrugged. "Sorry to disappoint you. I was born to be around greenery, not violence." If Rhona came in at the end of everything, she must not have seen any of my other displays of power. So secure in her own scheming, she'd ignored the threat I could potentially be, and Finn hadn't told her otherwise.

The question was, why would he do that?

"Even with your mother's power running through your veins, you're barely a blip on my radar."

I was going to kiss Hazel right on her pretty mouth next time I saw her for teaching me that trick. That and the tattoo she'd spent weeks correcting had given Rhona the wrong impression about me. On most magical "radars," i.e., scent or power sensing, I appeared as a hedgewitch or mid-level Floromancer, nothing out of the ordinary or too extreme. The thistle tattoo on my arm kept my Chimera blood hidden from all but the most powerful of senses.

Finn had damaged the tattoo last time we tangled, and Hazel had to slap a temporary magical bandage on it while she worked to find the fix. From Rhona's reaction, the thistle was back to full power and working better than expected.

But...there was one thing she shouldn't know. That Finn shouldn't know.

"How do you know my mother?"

Rhona's smile reached her eyes. "We go way back. Sometimes we find we have mutual interests."

"Like now?"

"You are of no use to me and have no need to know my plans."

With that rebuff, Rhona exploded into hundreds of crimson moths and swept out the door in a wave of blood-red wings.

I slid down to the floor, wrapping my trembling legs around my knees. My breath came in ragged and harsh waves, and I stifled the scream threatening to tear from my lungs. Another Chimera in Joy Springs, and it was all my fault.

A kiss of loamy forest and golden magic kissed the back of my neck. The scent of pine and wildness rose around me. I closed my eyes.

"Cernunnos."

A leather clad leg stepped into my field of vision. Craning my neck up, I beheld the vision of the fae king, in all his tanned, bare-chested, and antlered splendor. "Your timing is impeccable as always," I said dryly.

"You were wise not to show your hand," he said, folding his body into a cross-legged seat opposite me.

"She would have killed me." The woman was barely leashed rage, malevolence leaking from her every pore.

"Not today, unless you provoked her."

I buried my face in my knees. "Did you know there was more than one Chimera here to come fuck up my world?"

"The gods know many things."

I snorted and lifted my head to peer up at him. His eyes burned with emerald and golden fire. "No joggers today?"

"I'm afraid I'm on the clock."

I huffed a laugh. "No rest for the weary."

"There are more where she came from."

"All terrible?"

Sadness flashed over his face. "Are you terrible?"

"We both know I'm not a full Chimera."

"Is Caelan terrible?"

"He can be," I muttered.

"Evangeline," he said, disapproval simmering in his tone. "There are good and bad beings of every kind. Chimeras are naturally volatile, but it doesn't mean they are inherently evil."

"But Rhona is. I'd bet my left tit."

Cernunnos winced. Every time he did something like that, I moved a little bit closer to believing he was my father. "Please don't bet body parts. Especially..." His voice trailed off and he waved a floppy hand at me. "Those."

"The king of fae is uncomfortable talking about tits?" I teased. "I bet you've seen a million pairs."

His pained expression made me laugh.

"Is it time for you to tell me if you're my dad?"

Cernunnos sighed and shook his head. "You will find out when the time is right."

"Of course. Because knowing all the secrets of your heritage cannot possibly be advantageous against two Chimera shifters who seem to have an unhealthy interest in me. Totally under-standable."

"Sarcasm is a tool for the unintelligent," Cernunnos responded.

"Which is exactly why I should know about my genetic makeup. To figure out who made me stupid."

The fae king's lips tugged up. "You're a menace."

"I've been called worse."

We sat in the greenhouse in a companionable silence for a while. "I like this place," Cernunnos said. "Life brims in this small house. You've done well, child."

"*Your* child?" I fluttered my eyelashes.

"Menace," he muttered.

"Not that I'm upset by it, but why are you here? Is there a doom and gloom warning you're about to drop in my lap before you flutter away?"

"I do not flutter, Evangeline."

"Gallop then. On your wobbly little deer legs." I grinned at him unrepentantly.

Cernunnos shook his head and uncurled himself from the floor. He held a hand out to help me to my feet. "Cowering on the floor is beneath you. Rhona is a threat, but she is not an imme-diate one. Come. Make me a cup of coffee, and I will take some of that cake that goes with it if you have some."

I blinked, trying to remember what I gave him. "Coffee cake?"

"The cinnamon swirl thing with the delicious crunchy topping."

I looped my arm through the fae king's arm and led him toward the house. "You're in luck. I have half a cake left over from yesterday."

CHAPTER
Eleven

Cernunnos left after a large slice of cake, a cup of dark roast coffee, and a few more cryptic warnings thrown my way. A normal weekday for me by now.

I waited for half an hour to ensure I was completely alone before I went into the master bedroom, pulled all the shades down, and encouraged my plants to spread their foliage out, blocking all the windows and hidey holes where prying eyes might hide.

I sensed nothing, the house still and quiet, other than the soft susurrations of growing plant life, but being paranoid had kept me alive all these years. Once all the walls and ceiling were covered in glorious, thick growth, I brought the silence wards up and cast a glamour around the room. Any hidden cameras would see one thing while I worked on another.

I flipped up the large, colorful rug from the middle of the room and lay my hand against the warm, living floor. A sigil put in by Hazel glowed in greeting, and I settled my palm against the sigil, my fingers inside each of the small glowing circles on the edges. Five soft pricks and five drops of blood later, the sigil brightened, and the click of a large lock sounded.

A whir of a mechanical wheel and the floor slid open,

revealing a gray stone staircase. The flutter of wings sounded, along with the deep sound of a raven caw. I waited until Poe flew up and settled on my shoulder.

I stroked his silky feathers. "Haven't seen you in a while, friend. Would you like to fly?"

Poe dipped his head. "Fly. Stretch. Breathe."

"Mind walking down with me first?"

"Walk down. See Fee."

"Is it safe for her to fly yet?"

A violet shimmer of magic, Poe's strange power sweeping through my land. "Stay inside my wards. Fly."

"She'll like that." With the raven on my shoulder, I took the steps into the true beating heart of my home.

I usually came down here a few times a week to check on my treasures and ensure all my shade plants were doing well. Lately, I've been down here every night. Guilt flooded me at Poe being trapped down here, but the raven insisted. He took the duty of protecting Fee seriously.

It had taken a while for the egg to hatch, and when it had, magic had rocketed through the shop, bouncing around the warded store until it had flooded into each and every one of us and back into Fee, our brand-new baby phoenix.

This was the item I suspected Neit warned me about. My mother possessed three legendary birds, animals capable of extraordinary healing feats, their song capable of resurrecting the dead. But one of them had somehow managed to get one of their eggs out of Cliona's clutches and into the hands of a strange man who sold me duck eggs at the local farmer's market.

I knew the egg was magical the moment I laid eyes on it. But what I hadn't expected was what currently sat in front of me, nibbling its glowing feathers.

None of Cliona's birds could be considered extraordinary when gauging by appearance only. She had a goldfinch, a Eurasian chaffinch, and a starling. All normal, average birds one might see when they walked outside in certain countries.

This baby was none of those.

"Hi, Fee." The baby hopped onto the edge of its basket and flapped its way over to me, landing on my outstretched arm. Fee nuzzled my bicep, rubbing her brightly colored feathers against my arm. Her tail swept a full twelve inches down my body and was covered in the softest bright blue and purple downy feathers, pulsating with a deep, ancient magic. Her head and the rest of her body were covered in bright orange and yellow feathers, and her eyes were a deep, burnished gold.

She was the most beautiful animal I'd ever seen. I held power over fauna, though I rarely used the magic. Animals were deeply intelligent, feeling creatures, different from plants, though they held a strong sentience, too. A *different* sentience. I was careful with my plants and never pushed them in any direction they were resistant to going. But animals...I'd only used my power to heal them, never compel them, though they were drawn to me.

I'd never compel Fee to do anything other than be herself, but she required almost more protection than I could offer. I was not equipped to deal with a freaking *phoenix*, but here I was. About to sneak my legendary bird out for a flight I prayed to the gods no one would notice.

But how could no one notice such a majestic animal? And how could I keep her safe?

And the million-dollar question, how the hell did a common songbird lay a phoenix egg?

"Fly?" Poe croaked.

Fee jerked her head up. She didn't speak, and I never expected her to. Poe was an anomaly in a family of anomalies. But even though the phoenix never spoke, she understood when we spoke to her.

I'd formed a strong bond with her and would protect her with my life, but I had to find a way to protect her in a way that allowed her to live. Not live in a magical basement, only allowed to fly when I deemed it safe.

Fee bobbed her head and let out an adorable little cry.

"Come on, you two." Fee hopped on my left shoulder; Poe settled on the right. They waited patiently while I checked on my plants, giving them a healthy drink of water and a boost of nutrients. A double check to make sure all the protections were in place, and we were off to the kitchen.

"Want to eat first, Poe?"

The raven shook his head. "Fly! Fly!"

"Alright. Keep an eye on Fee. But don't take off until I double check the wards and put up the canopy, okay?"

"Make high."

"As high as I can," I promised, guilt flooding me. Poe could fly as long and as high as he wanted to, but he wouldn't. Not as long as Fee needed him.

Every time I let them out, I raised the canopy a little higher, but it was almost at its max. Any higher and people would begin to notice.

Both birds' bodies quivered with anticipation when I stepped onto the porch. "Be patient," I urged. "It will only take a few minutes."

Poe made a quarking noise and ruffled his feathers, his impatience evident in his motion.

I moved some leaves out of the way and sank onto the ground, digging the tips of my fingers into the soil. Closing my eyes, I sank into stillness and connected with the earth.

My land was well-sated and relaxed, no longer in a true growing season. Autumn was the time to slow down and begin preparing for winter. Joy Springs was colder than the Gulf Coast, but we rarely saw a hard freeze for long, if at all. But things stopped growing and slumbered.

I coaxed the ground to alertness and sent them a mental image of what I wanted and why. The land perked up when I showed them Poe and Fee, its attention snagging on the phoenix's incredible plumage. Slowly but surely, vines rose from the ground, hugging and curling around trees and structures, climbing toward the sky before they reached for each other to tangle in a camera proof canopy.

It took a little longer than I expected. Autumn moved slower than spring and summer, but soon enough my land fell into darkness. I sent several globes of light into the sky, interspersing them in a pattern Poe and Fee could use as an obstacle course if they wanted.

"Ready?"

Fee's cry was exultant, shattering the quiet evening.

Tears sprang to my eyes, and I wondered if I could ask for help to protect her. The Keep might be a good place. Caelan had a lot more land, but what would he do with such a treasure? Would he use it for his own gain?

"Go," I whispered. "Fly free."

Both birds shot from my shoulders in a sharp arc upward, their happy cries echoing through the land.

"Thank you," I whispered to the land.

A soft, warm pulse was its answer.

Once the birds were fed, they landed on the loveseat and curled around each other. I never kept them behind the locked doors when I was home, but I couldn't risk allowing them outside with cover. All the shades were drawn and double-checked for any other presence before I let them roam free.

After a quick dinner of tacos, I curled on the couch with my e-reader. Poe flew over and settled onto my lap.

"Fly tomorrow?" Poe croaked.

"Maybe." I stroked his feathers absentmindedly. "What do you think about me asking Caelan to care for Fee?"

Poe ruffled his feathers and cocked his head up. Intelligence gleamed in his dark eyes. "Like." He bobbed his neck like that settled everything.

"You think she will stay safe there?"

"Caelan predator." He snapped his beak a few times. "Eat prey. Fee safe."

Poe always had good judgment about people. "Poe visit."

"Are you sure he won't use her for his own gain?"

A shake of his feathery head. "Lord honor. Love Evie. Won't steal."

I stilled. "Oh Poe. He doesn't love me. He wants to use me."

He made a quarking noise. "Love Evie. Love Fee. Love Poe. Safe."

"Fee?" I called.

The phoenix popped her head up and burbled.

"Do you want the chance to fly free? High in the sky?"

She flew over and settled by Poe, nudging him with her tail to move over. Poe croaked at her but shifted. I grinned at their antics.

Fee bobbed her head.

It was still early. "Are you truly sure about this, Poe? We can't take it back."

"Lord safe. Fee fly."

I pulled my cell out and texted Caelan.

CHAPTER

Twelve

CAELAN

My cell beeped as Simone was leaving the room after a security brief. Garrett was in town trying to decipher the rumors swirling about Evie and the Chimeras.

Can you come over? I have a proposition and don't want to discuss it over the telephone.

I froze. Was this about the marriage? Hope wrapped a fist around my heart and squeezed.

Have you eaten? I'd fed her once before and was dying to do it again.

I made tacos. There's plenty left if you want them.

Evie was going to feed me? A dark sense of rage filled me as I thought about who else she might have fed over these last few months. I vowed to ensure I'd be the only one she offered food to in the future.

Shaking those possessive thoughts off, I checked the time. *I'll be there in twenty. Are the wards still keyed to me?*

Yes. The front door is unlocked. Come inside.

I didn't waste an extra minute. After I tossed Seymour some mealworms and patted him on the head and gave the turtle vine a little water, I got my shoes on and headed out the door without telling anyone where I was going.

Something about Evie's property relaxed me as soon as I stepped onto the land. An intense peace had settled into the plants and soil, and the wind smelled of fresh, green life. The wolf inside me inhaled and curled into a tight ball, falling asleep. The Keep was my home, but it had never given me this much peace. Evie's garden brimmed and overflowed with the gentle part of her power. On my land, some of her magic had aligned with mine, and the Keep grounds were much more relaxing than they used to be, but this was on another level.

Following Evie's instructions, I knocked once and pushed my way inside.

Evie sat curled on the couch, her lower half covered by a blanket. Her dark hair was up in a messy bun, and her hands held a steaming mug. An e-reader sat on her lap next to a massive dark bird.

I blinked. This must be the one I saw her with all those months ago.

Resisting the urge to sink beside her and pull her into my arms, I waited.

"Lord."

The bird's deep voice startled a laugh from me.

"Hello," I said.

Evie's fingers stroked the back of the raven's neck. "This is Poe."

"Poe. I'm Caelan."

The raven bobbed its head.

Evie pointed to the kitchen. "Everything is in there if you want to make yourself a plate. There's a bottle of red wine on the counter. It doesn't go with tacos, technically, but it's good wine and the tacos are good, so…" Her voice trailed off.

"Thank you." I went into the kitchen and made several tacos, my shoulders relaxing at the domestic task. Living in the Keep meant being catered to. Doing this small thing for myself and not having Evie scrape and bow at my feet was nice. Wonderful, actually.

I might be making my own plate, but Evie's essence had sunk into every part of the meal.

She didn't speak until I had settled into the chair across from her with a glass of wine and a heaping plate.

"You could have taken the rest if you wanted it. I know how much shifters eat."

"I had dinner earlier." Simone had brought a plate into the study before the security meeting and waited until I'd eaten every bite. The Keep had a chef, a great one, but I'd always preferred home cooking, simple meals that were filling and flavorful, and showed the effort someone had gone to.

"Go ahead and eat. We can talk afterward if you like." She wore an odd expression, one of worry and concern.

"Everything alright?" I picked up the first taco and bit into it. Flavor exploded in my mouth as I chewed. Cumin and chili powder, garlic and onion, the salsa Verde I'd spooned out of a pretty, chipped china bowl decorated with multi-colored flowers around its edge.

"Fine," she assured me. "I have a situation I need assistance with."

My eyebrows rose. "Evie Quinn asking for help? I can't believe it."

She rolled her eyes. "Don't make me regret this."

"Where did you get this meat? It's fantastic." And it was. Flavorful and tender and possessed of a wild note, there was no way this was grocery store meat.

"I have a good relationship with a lot of farms. One of them ships me a box every month filled with grass-fed and finished beef, heritage pork, and chickens." Evie smiled as she watched me devour the tacos. "I'll send you home with a few packs if you like."

"I like," I said with my mouth full. Every single bite on this plate would go in my mouth because Evie had made it.

She snorted. "I have an extra dozen duck eggs in the fridge too, if you'd like to try some."

I shoved down the magic threatening to burst from my body, the urge to lift her from the couch and wrap myself around her. It took me a moment to respond, and when I did, my voice was rough. "Duck eggs?"

I didn't give a shit about the eggs. What I cared about was this gentle, giving Evie. We weren't fighting or yelling or angry. Evie on a normal day was already dangerous to my heart. This Evie threatened to undo me.

Her eyes lit up. "Yes! The yolk is darker, richer than a normal egg. I use them when I bake and occasionally eat them for breakfast."

"If you have some to spare, I'd love to try them." And I would. My chef would try to run me out of the kitchen if I tried to cook, but in this case, she would need to bend.

Evie rose and grabbed the wine bottle, carrying it back to the sofa. Before she sat down, she waved the bottle and lifted her eyebrows in silent question.

My heart did a strange little trip as I held my glass up for a refill.

She smiled and poured some in mine and hers before re-taking her place.

Once I finished my tacos, I went to wash my plate, but Evie called out from the couch. "No need. I'll take care of it later."

Evie watched me carefully as I sat back down and waited. Whatever she wanted, it must be important.

"I'm not sure if it's a proposition or a favor I'm about to ask, but I think it leans more into favor territory."

I inclined my head. "Ask then."

"It requires secrecy on both our parts, as well as from everyone in your Keep."

My eyebrows flicked up. Interesting.

Evie's raven quarked and lifted its wings before it hopped off the couch and glided over, settling into my lap. I froze in surprise. Most animals didn't like wolf shifters, but Poe was a curious thing. He lifted his beak and studied me with intelligent, dark eyes. "Fee!"

"Wait, Poe," Evie said. "Lord—"

"Caelan," I growled.

Her lips quirked. "Caelan, I am in possession of something my mother wants. Desperately."

"Oh?" I lifted a hesitant finger and when Poe didn't move, stroked the back of his head, surprised by the silkiness of his feathers. "Did you steal it?"

Evie barked a laugh. "No!"

"I wouldn't judge you even if you had. Whatever you have must be important if your mother wants it so badly."

"It is an anomaly," Evie said. She sighed and took a sip of her wine. "I find myself unable to offer this treasure the…care it requires."

I lifted my gaze. "This treasure is living?"

"Fee! Fee!" croaked the raven.

"Patience, Poe."

My brow furrowed. "Fee?"

Evie leaned forward, intensity burning in her gaze. "I need—"

I set my wineglass down and rose, carefully lifting Poe. In a few steps I was beside her, mere inches separating us. "What is it? Tell me."

Evie's nostrils flared. She squeezed her eyes shut. "Fee," she said quietly. "Come on out."

A blur of orange and vivid blue swept through the air. I watched in awed fascination as a being straight out of legend swooped and landed right on Evie Quinn's lap.

"Well," I breathed. "Alright. This is what your mother covets."

Evie rubbed her fingers over the phoenix's chest. "Yes. Do you know much about my mother?"

The moment I found out who her mother was, I went home, scoured the internet, and sent Garrett out to find whatever he could about her. "She's ancient, part of the Tuatha, and she owns three legendary birds."

"But not this one," Evie said quietly. "Though I'm sure she wants to."

"What I don't know is why this one is a phoenix when none of her other birds are all that remarkable."

Fee's tail whipped around and landed on my leg, the glowing feathers pulsing with a type of magic I'd never felt before. "You are stunning," I murmured.

"I have no idea why Fee is a phoenix," Evie said. "Somehow, either the mom or someone loyal to my mother smuggled the egg out and it landed at the farmer's market with a man whose booth I frequent. He gave it to me and asked that I keep it safe."

"And this little girl came along a few months later."

"Yes. And I don't think I can care for her the way she needs. Not with all the current…scrutiny."

Scrutiny I'd put her under. Fuck. "What is it you need from me?"

"I'm not sure what I need other than a space for Fee to be safe. She needs to be able to fly free. I let her out when I can, but I have to put a canopy up that restricts how high she can fly. My property is too close to town, and she'll be noticed."

As Shifter Lord, I had an immense amount of land at my disposal. As Caelan, I held even more.

"What do you want from me in exchange?" Evie asked quietly. Her shoulders slumped, making me feel like utter shit.

"You've never asked for anything for yourself." I snorted. "Other than for me to leave you alone, which admittedly I am terrible at doing."

A slight smile tilted her lips up.

I brushed a hand over her cheek. "I will gladly do this for you and ask for nothing in return."

"There's one more thing."

"Poe!" the raven croaked. "Poe go!"

A wince. "My raven would like to accompany you and visit freely if you would allow it."

"Of course. Poe is welcome. I'm sure Fee would like to have a friend with her."

We chatted over the details, their diets, and what Evie needed, which was only that Fee be kept safe and allowed to fly whenever she wanted.

I let her in on a little-known secret. "The entire Keep is protected by a spy proof ward. That's why you never see news stories about any of the goings on there. The media has never been able to pierce our veil of privacy."

"Comforting, but what about magical means?"

"That too. Not once has any magic—" I paused at Evie's grin, "other than yours, penetrated the keep. And yours was not for spying. The Keep has many talented magicians who work solely on my security team. Your treasures will be safe at the Keep."

Evie watched me, a solemn expression on her face. "Caelan."

My heart clenched at the rasp in her voice when she said my name.

"I can't let you take them if you use them against me. Fee can't be a pawn in whatever this is between us. And Poe must be allowed to enter and leave at will."

"I swear to you, I will protect them both with my life." I laid a hand over my heart. "In this, we are agreed."

Evie swallowed hard. "Why?"

"For many reasons. The simplest one being for you."

Suspicion flickered in her eyes. "I'm still not going to marry you."

I laughed. "Maybe not tonight. Maybe not tomorrow. Maybe not even next year." I rose and offered my arm to Fee. Poe hopped onto the top of the couch and flapped onto my shoulder. "But one day, Evangeline Quinn, you are going to be my wife."

I turned and left the house before she could regain enough composure to scream at me, smiling all the way.

Caelan's words about being his wife still rang in my head the next afternoon. All four of us stood around the worktable putting together some ideas for the Keep holiday centerpieces using fake flowers while we practiced. The shop had had a steady stream of business the last week, but today was especially busy for some reason, so the brainstorming session stopped and started multiple times as Moira and Tess broke away to help with customers.

Worry about Poe and Fee churned through me, and I was about to text Caelan when my phone beeped. I opened the message to see a picture of Fee flying high in the sky, a riot of color against the afternoon sky. My breath caught.

"Evie?" Moira asked.

I flipped my phone around and showed them.

"She's stunning," Ash breathed. The dryad had never seen her in flight before, though he spoiled her with treats as much as he could.

"And you're sure she's safe?" Tess asked, her hands deep into a basket of succulents.

"Caelan promised me he'd protect her with his life."

Moira whistled low. "What did he demand in return?"

My stomach warmed. "Not a thing if you can believe it."

"I don't," Moira said immediately.

Ash snorted. "Me neither."

I held my hands up, flinging dirt around. "Me either, but he left without asking for a single thing. No demands. No contract. No nothing. Trust me. I'm as surprised as you are."

Moira's lips turned down. "It's dangerous to become indebted to him."

"I'm well aware. But I had no other choice. He is the only one powerful enough to keep her safe. Caelan has the means and the land to protect her." I shook my head. "Also, I've never seen him act needlessly cruel. Even Seymour has softened toward him."

Ash laughed. "I thought for sure Seymour would have everyone in that Keep paralyzed within the first month he was there."

"He popped about twenty-five percent," Moira said with a chuckle.

Tess pulled out a silvery gray succulent and tested it against the fall basket before frowning and putting it back. "Maybe we should try to sell some of those."

"Like Seymour?" Ash asked.

"Too much liability. If we accidentally sold one to a human, they'd sue us into oblivion."

"Not to mention inadvertently exposing magic to them," Moira added.

Ash's hands stilled. "I've been thinking about this for a while, and Tess's idea makes me think there's a market for an online-only marketplace for paranormals who want to shop for exotic plants."

"Plants like Seymour?" I asked.

"For a little of everything." Ash frowned. "But if I may say this, I don't think you should do more plants like Seymour. You poured a little too much of yourself into that one."

Tess nodded in agreement. "He's right. Seymour has too much

sentience to belong to the plant world anymore. He's something completely original now."

Moira grunted. "I'm with the rest of them. Boost them for health and growth and possibly some ability to communicate what they need, but don't go as far as you did with our bitey little friend."

"It takes too long, too," I agreed. "Seymour took weeks to create. But you're right. He has become something other than what he was meant to be. As long as Caelan cares for him, I won't take him back."

"Not that Seymour will let you," Ash added dryly. "He's just as violent as the Shifter Lord."

Seymour and I were permanently linked. I'd know if something happened to him, and I knew I could compel him to return to me if I wanted to. Not that I would. He'd found a better caretaker and companion in Caelan than he ever would in me.

"We'd have to find a website designer and sketch out some ideas, but I'm open to it."

"No need," Tess said. "I've sketched a few things out. I'll grab my tablet from my apartment after lunch if you want to see them."

My gaze flicked to Ash who wore a self-deprecating smile. "Tess and I have been talking about it for a while."

"Just ideas," Tess promised. "I like drawing anyway, so it wasn't a big deal to put something together." She ducked her head and focused on the succulents she was digging through. Tess was a staple in the shop and our friend, but I was beginning to realize Tess was much more complicated than she seemed on the surface.

And we still hadn't talked about what she'd done to Neit.

"Happy to take a look." Ash's idea was a good one, but I wasn't sure if I'd have the time to maintain it.

"Do you have a running list of what we could sell through the site? If we did one."

"My bonsais for sure."

"Your turtle vines were popular with the Keep," Moira said. "We'd make a killing with those on Valentine's Day."

"As long as they don't bite," said Tess.

"Evie saves all the biting things for Caelan," Moira said with a sly grin.

"Don't even start." I put the last fake flower into the foam and adjusted some of the wiring to see what it looked like when every plant in the office went quiet and still.

"Evie." Ash's brow furrowed as he stared outside. "There's something off about that woman."

I laid my wire cutters down and wiped my hands off. "Everyone stay here. There's a reason she's not coming inside."

"The wards?" Moira said.

"If it is, we know who it is." Little Shop of Florals was a public shop, and the wards were mostly used once we closed, though we'd blocked my mother and Finn from entering at all. Cliona wouldn't bother with a disguise, so I knew it wasn't her. She was far too in love with her own reflection to choose something other than the form she was born with.

But a Chimera, on the other hand, could and would choose another form, one of the many reasons they were excellent spies.

I gathered my magic close around me, funneling so much power, my eyes cast a light over the shop. Dimming it down so as not to freak out the humans, I steeled my shoulders and stepped outside.

The stranger made no effort to disguise their scent.

"What do you want?" I asked.

The woman was my height and blonde, resembling Gianna, Caelan's now deceased former fiancée. The nose was a little off and the eyes were a different color, but she still had that pale and icy hair and the aloof manner. But the scent told me exactly who stood before me.

"I'm not here to fight. Only to talk." The woman gestured toward a bench several feet away. "Mind sitting with me?"

I eyed Finn with suspicion. "Why should I trust you now?"

"Because there is a much larger threat out there than you or I."

"Rhona."

Finn's lips thinned. "Please, Evie. You will come to no harm."

The absolute last thing I wanted to do was be on the same continent as the Chimera who made me what I was, but I was curious. If he had information about Rhona, I'd squash down my disgust and listen to what he had to say. But if he tried to attack me in broad daylight, all bets might be off.

"Fine." I gestured for him to go first. No way would I turn my back to Finn.

He gave a smirk that looked odd on the woman's small face and strode over to the bench.

"Your female walk needs some work," I said.

Finn stiffened. "It's not a form I take often."

"Obviously. You look like a toddler trying to wear its mother's shoes."

Finn shot me a dark look as he sat down. "Your mouth is going to get you in trouble one day."

"My mouth gets me into trouble every day," I corrected as I sat on the opposite end of the bench, as far away from him as I could get.

"It wasn't long ago when you wanted to crawl inside my skin," Finn observed.

"Fuck off, Finn," I snapped. "Say your piece and leave me alone."

He clicked his tongue. "You are not the Evie I remember."

"That Evie died when you—" My voice broke, and I choked down my sob as the memory of that night under the stars played in my head in violent color. "You have five seconds to start talking, or we're done."

Finn sighed. "Fine. I wrongly assumed we were the only two Chimeras left in the world."

"Rhona implied there were many more of us. Do you have numbers?"

He shook his head. "You may think I'm cruel, but you have

not known true cruelty." Finn looked away, his eyes holding too much knowledge. "Rhona is the worst of us."

"I dunno, man. You're pretty terrible."

Finn blew out a breath and looked heavenward, as if I were the exasperating one here. "We are creatures filled with ancient magic. Sometimes our basest instincts control us."

I stared at him for a long moment, rage making me clench my fists. "Is this your idea of an apology?"

His jaw tightened. "Despite everything, I never meant to harm you."

I blinked. "Which time, exactly? Because I remember multiple murder attempts."

His dismissive snort pissed me off even more. I rose and stepped away from the bench.

"I never planned to kill you, only convince you that you needed me."

The sincerity in his voice was galling. People really thought the way Finn did, as if people were their property and they were somehow entitled to their time, their mind, their *bodies*. He'd found me at the lowest moment in my life, charmed me, and ruined what little self-respect I had left.

After everything I'd gone through, when I would have taken the smallest crumb of affection or genuine care, and Finn arrived and not only offered it but made me feel I was beautiful, cherished…well, I thought there'd been a boulder to step onto from my place at rock bottom.

And then as soon as I stepped onto that boulder, Finn kicked it right out from under me.

I chewed on the edge of my lips debating how much trouble I'd be in if I stabbed him through the heart in public.

Power rolled through the street, a punch of visceral, violent strength.

Finn froze as Caelan came into view from around the corner, Simone trailing after him.

The Shifter Lord didn't look at me. His eyes were trained on

Finn, eyes blazing with golden magic.

"Uh oh," I sang. "You're in trouble."

Finn glared and stood up, surprisingly not running away. "Your Lord needs to be in the loop as much as you do."

"Finn." Horror filled me.

"Do not worry, little Chimera," he whispered so low only I could hear him, "I will not tell your precious lover what you are."

"He's not my lover," I hissed.

"Tell that to the Lord," Finn drawled.

Caelan stepped up beside me. "Evie."

"Lord."

He shot me a golden-eyed look. I was not calling him Caelan in public. Not with other people around.

"Who's your friend?" he asked.

Finn grinned, the sharp-toothed smile completely out of place on those feminine features.

"You've met before."

A rise of a dark eyebrow. "Oh? I think I'd remember if we'd met before." He touched a hand to his chest. "I am Lord Caelan. And you are?"

But then his nostrils flared and that golden magic punched out in a wash of painful prickles that touched every inch of bare skin. "Finn," Caelan snarled.

Wisely, the Chimera took a step back. "I'm not here to fight."

"I don't care why you're here," Caelan growled. He glanced at me. "Are you alright?"

"Your lovely witch is just fine. We were having a great chat before you interrupted." Finn grinned as Caelan began to glow, his power an unearthly shimmer around him.

"Stop antagonizing him and tell him why you're here."

Finn rolled his eyes. "You used to be so much fun."

A small whisper of power and a row of thorny rose bushes directly behind Finn grew and popped him on the back of his thigh. He hissed in pain, eyes flaring with crimson before he let out a harsh crack of laughter. "If I knew you were into pain, things might have been different all those years ago."

Quick as a lightning strike, Caelan's fist slammed into Finn's face, the crack of bone breaking loud as a gunshot.

Finn let out a bark of pain and backed up, straight into the rose bushes where he hissed again as he struggled to free his clothing. Blood streamed down his face.

"Oh shit," I breathed.

Several people on the street had their phones raised, recording Caelan striking a defenseless *woman* in public.

"Lord," Simone urged, reaching out to touch him on the arm.

Caelan's chest heaved with anger. "Say one word against Evie again, and I will destroy you."

"Just like you did last time?" Finn taunted, though it came out like, "Juh ike ooh did ast time?"

"Lord Caelan, you can't hit her again. Striking her once is bad enough. We'll have to activate the team to destroy the footage." Her gaze swept over the town square. "Maybe even pay some bribes," she muttered under her breath.

"That is not a *she*," Caelan barked.

"Finn. Stop being a dick." Exasperated, I threw my hands up in the air. "I don't care what you say about me. We both know what you did to me, and your jokes and digs about knowing me back then are only designed to make me break. I don't care about you, Finn. That means I don't give a shit whether you live or die—"

"I do," Caelan interrupted.

"But if you don't spit the reason you're here out, I'm going to eviscerate you myself."

"I'll help," Caelan said.

Finn's lips quirked as Simone dug her cellphone out and frantically texted someone at the Keep, no doubt to start immediate damage control.

The optics did look bad, but there was no way to tell anyone what Finn actually was without making things a thousand percent worse.

"A new Chimera is in town. She's intelligent, dangerous, and crafty. If you're smart, you'll take her for the threat she is. Not only to you, but to all of us. She has plans, and your Floromancer is part of them." A faint smile tipped his lips up. "One final tip before I leave. Consider this a gift for taking good care of my Evie while she waited for me to return." Caelan's deep snarl made Finn laugh. "So grumpy," he said in a high-pitched voice.

"Speak or die." Caelan's eyes washed the sidewalk in golden light.

"I see why you like him," Finn said to me. "He's less fun than you are."

"Finn." For the gods' sakes.

He winked, and I remembered why I'd taken a chance on him that long ago night in Scotland.

"For a while there, she had more than a *passing* resemblance to your missing fiancée. I'd say for maybe two weeks, Rhona was a spitting image."

Caelan froze. "Gianna. Do you know where she is?"

Finn's gaze flicked to me, and I knew he was about to screw me over. "You should ask your lovely little flower girl." With a quick look around, he grinned and disappeared in a flash of crimson light.

Fucking Finn.

CHAPTER
Fourteen

Simone, usually so unflappable, gaped like a fish. "I—uh. Lord, with your leave, I'll head back to the Keep, to start damage control."

He waved a hand at her, not bothering to respond.

With a final wide-eyed look at me, Simone spun on her heel and hurried away, leaving me and the Shifter Lord in the street.

"No one saw Finn leave," I said quietly. "The street went empty after you broke Finn's nose."

"Would you like to talk here or in your office?" Caelan said in a toneless voice.

His eyes still glowed that perfect, golden hue, telling me I was in deep shit.

"Um. Let's go…elsewhere."

"Lead the way," Caelan said.

I poked my head into the shop to tell them I'd be back in a little while, but everyone waved me away the instant they spotted Caelan looming behind me.

"Be careful," Moira mouthed before tossing me my purse.

I dug out my car keys and was about to click the lock when Caelan snatched them from my fingers.

"I'll drive. Your house?"

"Sure."

We drove the entire way in silence, Caelan's eyes glowing the entire time. He unlocked the door, held it open, and didn't slam it shut.

Even when furious, Caelan was a gentleman.

I, on the other hand, felt like I had four feet and five arms. I tripped on the steps going inside my house, dropped a coffee mug on the kitchen floor, shattering it into a hundred pieces, sliced my finger on one of the glass shards, and was about to slice another when Caelan gripped my hand firmly in his own and crouched down beside me.

"Evie." Quiet words laced with tension. "Go sit down."

"But I have to clean it," I protested.

"Sit. I'll make the coffee." He reached up for the roll of paper towels and tore one off, pressing it to my bleeding finger. "Hold pressure there."

He helped me up and took me over to the couch where he sat me down.

I stared at him open mouthed. "You don't have to—"

Caelan's shoulders stiffened. "Can't you stop arguing with me for one second, please?"

"I—" Shit. He was right. "Fine," I said with a sigh.

His chuckle was soft, almost silent.

Why was I always an idiot around him?

"You need a better coffee pot," Caelan grumbled as he filled the cheap glass carafe. "With all the money you charge me, you could afford to buy a damn coffee shop, and yet you keep this cheap monstrosity and drink whatever terrible swill it produces."

"It works," I said simply.

"Lead pipes work inside old homes, yet the water still poisons you."

"That's a massive leap from cheap coffee to lead poisoning."

"Cheap coffee *is* poison," Caelan pointed out.

"No. It might taste like shit, but it's not poisonous."

"It's poisonous to my sensibilities," Caelan grumbled.

"That's because you're rich as Croesus and sleep in a bed made of gold where servants wearing pristine white offer turn down service and leave expensive candies on your freshly fluffed pillows."

Caelan laughed. "Don't knock turn down service. Besides, you're rich, too. Or you will be, if you charge every Lord the same way you charge me."

"I don't do work for other Lords."

He turned but not before I missed the pleased smile on his face.

I rolled my eyes. Men.

Once the coffee finished brewing, he poured us both mugs and brought them over to the coffee table, setting mine before me.

Instead of taking the chair opposite, he kicked off his shoes and sat right beside me, turned to face me, one leg propped sideways on the couch. It was the most relaxed I'd ever seen him.

But...his eyes were still golden. He might look calm and composed on the outside, but the Shifter Lord still fumed.

I kept my eye on him as I picked up my coffee.

"Is she dead?" he asked.

Coffee sloshed over the edge of the mug and burned my fingers. I hissed in pain and set the mug down with a loud clack. Caelan reached over and took my fingers, lifting them to his lips.

Cool breath washed over them, golden eyes locked onto mine. My blood thickened, pulse slowed to a thud.

"Is. She. Dead." Each word clipped at the end, my face awash in golden light. Caelan's power rumbled through the room.

I swallowed and considered lying, but he'd smell it on me. We were in close quarters and would scent the untruth on me before I finished telling it. "Yes."

Caelan's eyes shut for a long moment. He still held my hand, his warm calloused thumb stroking the back of my hand, sending tingles down my spine with every touch. "How?"

His behavior was weirding me out. Was he pissed? Was he about to kill me? Happy about her death? Sad? The glowing said one thing, him rubbing on me said something completely different.

And men talked about women giving mixed signals!

"I don't know," I said finally.

Caelan's brow furrowed as he digested that. "You aren't the one who killed her," he murmured after a moment, his expression clearing.

I blinked. "What? No!" I yanked my hand away. "You thought I *murdered* your fiancée? What the hell, Caelan?"

He sipped his coffee and studied me. "I thought it was a romantic gesture. Violent and unexpected. Just like you."

What was happening right now? "I've never killed anyone! That's not how my power works. Murder is the antithesis of Floromancy." I shook my head. "And you're the only one who makes me violent!"

If I had a pillow, I'd strongly consider smothering myself to get out of this bizarre, maddening conversation.

"Finn makes you violent," he said, the glow in his eyes turning deeper, a warmer molten gold.

"Because Finn is trying to murder *me*. You just...piss me off."

Caelan's delighted grin made me want to smack him. "Can we please be done with this conversation?" I begged.

His rumbling laugh made my lips tug into a hesitant smile.

"Where is she?" he asked.

That I could answer truthfully with zero hesitation. "I gave her back to the earth."

Caelan's head tilted in curiosity. "Explain."

"Floromancy is magic deeply rooted in the natural world. If you follow the lore, we were created from dust and when we die, to dust we return. My powers are inherent with life, but death is just as much a part of the cycle as life."

"You turned Gianna to dust." No judgment in his tone, just a thoughtful note.

"I did. For what it's worth, I'm sorry about the way this ended." I left Cernunnos out of the conversation. We were dancing far too close to the truth on many things concerning my life, and he already knew about my mother. The king of the fae was another ballgown.

"How did you discover her?"

"Magic," I said, careful to toe the line of the truth. "When I found her, she had been gone for a while."

He sat back; tanned fingers curled around his mug. "You could have called me."

"We don't seem to have the kind of strong relationship bond where we'll hide bodies for each other." I softened the words with a sad smile. "I couldn't have done anything for her, nor was I willing to risk being framed for murder."

I frowned. "Because that's exactly what Finn would do. Nor did I want the Lord to find out, so I sent her back to the earth."

Caelan rubbed his face. "This complicates things. Her family is looking for her and has been for a while." He tilted the rest of his coffee back and rose. "Can you show me where you found her?"

"Let me get another cup of coffee."

Caelan stared down at the spot where Gianna once lay and said nothing for a long time. I ran my hands over my arms to shake off the chill. Coming out here creeped me out. Gianna was no longer here, but a residue lingered around the space, silently screaming something terrible happened there.

"I'm going to shift," Caelan said.

Before I could say anything, a flash of light cracked in the woods and a large wolf stood before me. His coloring could best be described as dark, not quite black, not quite gray. Deep charcoal, the color of roiling smoke from an out-of-control fire, Caelan leaned forward, dropping his massive chest to the ground. He dug his nose into the leaf litter around the tree that rose from the spot and sniffed around for a while before standing and walking around her hasty grave, nose still to the ground.

I didn't interrupt, only went to the ground in a cross-legged position, watching Caelan as he investigated. Finding something, even a hint of a scent trail would surprise me, but maybe he'd pick up something other than Gianna's. There was no doubt in my mind Rhona was the one who took her out, but I had zero solid proof. A shitty personality wouldn't get someone convicted in court, so if Caelan needed real proof, he'd have to find it the old-fashioned way now that I'd destroyed every shred of evidence Gianna was ever here.

When he went for several minutes with no signs of stopping, I decided to connect with the land to see if I could wash away the dark feeling in the area. It shouldn't disturb Caelan, and it'd give me something to do while he investigated. Once my feet were bare, I dug my toes and fingers into the cool soil and closed my eyes.

CHAPTER
Fifteen

CAELAN

I'd never get tired of watching Evie commune with the earth. Her hair fell dark and loose around her shoulders, a wind I couldn't feel making the strands dance in the air. Magic the color of watermelon tourmaline swirled around her, roots snaking from the ground to curl up her calves. She was Earth incarnate, Mother Earth given form. A serene smile stole over her face, her lips slightly parted, and her cheeks flushed with color.

Goosebumps had risen over her skin, the chill in the air growing as the sun set.

I shifted back to human form, careful not to disturb her communion.

No trace of Gianna existed in this place. Yet an odd resonance pulsed through the land, warning trespassers something terrible had occurred here. Whatever Evie had done, she'd succeeded. It was almost like my short-term fiancée had never existed. I never liked the woman, and she'd never liked me, but many powerful partnerships were formed regardless of whether the spouses liked each other. Pity was my dominant emotion.

Her family would never be able to lay her bones to rest, but Evie had given her a warrior's send-off, returning her bones to the world that had borne her.

I dressed quickly and sat before Evie, not close enough to disturb her, but close enough to make her bitch at me when she opened her eyes. A smile curled my lips. Magic washed over me, strong enough that my sleeping wolf cracked an eye open in curiosity and stretched languidly.

Her power always soothed the wild beast living inside my body, bringing me a peace I'd never felt before. Hers was the magic of green things of life and growth, where mine would always be rooted in violence and power.

I shifted position to watch as Evie's magic soaked into the place that once held Gianna's violent grave, tourmaline colored magic spiraling up around the surrounding plant life before shattering in a rainbow of light.

Storm clouds rolled over the sky, stopping to center over our heads. The wind stilled, but Evie's hair kept dancing. An unnatural rumble of thunder sounded through the clearing, and a chill touched my spine at the power such a small woman could hold within her body. Did she know she could command the skies, or was this an odd side effect of what she was doing?

A cool drizzle touched my skin, soft but steady. Evie's brow furrowed, magic swirling around her like a maelstrom. She lifted her head, neck tilted back, water pouring down her skin.

I swallowed hard, desire roaring through my veins at how primal she looked.

Thunder clapped, a crack of sound in her woods. Seconds after, lightning streaked through the sky, arcing right toward Evie.

Sixteen

Today felt different. The leftover magic saturating the soil around Gianna's grave tainted my land. I couldn't believe I failed to sense it before, but neither had I communed with the land here, not so deeply as this. I sent power through the soil, destroying every tiny trace of foul magic I could find. Deeper and deeper I went, spiraling down toward the heart of the world, seeking and cleansing every piece of darkness away.

Whatever happened to Gianna had been terrible. The land gave me no visions, but a phantom pain pulsed through my bones, a lingering trace of terror resonating in my heart. Cool rain struck my face, but it wasn't enough to drag me from this task. I wouldn't stop until the land was fully mine once again.

Thunder rumbled through my body. A sharp metallic scent hit my nose, reminiscent of burnt electrical wires. But I kept going. I was almost there, had almost cleared away the scourge rotting the land around this place of death. The air went still and just as I touched the last piece of rot, white, burning light seared my vision.

Electricity snapped through my body, every muscle and nerve crackling with power. My body bent into an impossible arc as I sent that light down into the ground, and the last piece of that dark magic dissolved with a disturbing pop.

"EVIE!" A roar of sound and a solid body hit mine, separating me from the lightning.

I wrapped my arms around Caelan, protecting him from the backlash as the electricity roared around us, and opened my eyes. My toes were still locked into the dirt, and I let my magic pool out of my body, releasing all the extra power into the ground.

We lay tangled together in the middle of a storm, the once gentle rain beating around us in sheets. Caelan rested his forehead against mine, his breath coming in sharp heaves.

"You idiot," I croaked. "Don't you know you never touch someone who's being electrocuted?"

Caelan huffed a pained laugh. "It wasn't natural lightning. I thought I'd be safe."

"Even magical lightning can electrocute you, dummy." We lay smashed together, Caelan's heavy weight on top, his arms wrapped around my waist and mine around his. He wasn't wearing a shirt, my fingers touching lean, muscled, bare skin.

"We should get up," I said quietly. "The storm is dying down, and it's safe to move."

"Mmm," Caelan said. One of his dark eyebrows rose. "Or we could stay here for a little while and see what happens." His grin was contagious.

A laugh escaped me. "Get off, you oaf."

"Last chance, Evangeline. We're alone. Soaking wet, giving us the perfect excuse to slip out of our clothes." His lips hovered just above mine, his warm breath caressing my face.

I wanted to. Gods how I wanted to. But this was Caelan, a Shifter Lord, not a faceless man I could enjoy for a little while and never see again. He smelled of a winter forest and wild things, his eyes molten gold with desire.

Caelan brushed a wet strand of hair from my cheek and bent to nuzzle my neck. "Say yes, Evie." A hot kiss at the hollow of my throat, my collarbone, behind my ear. The slide of his hand down my waist, leaving a trail of heat in its wake.

I'd stopped being driven by most emotions years ago, though anger still got me these days. "We both know it's a bad idea," I said a little breathlessly.

Caelan smiled against my neck. "It's not bad right now, is it?"

Ass. We both knew this was great. "Getting involved with you would undermine everything I've built and put me under the Lord's control."

Caelan stilled. "You think I'd control you if we took this farther?"

"I think you'd try."

He grunted and popped his head up, a chill left behind where his lips had lingered. "Why are you so resistant to what's building between us?"

"Because you are who you are, and I am…me."

His eyes narrowed. "I think we both know that's only a small part of the reason." Caelan shook his head and sighed. "Then how about we get married?"

I laughed out loud. "You think getting married is better than a physical liaison?"

"I think if we get married, we could have more than one liaison." He grinned. "We could have liaisons multiple times a day."

Everything tightened inside of me. "Well, my point stands. And Cernunnos outlawed forced marriages, so once again I'm telling you no."

Caelan rose in a lithe movement and held his hand out. "You're right, but the Lords have not given up. They're wary of you and your involvement with the Chimera."

I wrung my shirt out and grimaced. "If Finn would stop coming around, I'd have no involvement with him." Or anyone else, I didn't add.

"Walk with me," Caelan commanded.

I bristled at his tone, but I wanted to get out of my wet clothes, so I dutifully followed him back to the house. Once we were inside, I tossed him a pair of joggers and an old t-shirt from the small pile of clothes I'd kept after my divorce. They wouldn't fit him well, but he'd be covered.

Caelan caught them and frowned. "More of your... husband's?"

"Would you rather be naked?" I snapped.

A slow grin curved his mouth. "Yes."

I couldn't stop my snort. "No! Get dressed. I'm going to get changed."

I hid my grin at Caelan's loud sigh of disappointment .

WHEN I RETURNED to the living room, Caelan was dressed and parked on the couch with a fresh cup of coffee in his hands and one for me sitting on the table.

"Is there anything else you want to tell me?" he asked as I curled into the opposite chair.

"Why would there be?"

His stare pinned me in place like an unfortunate bug in a science experiment. "No woman has ever been so resistant to my considerable charms."

My brows flicked up. "How unfortunate for you."

"This naturally means you are hiding something."

I counted to five in my head to stop myself from commanding one of my plants to stab him in the kidney. "And if it does? Are you not keeping secrets from me, Lord?"

His eyes darkened. "Yes, but I am a Lord. Secrets are a job requirement."

"And I am a person who doesn't divulge things about myself until I am in a committed, loving relationship, and I am secure in my trust of the other person."

Caelan studied me for a long moment. "And yet you resist this when I offer it to you."

I blinked, struck stupid by his words. "You have never offered this to me," I said slowly. "You've offered me sex, and you've offered me marriage."

The Shifter Lord sipped his coffee, a slight furrow between his brows. "I agree the sex offer doesn't include what you need, but why wouldn't the marriage offer?"

A crack of laughter escaped me. "Because you're offering so another Lord will think twice about doing the same thing!"

"So?"

My fingers tightened around my coffee mug, the urge to throw it at his smug face burning like a supernova in my veins. I took a deep breath and slowly let it out. "Have you ever had a long-term girlfriend?"

He frowned at the abrupt change in tactic. "Why?"

"Just answer the question before I plug you with a face full of ceramic."

Caelan grinned. "I wondered how long it would take you to get violent."

"Caelan!"

He sat back and studied me. "Fine. No. Not for any length of time."

"What was the longest relationship you had?"

His forehead wrinkled in concentration. "Three months."

"Would you have asked any of those women to marry you?"

"No," he said with zero hesitation.

"Why not?"

He shook his head. "I don't understand this line of questioning. Are you trying to get to an aha moment or something? That doesn't seem like you, not in this capacity."

I waited.

Caelan threw his hands up. "Because they never ticked my boxes. A Shifter Lord cannot marry just anyone, Evangeline. There are certain things a woman must possess to take a Lord as a spouse."

"But what about Caelan?"

His lips tightened. "What about me?"

"Think of yourself as only a man. Would the man have asked any of those women to marry him? If he wasn't a Lord or had any boxes he had to tick?"

"You are infuriating," he muttered. "Like a godsdamn mosquito buzzing around my face and biting me over and over and I'm too slow to kill it."

"Nice," I said dryly.

He let out a growl, his stormy eyes flashing with hints of gold. "I'm not sure what you want from me here, but no, I would not have asked any of those women to marry me even if I wasn't a Lord."

"Those women were temporary distractions, then?"

"I'm going to strangle you slowly," he snarled.

"I'm not asking because of jealousy or anything of the sort." And it was true. The thought of him being with a ton of women made my stomach tight, but I held no claim over him.

"Yes. I knew I'd never marry any of them."

"Then why on the gods' green earth would you ask me to marry you if not for the reasons I said? We have no relationship other than my contracts with the Keep. We've never been on a date or gone to dinner without wanting to strangle each other. On what planet do you think that makes us compatible? Admit it, Caelan. You want me because of my power. You want me because you see the other Lords coveting me. I'm in your territory and if I accept one of their offers, you will lose me. You see me as a boon to your own grip on this land, and if you secure my allegiance through marriage, you could be unstoppable."

Caelan's eyes narrowed. "You have a high opinion of yourself."

I almost laughed. "You know I can stand toe to toe with you."

"You haven't seen what I can do, flower girl. I've always shown great restraint with you."

I gave him a sharp smile. "Who says I haven't done the same?"

A considering look stole over his face. "Told you I knew you were keeping secrets."

"You aren't denying anything I said."

He sipped his coffee. "Because you aren't wrong."

Hurt stabbed me, a sharp knife in my gut. I fought to keep my expression neutral.

Caelan set his mug down and took mine from my hands. "But those are not the only reasons."

"Gosh. The romance. It burns."

Caelan snorted. Sliding calloused thumbs over the top of my hands, he looked into my eyes. "I am a Lord and always have to consider the good of my territory. So yes, you'd be good for me and my land. You already have been."

"Debatable."

"But you refuse to recognize there is more between us than duty. You cling to your identity and your secrets and refuse to believe I care or that I would stand beside you when you choose to reveal them."

"Some secrets are too terrible for another to bear."

Caelan froze. "Evie?"

I slid my hands from his and rose. "I'm tired. It's been a long day, and I still need to check my greenhouse."

"Just like that, this discussion is done?" Disapproval shimmered in his eyes. "Do you want pretty words, flower girl? Lovely words of adoration? Poetry written in the sky? Roses strewn at your feet, perhaps? Do you want to be wooed? Showered with diamonds and emeralds? Is that what you require?"

Every word he said was another dagger to the heart. I could not care less about any material thing. All I needed to be content was a few close friends and a plot of land to make my own. I wanted to walk in the woods and trail my fingers through fern fronds and run them against a tree's rough bark. But if I ever took a husband? Another one? I wanted; no, I needed so much more than I ever had before.

And so I laid my soul bare to Caelan for this one thing because he needed to understand I was not someone he could shove into a loveless box and abandon. "I want to be loved in a way that leads to madness. I want someone who cares more for me than anything else in the world. Someone who will choose to stand with me against the world when it comes for me. And it will, Caelan. Soon enough, my secrets will lay bare. Will it be you who stands with me? Or will I stand alone?" An eternity of sadness sank into my bones. "I know the answer, Lord. It's the same no matter who answers the question."

Caelan rose, his face a blank mask, and came so close our noses almost touched. "How little you think of me, flower girl." A snort of disgust and he was gone, out the door and off my property in a blur of speed that sent a spiral of fear through my bones.

CHAPTER
Seventeen

CAELAN

I sent the edict down less than twenty-four hours later.

All Shifter Lords were to be out of the Lord of Texas and the Borderlands' Territory within eight hours of receiving notice.

Soren sat in my study watching me carefully. "What happened?"

"Evie happened," I snarled.

"All terrible decisions do seem to stem from a woman," the other Lord said dryly.

When I sent him a dark look, Soren merely laughed. "I'll be out of your property within the hour, but this edict will raise some eyebrows among the others. Maybe not your precious Rowan, but Donovan will come sniffing around."

"Let him come." I was itching for a good fight anyway.

Seymour sat beside me, traps waving around like he was at a rave. He hadn't lunged for Soren, surprising both of us, though Soren knew better than to reach for him. The Red Dragon flytrap had shown a disturbing sentience and grew more intelligent as the days passed.

"Would you like to talk about it?" Soren asked, the whiskey tumbler he held glinting iridescent as the light hit the crystal.

"She flat out refuses to have anything to do with me," I said before I could zip my lips.

Evie was the most frustrating woman I'd ever met.

Soren's brows flicked up. "Even a carnal relationship?"

"She'd just as soon I never darken her doorstep than let me show her my dick."

Soren's laugh made me snarl softly. "Maybe your Floromancer needs a gentler wooing."

I told him what Evie said to me. Even repeating the words sent pain through my soul. What had happened to her to make her think such things? After everything, why would she think she'd stand alone?

Soren's expression sobered. "Someone has profoundly hurt your Evie. Do you know anything about her ex-husband?"

I didn't think her ex had everything to do with it, though he probably held some responsibility. "Not much on record. They were married for a while. The divorce was abrupt and went fast. Evie left without much of anything other than the clothes on her back."

"And now?"

"I believe he's remarried and has children."

Soren studied me. "How old are those children?"

I stilled as the dates clicked together in my head like the last puzzle piece, and a low curse tore from my throat. "That *sonofabitch*."

He held up a hand. "Infidelity can leave anyone heartsore for the rest of their lives, but a spouse having children with their affair partner can break someone." His face softened. "Especially if Evie wants children."

I was such an asshole. This wasn't everything. Evie's secrets were deep and held tightly, but this was yet another hit to her psyche.

"When did you become such a good person?" I groused.

Soren laughed. "I promise I'm no such thing. You see this on the inside, and I'm looking from the outside. I am not emotionally tied to your Floromancer. Not like you or Rowan."

My attention was a jagged thing. "Rowan?"

He grinned. "Murder lurks in your eyes, Caelan. Tone down the glow, please. Rowan has no designs on Evie that I can see, only a deep-seated need to protect her." Soren frowned. "From us, no doubt."

He scrubbed a hand over his face. "When did we become such insufferable jerks?"

"She likes Rowan best," I growled.

Soren rose and set his glass down. "Because he's not insufferable. Perhaps we should try it."

"Good luck trying that with the vampire," I said.

"Moira has no idea of the charm offensive coming her way," Soren said with a wink. He paused at the door. "Even I can see your Floromancer has a tender heart. She might possess a spine of steel, but it doesn't mean she is not vulnerable. If you wish to win her, you must first understand her. That is the way to her heart. Gain her trust, Caelan. The rest will follow."

I thought I had it, but apparently the gods were laughing at me for my blind assumption.

Soren slipped out, leaving me in a silent study, staring at the wall as I mulled over his words.

Gain her trust. The rest will follow.

CHAPTER
Eighteen

I awoke the next morning to a new shadow over my bedroom windows. Frowning, I reached out with my magic and probed the shadow, only to realize they were roses.

I had no roses on that side of the house. Confused, I rolled out of bed and opened the window.

A heady scent teased me as I peeked out, gawking at the insane growth of a pink double rose. "What the hell?" I whispered.

Careful not to shut any part of the plant in the window, I shut and locked it, then went to the kitchen to turn the coffee pot on. Thinking was hard without caffeine.

Once I was dressed and had a travel mug of coffee ready, I headed outside to track the errant growth.

As I came around the corner, I sucked in a breath. The entire side of the house was covered in blooms. The sight was stunning. Gorgeous multi-petaled roses grew up the siding and curled onto the roof, stems dripping with multiple flowers.

I touched the side of the house to check on the stability. While flowers and vines growing on a house can look beautiful, the weight can damage a dwelling quickly.

But the wood sighed with contentment. For now, it was happy, but where had the new growth come from? The only roses I had were by the green house. Carrying my coffee, I headed over only to stop in my tracks. Plants and vines poured from the greenhouse windows, the glass scattered all over the ground.

"Shit."

I held up a hand to open the door, only to see my palm flickering in and out of existence. What was happening to me? Willing my hand to stay in human form, I entered the greenhouse, almost surprised I had a clear path to walk through.

The place looked like a jungle. Every single plant inside was four times larger than it should be, even the new seedlings I'd planted only a few days ago.

Another side effect of merging with the Chimera. Yay. Fun.

With a sigh, I set my coffee mug down and got to work.

A FEW HOURS LATER, a vehicle pulled up. Moira, Tess, and Ash got out of the car and came to the greenhouse. Ash's eyes were wide.

"How much have you gotten done since this happened?" he asked.

"Twenty-five percent," I muttered. The most important thing was getting the plants away from the glass so I could have the windows repaired to keep the temperature regulated. The plants would be fine for now. Outdoor temperatures were dropping, but there was no chance of a freeze for at least the next several weeks.

Moira whistled low. "Did you lose control?"

"I woke up to this."

Tess floated around, investigating everything with her pale gaze. "Your magic is fluctuating. I can feel it pulsing around this place. You spend the bulk of your time here, soaking your plants in your power. I'm surprised this hasn't happened sooner."

"A hint would have been nice," I grumbled at Tess.

She sent me a serene smile. "I am a banshee. Not a magician."

Ash ducked to hide his grin.

"Right," I said. "How silly of me to forget."

Moira laughed. "I feel it too. This place is vibrating with power." She sent me a suspicious look. "How much more powerful are you now that you've opened yourself to the Chimera?"

I looked around at the greenhouse and shrugged. "I have to be extremely conscious when I'm working at the shop, but this was done during sleep when I have no control." I frowned. "Though I've never had such a slip during rest before."

Ash touched the side of the greenhouse and frowned, though he didn't look over at me. "Stand back," he said.

We obeyed instantly. Ash's magic was similar to mine, though his main domain was trees. My greenhouse was made of gathered oak that had fallen naturally. Ash's eyes glowed emerald, his power groaning into the wood.

A pop sounded in my ears before the pressure I hadn't realized was building up slowly drained away.

Ash patted the side of the greenhouse. "Poor thing. She was bloated with magic."

Too focused on the glass and the extra growth, I hadn't thought to check on the structure. "Thank you. I don't want to kill anything, so I've been trying to transplant most of the extra growth. If any of you want anything, feel free to take it."

"Have you called Simone?" Moira asked as she bent to size up an overgrown patch of French thyme. "She'll want some of these."

I thought about it. "I'll transplant some into pots and bring them to the Keep. I don't want her reporting back to Caelan about the current state of my jungle."

"I'll take whatever is left over," Tess said. She reached a pale finger out to touch a moonflower blossom, one that shouldn't be blooming this late in the morning.

"If you want some moonflowers, I have a massive bag of seeds in the house. You can take whatever you like."

We worked in silence for a while, everyone rolling up their sleeves to help me get things under control. A warm feeling settled into my chest as they helped carefully cut all the growth back and painstakingly pot each new plant baby.

By the time we finished, the sun was setting, we were all covered in dirt, and my magic had settled into a happy, contented hum. Maybe the problem wasn't that I was having issues with the new Chimera power. Maybe the issue was I was failing to burn off some of the excess and it was causing the excess to escape when I was unaware.

I sank onto the ground with a groan. "Wow."

Moira, Tess, and Ash all found a seat. "That was fun!" Moira said. "We haven't worked like that in ages." She wiped her dirty forehead with the back of her arm, leaving it worse than it was to start with. "Being at the shop is always fun, and I love working with all the smaller plants, but this place was a jungle!"

Ash grinned. "You're right. Maybe we should consider that when we talk about new offerings in the shop." He eyed me. "How are you feeling?"

"Ugh. I knew you'd sense it." I picked up a clod of dirt and tossed it at him.

Ash laughed and easily batted it away. "You look like your old self again. Dirtier, but healthy."

"I feel good," I admitted. "Really good."

My muscles were the kind of sore you get after a good but not too intense workout. The unending well of magic inside me slumbered like a tuckered-out kitten, and even the vicious Chimera's power felt quiet and still. Ash was right. I did feel like the old me, the one who existed before the Lords had come into my life.

But today I was less afraid, and I couldn't explain why. Maybe because I was coming to accept that I wasn't just one thing. I wasn't only a Floromancer, or only a demi-god, or only a Chimera. I was Evie, mixed up and still learning as I went.

And that was okay.

I'd spent the entire day avoiding thinking about Caelan and the hurt in his eyes when I told him what I needed. But I wasn't sorry about it. My confession was the truest thing I'd ever said to him. I wouldn't marry someone who didn't know me. But I wouldn't allow someone to know me until I had complete control of this thing living inside me. Even then, I wasn't sure I'd ever relax and open myself to trusting again.

Not after the divorce and Finn, and what happened to me afterward. Too many terrible events in such a short time had left an indelible mark on my soul.

Maybe in another life, I would give into my impulses with Caelan.

But not this one. Not now.

Ash reached over and touched my arm. "You're going to be okay."

I put my hand over his. "As long as you guys stick around, I'll be great."

Moira scooted closer. "You're never getting rid of us. We're like ticks, burrowed inside you."

"Gross," Tess said with a shudder. "Ticks live in my nightmares."

"Mine too," Ash said.

"I get what you're saying and thank you. You're stuck with me, too. Like peanut butter and jelly."

"Much better!" Tess grinned.

A shimmer of magic appeared in the air before us seconds before a scroll dropped into the middle of our grouping. Everyone froze.

A red satin ribbon with a thistle and a small bone kept the scroll together. The scent of a familiar woman floated up.

"Shit. It's from Rhona." But I made no move to collect the scroll.

"Can we ignore it?" Ash asked, brow furrowed in a wrinkle of distaste.

Tess reached over and snatched the scroll, carefully unwrapping the parchment.

"Broken keys still open doors," she read.

When she said nothing else, I frowned. "That's all it says?"

Tess turned the note around and showed us.

No signature. Only those few words. "I'm not sure what to make of that. Is she threatening me?"

Moira's lips pursed. "A broken key. Do we have one of those?"

"Not that I know of. Everyone has keys in their junk drawer to doors they no longer use. But keys are hard to break, aren't they?"

"Unless she's not talking about an actual key," Tess said. "Maybe Rhona is trying to open something."

A contemplative look stole over Moira's face. "Spells open things," she mused. "What could Rhona want to open and why would it concern you?"

The sound of breaking ceramic clattering in the greenhouse halted their conversation. I rose to my feet and put my finger to my lips. On silent feet, I crept to the greenhouse. The door was still open, and I poked my head in. Rustling greenery to the left caught my attention.

I stepped inside and used my magic to move some of the greenery aside. A rhythmic thumping came from deeper within until a deep red trap lined with "teeth" appeared above the greenery.

"Seymour?"

The thumping stopped abruptly, the plant's traps snapping shut.

I peered closer. "Oh no. You aren't Seymour at all, are you?"

There was a faint stripe of green atop its main trap. "Aren't you a pretty thing?"

Thump, thump, thump. In a few short moves, the flytrap stood before me, opening and shutting its trap. I reached for its pot only to realize it was broken.

"You tried to plant yourself," I whispered as I spotted its roots spilling out from the bottom of the ceramic and other roots gripping the sides to move itself. "How about I help you?"

Quivering traps told me yes; it would like that very much. I scooped up the flytrap and cradled it in my arms. Before going to the potting bench, I poked my head out the door.

"All good!" I called. "A new friend popped in to say hello."

Everyone cooed when I held out the new flytrap.

"That's not Seymour!" Ash said.

"Did he have babies?" Tess asked, floating over to take a closer look.

"I don't think so, but I'll ask Caelan. Give me a few. I need to repot this poor little guy."

"I want to watch!" Moira said.

In the end, the new Red Dragon flytrap found itself in an adorable blue and white ceramic pot dotted with flowers. And I was left wondering how the hell another sentient flytrap had found its way to me when I hadn't created it. Not technically. My magic burned inside the plant clear as day, but another whisper of power clinging to its roots held me in awe.

My power dominated, but Caelan's power was somehow mixed in its roots.

How had this happened?

Moira and the others had gone home a little while ago, leaving me in the greenhouse finishing up a few things. The flytrap kept me company as I swept up the rest of the glass, occasionally thumping its pot when I got too far away.

When I finished, I scooped the pot up and headed back to the house.

"You have to be careful," I lectured the flytrap. "Your pot will break if you jump too high and land too hard. I need to put you on the shelf where there's extra light. Okay?"

It waved its traps in agreement.

Suddenly, I realized where it had come from. "You little minx. Did you escape from the Keep?"

More trap waving. Shaking my head at its naughtiness, I reached for my cell and sent a message.

I have something of yours.

The response came quickly. *My heart? My soul?*

I couldn't stop my laugh. Instead of responding, I snapped a quick picture of the flytrap and sent it to him.

How did it get there?

No idea. I found it in the greenhouse.

It's not an it. She's a girl.

I smiled. *Oh?*

Strong feminine energy. Jealousy when Seymour came around. It makes sense. She couldn't take not having me all to herself anymore.

Idiot.

It's true. Want me to come around and get her?

If you want her back, you're welcome to send Simone by the shop tomorrow.

The response took longer this time.

If I choose to come myself?

You can come if you want. But she's in good hands.

I'll see you tomorrow, flower girl.

I didn't respond. And the leap my pulse took was merely due to the a/c being turned down too low.

Nineteen

On my way out the door the next morning, I scooped the flytrap up and settled her into a small plastic tub, tucking old newspaper around the pot to keep it secure. But as I carried the tub to the car, the flytrap wiggled and jumped clean out, landing with a hard crack on the ground.

I gasped and dropped the tub. "No! Are you okay?"

But the plant ignored me and thumped over to the edge of the greenhouse where it reached down with one of its traps and nudged at the ground.

I hissed. "Be careful! What's wrong with you?"

Bending, I gently scooped up the plant and brushed away the dirt where she'd been digging. Something small, round, and iridescent glinted up. At first, I thought it was a pearl, but when I reached for it, a living hum of magic pulsed from the ground.

Curious, I carefully picked up the round object and held it in the palm of my hand.

"A seed," I murmured. A kind I'd never seen before.

"Why'd you bring me to this?" I asked.

No response from the flytrap. "Come on, then. Let's get to the shop. Maybe someone else will know what it is."

The drive to Little Shop of Florals was uneventful, though the plant vibrated the tub in excitement. I reached over and stroked her traps.

"Hannibal is a good name, but you aren't a boy. At least according to Caelan. How about Hannah?"

More quivering traps. I laughed and pulled into the parking spot right in front of the store. "Hannah it is then."

Moira held the door open and locked it behind me when I walked in. She greeted Hannah with a smile and a wave. Tess floated over and scooped Hannah up, taking her over to the shelf by the window. "You can't jump around when people come in, okay? Not if they're human. Do you know what a human is?"

Hannah bounced her pot.

I grimaced. "Maybe it was a bad idea to bring her here. If she starts thumping around the shop, we might have an incident on our hands."

"She understands," Tess said.

Moira and I exchanged a look that said, is it me or is she getting stranger?

"How do you know?" Moira asked.

"She was created from a piece of Evie, and I know Evie's soul." When Tess glanced back, her eyes shone silver.

Yep. Definitely stranger.

"Well. Alrighty then," Moira said. "Thumper, no thumping."

Hannah waved her traps around as Tess adjusted her position so she could get more light. "There you go. That should be perfect for you."

Ash came in from the back and stopped abruptly. "What is that?" His words weren't a question.

"Hannah?" I pointed to the shelf. "She's hanging out for a little while until Caelan comes around to collect her."

"No. Not that." His eyes glowed. "You brought something into the shop. Something new. What is it?"

I blinked. "Um. The tub? It's plastic which I normally don't use, but it's good to transport plants around in."

Ash came closer, his gaze sweeping over my face. "No. You've brought something dangerous into this store, Evie."

"Dangerous?" I laughed and flexed my biceps. "Just these two guns."

"Evie. I'm serious."

He rarely sounded so grim, so I stopped joking around. "Um." I patted my pockets. "Oh! I forgot." I dug into my pants pocket and pulled out the small seed. Perfectly round, a shimmer of magic surrounding its hard shell. "Hannah dug it out from close to the greenhouse."

Ash sucked in a breath. "Evie. Do you know what you have?"

"A seed, but I've never seen its type before."

"Because there's only one." He tipped his hand palm up. "May I?"

"Of course." I carefully tipped the seed into his hand.

Ash's lips pursed into a silent o. A boom of sound came from outside the shop.

"Say nothing," Ash hissed, the seed gone in the blink of an eye.

I opened my mouth to speak, but the door crashed open, glass shattering into fine powder. Moira barked a command, an impenetrable, transparent wall appearing a split second before we were sliced into a million pieces.

No one said a word for a long moment.

My mother stood right outside the doorway.

I needed more coffee for this.

"Invite me in," the goddess Cliona said. No good morning, no platitudes, no pretending she was here to see how I was doing.

Mom was pissed.

I responded accordingly. "You just broke an expensive door, and you want to sit down for tea? That's not how it works."

"Evangeline. Drop your wards and invite me in. We will not have this conversation with me standing in the street."

Cliona was a stunning goddess. Dark shining hair spilled down her shoulders, and her azure eyes, the same as mine, sparked with both magic and temper. Her face looked like the work of a master sculptor, every part of it smooth and lovely.

Too bad she was a massive bitch.

"Again. No. If you cause a scene, you'll scare the humans. What do you want, Mother?"

Cliona's delicate nostrils flared. "You have something of mine."

Fee. Had she found out about the phoenix? "I'm not sure what you're talking about. I covet nothing of yours."

"Open the door," Cliona growled, the first real sign of anger she allowed herself to show.

"I don't have anything of yours. There. See? No need for us to sit down and chat."

"Where is it?" Magic glowed around my mother.

The first stirrings of real unease churned in my stomach. I was very glad it was early enough for everyone in Joy Springs to still be tucked into bed. If Mom got it in her head to destroy my wards, she'd have a chore on her hands, but they would fall.

I wasn't a goddess. Mom was ancient, extraordinarily powerful, and pissed off at me.

"Tell me what you're looking for, and I'll tell you if I have it." A dangerous game, but I'd perfected my lying game over the years. Even she could rarely tell when I was lying through my teeth.

"A seed," Mother said. "It is *mine*."

What in the actual hell had Hannah unearthed? I frowned. "I have a ton of seeds in the shop, but none of them are important enough for a goddess to seek."

"Do not play games with me, child. I am your mother. You belong to me."

"Ah. I was wondering when you'd drop all pretense of being a loving, caring mother. I don't have what you seek."

"I tracked it here!" she snapped.

Note to self. Do not pick up shiny seeds and bring them to work.

Moira stepped forward. "There has been more car traffic than usual this morning. Do you still sense the seed?"

I stepped closer to Moira in case Mom struck out at her.

Mom's brow furrowed. She tried to step into my shop and was repelled by the warding.

Her eyes glowed with rage. "Evie! Let me in!"

I stepped in front of the vampire. "Answer Moira's question. Do you still sense the seed?"

Mom's jaw tightened. "You are hiding it from me. Do not make me hurt you, daughter."

"Over a seed?" I laughed even as horror sparked in my veins.

"It is not—" Mom pressed her lips together and went silent.

What the hell was this seed and why was it so important to her? If Mom wanted it so badly, I knew she could never have it.

"I'm hiding nothing. Whatever you sensed must have passed by the shop. There's nothing in here but the plants I've nurtured and created." I held a hand out and swept it across the shop. "You're welcome to scan if you'd like."

I hoped and prayed Ash had hidden the seed well enough to escape her notice. When the dryad didn't react, the first stirrings of hope unfurled within me.

Mom's cold magic brushed over my skin, the power seeking something I no longer had. She did the same with Moira, but when she got to Ash, I held my breath until her power slipped away and swept through the shop. When she pulled her power back, no one said a word.

"I know you have it," she said in a cold voice.

I lifted both arms in a casual shrug. "Whatever you're looking for isn't here."

Another boom of sound from outside. Cliona stiffened and slowly turned.

"There you are." Neit's masculine drawl from somewhere on the street. "If I didn't know better, I'd say you were avoiding me."

My mother's posture went liquid, her magic silent. "Neit. How wonderful to see you."

His snort of disgust made my mother's slim shoulder stiffen.

"You've always been good at pretty lies, Cliona."

Neit came into view. His dark eyes were filled with lazy amusement as his gaze raked over me first, then settled on my mother. "Your daughter has your eyes," he mused. "Though her temperament is far different from your cool grace."

Um. Thanks. I think?

"Evie has always been full of fire," my mother said. "But you aren't here for Evie."

"No," Neit agreed. "I am not." He held out his arm, elbow crooked at ninety degrees. "Come, Cliona. It is time for us to catch up."

Mom didn't take his arm right away. Her posture stiffened. "This is not a good time for me."

"Whatever it is you're looking for, Evie said she does not have it. She has no reason to lie." His head cocked, a violet spark in his eyes as he turned his attention to me. "Is there?"

I swallowed. Mom was turned away and couldn't see my face, thank goodness. But Neit somehow knew I was lying through my teeth. "Of course not."

"See?" he said to Cliona. "Now come. There are things we must discuss."

When my mother still resisted, Neit's eyes tightened. He moved close to her and leaned in. "Do not make me force you in front of your child."

Mom turned, her face in profile, and for the first time in my long life, a touch of true fear touched her face. "Very well," she said, not an inch of the emotion in her voice. "Since you are so insistent."

Neit's lips tilted. With a lingering look at me, he disappeared with Cliona, the overwhelming power stifling the air finally gone.

I spun. "What the hell is that seed?"

"Not here," Ash said quietly. "We'll meet you at your house after work."

"Where is it?"

Ash's eyes glowed. "Safe."

He refused to answer any other questions and finally said he was going to get more coffee, leaving us standing there staring at each other with befuddled expressions.

"He doesn't want us to talk about it, so we should respect his wishes." Moira shook her head when I opened my mouth. "Ash rarely gets so serious."

"Tonight then. I'll order pizza."

Tess floated after Ash without responding.

"Neit is hot," Moira mused.

"Mmm. They're all hot, aren't they? Everyone with magic rolling through their veins is hard to look at." I rolled my eyes. "The men are so pretty. It's ridiculous."

"The women are too."

"The men have a dangerous edge, though. We're just pretty."

Moira laughed. "That's because we don't use violence unless we have no other choice. Men are just naturally pissed off all the time."

I rubbed a hand over my face. "Moira." The urge to spill all my secrets rose. I was keeping so many things held tightly inside and more and more anger rose every time a situation I was involved in spiraled out of control.

The vampire leaned forward and put her hand over mine. "Do you want to wait until tonight? Or is this something you only want to share with me?"

I'd always been closest with Moira, but what was happening with me affected everyone. "Alright."

Moira rose and brought me in for a tight hug. "Maybe add some booze with the pizza," she said against my hair.

"Another doozie of a night," I agreed.

Twenty

Full of pizza and beer, I dug my bare toes into the carpet and stretched. Ash and Tess lay tangled together on the couch, the dryad trailing a lazy finger through Tess's hair. Moira sat cross legged on the lounge chair, and I'd chosen the loveseat because it had a cup holder.

And I was currently on my fourth glass of wine, mentally applauding my foresight because the others had to shift position or, *gasp*, sit up to reach their booze, and all I had to do was pick it up and shift it a few inches to my mouth.

Music played through the Bluetooth speakers, one of Moira's numerous playlists, this one with hours of mixed genre music. We needed tonight, the chance to get together and take a load off for a little while.

The seed's shadow hung over us, no one wanting to broach tonight's peace. But we needed to talk about it. Whatever this was felt big. A portent of doom hung over our heads. Overdramatic? Six months ago, I would have said yes. Now? Everything felt like a portent of doom these days.

"Got any dessert?" Moira said.

Ash snorted. "I'm convinced your stomach and the Mary Poppins purse are related."

Moira patted her flat stomach. "It is bigger on the inside."

"You're lucky it's not bigger on the outside," Ash said, laughing when Moira tossed a napkin at him.

He shifted Tess and sat up. "Thanks for this evening. It's been far too long since we've all hung out like this."

"We see each other every day," Tess said. "But that's work. This is…friendship." She blinked owlishly. "It's nice."

I made a mental note to gather everyone at the house at least once a month in the future. "Then we'll do it more often," I vowed.

"I'll bring the wine!" Moira grinned and reached for her glass.

"Snacks are on us," Ash said, winking at Tess.

"Oooh, you're officially an 'us' now?" Moira teased.

The dryad tugged Tess closer. "Official," he confirmed.

"Yay!" I lurched from my seat, swayed, and reached for Ash and Tess, dragging them into a sloppy hug.

Moira snickered. "Oh yeah. I'm definitely bringing the wine next time." She uncurled herself from the chair and plopped beside me, throwing her arms over us.

We sat hugging each other for a while until Ash groaned and waved us away. "Let's put the wine down and chat."

"No," Moira whined. "Let's keep drinking and order sundaes."

I raised my index finger in the air. "Seconded!"

Ash rolled his eyes. "Next time we won't have such a serious thing to talk about. But tonight, we must discuss your finding."

"Not mine." I jerked a thumb over my shoulder to the flytrap gnawing on my hair. "Hannah uncovered it. She sensed something there and went straight to it."

The flytrap had proven adept at getting herself from point a to point b, and I didn't always see her move. Nor did I hear her either, but when I did, the thump, thump, thump of her pot was easily identifiable. It was when I didn't hear her, and she suddenly appeared somewhere that made me nervous.

"She's an extension of your magic," Ash said quietly, eyes

intent on the plant. "I believe you might have eventually sensed the same, but your attention has been divided. For months now."

I grimaced. "True. Sorry."

"No need to apologize. It is what it is. You don't commune with your land as deeply as you used to, not all of it."

I glanced at him sharply. "How do you know that?"

"I sense it."

At my freaked-out look, he laughed. "Your land is content and healthy. No need to worry there. What I'm saying is the land is hungrier than normal, and you might have sensed the seed sooner if you communed as often as you used to."

"You are really good at making me feel guilty," I muttered, even as I knew he was right. I communed with my land as often as I could, but I still felt its yearning. Part of me felt like I might sully my property with my Chimera magic—a foolish thought, but shaking it proved more difficult than expected.

Magic was magic was magic as Ash so often reminded me. It wasn't the power itself, only the wielder. Finn was evil in a way, but he'd also shown up to warn us about Rhona's presence. Probably to save his own ass, but by extension, he was saving ours, so I guess that would be a good deed. The jury was still out.

"You're an excellent steward of the land," Ash said. "It will always hunger for your presence no matter how often you feed the property. I'm only saying the seed appeared when it needed to. Perhaps it would not have appeared to your senses sooner. I'm merely speculating."

Moira leaned forward. "Tell us why you're being so cagey about this seed."

"And where it is," I added, promising myself I'd do better when it came to my Floromancy. I had some ideas about that, thoughts brewing in the back of my mind after I'd woken up to my greenhouse in chaos.

Ash was right about the magic, as he was right about most things, and I needed to siphon off my power more often now that the Chimera was rearing its ugly head more often.

Ash shifted, his eyes glowing emerald. "You may want to shield your eyes."

"Absolutely not," Moira said. "We've never seen you do what I think you're about to do!"

I shook my head. "Blind away, tree boy."

"Don't say I didn't warn you."

Ash's chest exploded in brilliant, verdant light, searing my eyeballs. Lifting his left hand, he reached inside the opening in his heart and pulled out a pearlescent, perfectly round seed.

"Holy shit," Moira breathed. "You stuck it in your *heart*?"

"Bad ass," Tess murmured.

"It's connected to your heart tree." As a dryad, Ash had a special connection to his main tree and had to return periodically to refresh his physical and emotional health, boosting his magic each time he went. Its location remained a tightly held secret, and none of us asked. If Ash's tree were damaged, the dryad would sustain the same pain. If the tree died…

None of us would ever ask its location because we loved Ash, and we wouldn't risk a slip up or being used against him.

But to be able to store something inside of what was essentially a magical storage chest that doubled as a teleporter was so cool. I didn't have a heart tree or anything of the sort, but I could hide something so deep in the heart of the earth even a mole couldn't find it. Not exactly the same as pulling something from my freaking heart, but pretty cool, nonetheless.

The seed lay on Ash's palm, glowing but inert. We all leaned forward and peered down.

"What does it do?" Tess asked.

Ash's expression sobered. "This tiny seed has the potential to end the world."

I sucked in a breath. "What?"

Moira gave him a considering look. "It's not like you to be dramatic, Ash."

"I can't be completely sure, but when your mother showed up, I had a good feeling I knew why she wanted this little guy."

I had no idea why she wanted it. All I knew was if she sought it, I wouldn't give it to her.

"The tree to the other worlds must be dying," Ash said. "If this seed has arrived, it foretells the death of the world tree."

A long moment dragged on as I stared at him in stark disbelief. Everyone was aware of the world tree in a roundabout way. The tree represented interconnectedness and held the doorways to the other realms. If the world tree died, it would shut the other gods away, trapping them in their realms.

No wonder Cliona wanted the seed.

I held my palm out. "May I?"

Ash tipped the seed into my hand.

My breath caught and held. The seed shimmered as I rolled it around my palm, the amount of magic inside its shell staggering.

I brought both hands together, closer to my lips.

"Evie—" Ash warned.

Closing my eyes, I sent a frisson of power out, seeking to connect, to understand.

Every plant in the house responded, a verdant scent of life growing throughout the room. Vines stretched and flowers bloomed, healthy dirt and greenery a sharp tang in my nose.

The seed pulsed with a royal blue light, peaceful and calm. Vines crawled over the ceiling and the couch, seeking to connect with its power.

"What do you want from me?" I whispered.

An astonishing amount of natural magic flared through the room. Familiar power.

"Gird your loins," I murmured.

The king of the fae appeared in the room, his presence larger than life. Cernunnos was massive, well over six feet. His hair was the soft color of doeskin, cascading past his shoulders and twisted with moss and several varieties of mushrooms. The fae king's eyes glowed with ancient power, his irises swirling with gold and silver sparks. Even though I'd known he wasn't of this world by his physical appearance, it was the antlers, twisted with moss and greenery, drops of dew on the tips, rising several feet above his head that marked his identity.

How he hadn't torn a hole in my roof by his arrival was one of those unexplainable miracles.

Ash's face paled. He went to his knees and bowed his head.

"Rise," Cernunnos demanded. "My people do not supplicate or worship, dryad. You are a loyal steward of my lands, and I am proud to call you one of mine."

Ash rose, his hands trembling. Moira and Tess had already stood. I still sat on the loveseat; the seed curled in my palms.

Cernunnos made his way over and sat down beside me. Ash and the others retook their seats.

The seed pulsed bright green before fading back into deep blue.

The king of the fae smiled. "You've chosen a loyal vessel."

I blinked. "Are you speaking to me or the seed?"

He held his palm out. Wordless, I passed it over, the color switching from blue to emerald-green. "Does it change color based on who holds it?"

"The seed is sentient. It does what it wishes. But…in a way, I suppose it does. Your magic comes from different places. Mine has always belonged to the soil and skies."

"What is it?" Moira asked, her eyes glued to Cernunnos' antlers.

"This," he announced, his voice rumbling like a summer thunderstorm, "is our beginning and our end."

Cernunnos coaxed my plants to come closer, the fae king's magic a brush of warmth over my shoulders. A soft hum of music floated through the air, and I smiled.

Tess gasped. "Is that—"

"The natural world," Cernunnos said. "Plants and trees communicate via sound and vibration. Evangeline's plants are tended with care and well-loved."

One of my older pothos brushed against Cernunnos' cheek,

making the king chuckle. "And very curious." He reached a tan finger up and brushed the underside of its leaves.

Several vines stopped inches away from the seed, the greenery vibrating in anticipation.

"Do they know what this is?" I asked.

"Oh yes. The seed is from the heart of the universe. Everything from the natural world will recognize what this is."

Cernunnos' attention lingered on the door. "You're about to have a visitor."

Two sharp knocks sounded.

"It's creepy how you do that," I muttered.

Cernunnos's toothy grin made me laugh. Moira waved me away as I started to rise. "I'll grab it."

A moment later, Moira stepped away from the door.

Caelan walked in, and silence so thick you could cut it settled around the room.

"Don't be rude, Evangeline," Cernunnos said quietly when I stared at the Shifter Lord dumbly.

Nothing could extinguish Cernunnos's raw power, but Caelan's magic thundered through the room, his violent nature rearing its head as he spotted the Fae King next to me. A golden sheen rolled over Caelan's eyes.

"Why are you still here?" I hissed to the fae king. "Don't you disappear when things get weird?"

Amusement glimmered in his ancient eyes. "Your Lord needs to hear this as much as your friends do."

Caelan's gaze dropped to the king's cupped palm. His eyes narrowed. "What are you holding?"

"A nuclear bomb," Cernunnos said, a toothy smile crossing his handsome face.

Caelan came closer. A soft thumping sound came from behind before Hannah leapt from the back of the couch, straight at the Shifter Lord.

A soft oof, and Caelan caught Hannah's pot, cradling the flytrap against his chest. "Well, hello there."

"I meant to text you, but the day got away from me. "

"She has a brand-new pot, so her journey worked out, I suppose." Caelan walked to the kitchen table and pulled a chair away, carrying it over to the living room. "When I saw the shop closed, I figured I'd head here."

Hannah waved her traps around.

"She's happy to see you." I frowned. "Hannah is much happier than Seymour was when he was young."

Caelan's gaze rose to me. "Hannah?"

"Evie named her after Hannibal Lecter." Moira grinned.

Caelan's laughter was deep and genuine. "Little cannibal." His voice held genuine affection.

Cernunnos gently clearing his throat made us all still.

"Sorry," I hissed. "But look at how cute Hannah is."

"She's very cute," Cernunnos confirmed. "But let's get back to the nuke I'm holding."

Caelan set Hannah down. "You're holding a seed. I'm supposed to believe that thing holds enough power to destroy us?"

"Your power belongs to the animal kingdom, Lord." His lips curved up. "And elsewhere, doesn't it?" Cernunnos tipped the seed back into my hand. "I know you sense the magic, but your kind can never feel its innate power."

"If I can't sense the power, how am I supposed to assist?"

Another enigmatic smile. "You are here to assist Evangeline."

My attention snapped to Cernunnos's face. "Excuse me?"

The fae king rose, moss swinging from his antlers. "No one is safe while your mother searches for the seed. You must keep it safe."

A sudden, horrific thought occurred to me. "She doesn't want to plant this, does she?"

Cernunnos's eyes flashed. "Your mother is no Floromancer. The seed came to the one being who holds the power to nurture and care for the power. Evangeline, you've been entrusted as a steward to hold the power of the gods."

"No pressure," Moira muttered.

I kept my pulse as steady as I could with that earth-shattering comment. "You said something earlier about being a vessel. What do you mean?"

Golden magic shimmered around the fae king. "When the time is right, you will know what to do. In the meantime, keep our power safe."

Caelan shook his head. "Aren't you the best steward? You're the fae king."

Cernunnos's form began to shimmer. "It hasn't chosen me, Lord. Even if I took the seed from Evie, it would come back to her sooner rather than later." His ancient gaze fell on me once more. "Trust only those in this room, Evangeline."

He winked. "Even your Shifter Lord."

A second later, he was gone.

No one said a word for a long moment.

Caelan shifted. "So…I guess I'm a member of the club now?"

CHAPTER
Twenty-One

"Just because Cernunnos told me to trust you doesn't mean I'm going to." I stared at the troublemaking seed in my palm and wondered why in the world it had chosen me. There were hundreds, maybe thousands, of people more capable than I.

All I needed was a break, not world-shattering trouble, and I had a feeling I wasn't going to get any kind of break for a long, long time.

"Should Ash store it again?" Moira asked.

I thought it over before shaking my head. "No. It's too dangerous. Ash's tree is too important for us to risk letting him store something this important."

"What about the Keep?" Caelan asked.

"As fortified as your Keep is, my mother can sense the presence of this seed. My wards are the only thing keeping her out. It's safest here."

Caelan frowned. "Unless you provide the same wards for the Keep. We have a lot more places to hide something of this power. My Pack will guard it with their lives."

"You already have Fee."

"Yes," he agreed. "And she's having the time of her life in the skies with Poe. But those two things are not alike."

"Right. This one might blow up the world." I closed my fingers around the seed. "It's not a good idea. If she discovers Fee, she'll discover the seed. Vice versa. I can't put you in that kind of danger. Asking you to keep Fee was bad enough."

Caelan took Cernunnos' place, an odd look on his face. "You aren't the only powerful thing in this room."

"That isn't the point. Cernunnos said the seed would return to me. Even if I gave it to you, it wouldn't stay."

Ash had been suspiciously silent until now. "She's right. The seed will return to her. Evie is the only one who can keep it safe."

Caelan's jaw tightened. "Then what do we do?"

Moira's brow furrowed. "Can you disguise it somehow? Hide it in an arrangement and ward the shit out of it? Or maybe put it in a piece of jewelry so your magic will disguise its power?"

"Mom knew where it was not long after I brought it into the shop, even with the warding up."

Excitement lit her eyes. "Because you brought the thing in unprotected. But if we ward the seed, wrap it in so much magic its signature is disguised by your magic and by ours, I think we might be able to pull it off."

Ash was nodding to himself. "It could work. We'd need to find a piece of jewelry—"

"I'll take care of it," Caelan said.

Moira pressed her lips together, eyes sparkling with mirth.

"Nothing ridiculous," I snapped. "Something simple, Caelan. Cheap. Something I can wear on a day-to-day basis. Alright?"

He held both hands up, his face screaming innocence. "Of course. I am yours to command."

"No diamonds or rare stones or anything to make me stand out. Simple and elegant and on a chain or ring or bracelet that I won't lose."

Caelan's nostrils flared. "A ring?"

I pinched the space between my brows. "Do not make this weird."

"Oh, he's going to make it weird," Moira said with delight.

"So weird," Tess said. She leaned closer to Ash. "Can you use my magic too?"

Ash blinked. "Of course. Why wouldn't we?"

Tess dropped her eyes. "Mine is volatile. My true magic. Not the small things I do around the shop."

"Tess. Yes. We'll infuse the jewelry with a part of each of us, and you are always included."

A pretty pink blush colored her cheeks. "Thank you."

"And me?" Caelan growled. "What about me?"

I opened my mouth to say absolutely not, but there was a look in his eyes, and a hopeful look on his face that gave me pause. Caelan made me so snappy all the time, it became my first instinct to deny him. But this was a small ask. And Cernunnos had told me to trust him.

"Do you want to be included?" I asked quietly.

The Lord swallowed. "I do."

I felt like I stood on the opposite side of a chasm from Caelan, and this moment would start building a bridge between us. Whether that was good or bad, only time would tell. "Then consider it done. Procure the jewelry and once we have it and see what we're working with, then we'll put together the spell."

I turned to the others. "Will that work?"

Ash and Moira gaped at me. The vampire was the first to recover. "Uh. Yes. Caelan will need to be there for the spell. Right, Ash?"

"Yes. Until then, I don't think Evie should leave her land."

At my strangled protest, Ash shook his head. "This is too important, and we can't risk Cliona coming back to the shop. We'll open the store tomorrow."

He focused on Caelan. "It's a lot to ask, but can you have something ready by tomorrow evening?"

The Shifter Lord didn't hesitate. "Yes. Meet here at seven?"

Everyone agreed and started cleaning up the remnants of dinner. Ash, Tess, and Moira headed out, Caelan lingering behind. He stopped on the porch, right by the front door.

The warm light of the porch picked up the gold highlights in his eyes; the smoke blue of his sweater, setting off the stormy gray irises. His dark hair brushed against the collar, and he shoved one hand into the pocket of his dark blue jeans, the other holding Hannah.

"Thank you."

I tilted my head. "For what?"

"For not dismissing me. I want you to know you can trust me and my Pack. It's not often someone in town has the ability to take us all on, and we'd rather work together than be enemies."

How much of this was sincere and how much was him trying to placate me? Or force my hand? I hated how suspicious I was all the time, but the paranoia served me well most of my life, and it was difficult breaking habits. Especially since I wasn't sure of his angle, if there was one at all.

"You normally kick people out of town who have the ability to challenge you, don't you?"

He slowly nodded. "I do. But those people also want my power. They aren't content to run a flower shop."

"You aren't afraid I'll one day grow mad with power and come after you?"

Caelan's teeth glinted. "I'd like to see that. Could be fun."

I leaned against the door jam. "You're right. I don't care about amassing power. I'd been here for years before you came into my shop."

Caelan fished his keys from his pocket. "I wish I would have known you sooner."

My heart did an annoying little skip thump. "So we could be fighting for years instead of months?"

His lips tipped in a smile. "I don't think we'll be fighting for years, flower girl. Something's gotta give before then."

I watched as he turned and headed toward the vehicle. "See you soon, Evangeline."

Shaking my head, I went back inside and shut the door. Freaking shifters.

Twenty~Two

CAELAN

I'd made it all of three steps before the Fae King appeared by my vehicle, his antlers gone, dressed in a pair of joggers and a t-shirt. My footsteps slowed, and I watched him warily.

"Lord," Cernunnos said.

"Why'd you do it?" I asked, unable to keep the question to myself.

"Why do the fae do anything?" he said, wearing an enigmatic smile.

I shook my head and kept walking, eager for a shower and my bed.

"Evie has many challenges coming her way," Cernunnos said when he realized I wasn't going to answer his question. "She needs strong allies in her corner."

"I would have gained her trust eventually." Believing that was one of the few things keeping me going. Now that I knew more of Evie's background, her reticence made a lot more sense.

"Not soon enough." Cernunnos jerked ahead toward Evie's house. "You love her."

It wasn't a question. "And if I do?"

"She isn't ready to accept how you feel about her. Evie is... damaged."

My lips pulled away from my teeth. "She is not damaged goods," I snapped.

Cernunnos's eyes swirled with unfathomable magic. "You misunderstand. Her heart is damaged, and she does not trust people, with good reason. If someone is to be with her, they must accept all of her."

The fae king tilted his head and studied me, his power cleaving me to the bone. Cernunnos didn't harm me, but I stood there under his judgment, knowing he saw everything about me. "You are not ready to do so."

"You don't know a thing about my heart."

Cernunnos straightened to his full height, the antlers reappearing on his head. Above us, the sky opened, revealing a host of transparent warrior riders and animals the likes of which I'd never seen before.

The Wild Hunt. I stood there awestruck by his simple display of unfathomable power, knowing if Cernunnos ever decided to strike me down, I was helpless to defend myself.

"I know everything about you, Shifter Lord." His voice rumbled across Evie's land. "And I know you will lose her if you aren't ready to bear her pain."

"You know what she's hiding." I stopped at the driver's side door, watching him carefully. "Why would she tell you and not me?"

Cernunnos laughed. "She told me nothing, young child. Evie clings to her secret as a child would their blanket."

"Why are you so interested in her?" I'd been wondering this for months now and hadn't come up with a single thing other than Evie's powers. Cernunnos ruled over green things and Evie was a Floromancer. Was she under his rule or was there something else going on?

"Humans have a custom. I think you call it meddling in-laws. Is that correct?"

I stilled. "In-laws." He couldn't actually be saying what I thought he was saying.

"Consider me a meddler," Cernunnos said.

A moment later, a massive stag stood before me, its antlers dripping with moss and magic. Before I could respond, the stag leapt into the air to rejoin the Hunt, and the skies closed, leaving me alone in Evie's driveway wondering what the hell was going on.

In-laws. That meant...

No. Surely not.

Twenty~Three

I spent most of the day in the greenhouse, doing my best to clear my head of any stress and worry over the seed and what its appearance in my life might mean. It worked, for the most part, but when the sun began to set over the horizon, all the worry crawled back into my heart.

Everyone would arrive in a couple of hours. I stomped my boots on the outdoor rug and shook out my hair and jacket before heading inside and straight to the showers.

I had a lot of spell-woven protections against ticks and other bitey things, but I could never protect against everything. Occasionally a spider or some other creature ended up hitching a ride back to the house.

After a delightful shower and a scrub that left me pink from head to toe, I dressed, leaving my hair wet for now, and went into the kitchen to start dinner. Magic expended a lot of energy, so I planned something protein and carb heavy: chicken fried steak, homemade mac and cheese, and balsamic-glazed, roasted Brussels sprouts. We'd eat first, then cast the spell to ward the seed until I knew its purpose and how it wished to be used.

The next hour passed in a blur. Folk rock poured from the Bluetooth speaker as I finished the last of the food prep. Everyone would be here in forty-five minutes which gave me enough time to finish drying my hair and put some magic appropriate clothing on.

Once that was finished, I went and unlocked the door for Moira, who always arrived early. I took care of some necessary plant maintenance, and when that was done, I prepped a large skillet, dipped the first steak into the egg wash and batter, and started the main course.

Ten minutes later, Moira breezed in holding a bulging canvas bag that clinked when she walked.

"We are not drinking all that tonight!" I yelled.

"Party pooper," Moira said with a grin. The vamp wore similar clothing. Loose, flowy pants, sandals, a tank top, and a long cardigan.

I'd texted Caelan earlier to tell him. Magic required freedom in all things and restrictive clothing tended to stagnate magic. I'd put on a pair of wide-leg cotton pants, a t-shirt, and also wore sandals I could slip off. My hair was arranged in a messy bun, and I wore no makeup or jewelry.

What we planned tonight was different from the other magic I used daily. Most Floromancy was intuitive, but I had the ability to perform ritualistic spells, though I usually chose not to. Such spells required strict adherence to the rules, and I much preferred natural magic, which had few rules.

Ash spent much of the day working on the spell's wording, and I had gathered almost all the spell's ingredients from either the greenhouse or around the property. What I couldn't gather, Tess had stepped up to bring.

"You ready?" Moira asked, peering over my shoulder at the bubbling steak.

"Whatever gets Cliona off my back."

She squeezed my shoulder and claimed one of the stools to perch on. "Are you worried about what jewelry Caelan is going to bring?"

At my dark look, she grinned. "Maybe it will be a huge engagement ring."

"Perish the thought. He knows I'd stab him."

"I don't think Caelan would hate that. He seems to like feisty women."

My stomach dropped at the thought of him with any other women, and wasn't that annoying? "Well," I said lightly. "I'm sure there's a lot of them in Joy Springs."

Moira rolled her eyes. "Keep denying your feelings and you'll lose him."

"I don't want him." I flipped the steak over, pleased to see the batter turned a crispy, golden brown.

"Uh huh," Moira said. She cracked open one of the bottles and poured us each a glass. "What's up with Cernunnos hanging around these days?"

"No idea." He hadn't denied being my father, but he hadn't confirmed either. If he was more than an annoying god hanging around, my heritage might end up being the biggest lie my mother ever told me. I'd no longer be a demi-god. I'd be something much more.

The thought of being a full god and part Chimera unsettled me.

If Cernunnos was my father, I'd be far more powerful than I ever expected.

Shaking my head, I peeked at the Brussels sprouts. Satisfied they still had some time to go, I reached for my wine glass and took a long swallow.

"He seems interested in you, and we all know it's never a good thing when the gods start knocking."

"I'm well aware," I said dryly. "Having Cliona for a mother is hard to forget."

"True." Her dark eyes shone. "I'm worried about you Evie. That's all. Things haven't been right since the moment Caelan showed up in our shop. You haven't been right."

I took the first steak out and battered the next, smiling when the oil sizzled and bubbled when the steak hit the surface of the pan. "We're all doing our best. You know I can't get involved with anyone."

Moira grunted. "I'm not sure that's true anymore. Caelan seems willing to deal with anything when it comes to you."

"Only because he doesn't know about the Chimera part."

I sank onto the stool opposite her. She looked heartbreakingly young with her bare face and ponytail. Long, pale fingers toyed with the colored, decorative knobs on her glass.

"His line is too pure to sully with Chimera DNA."

Moira blinked. "Evie! That's awful. Your DNA is not poisonous."

"Everyone else won't agree. There's a reason the Chimera were wiped out. I might not be like them, but it won't matter."

Moira's face softened. "You underestimate how much people care about you."

I pulled the second steak out and battered the next. "You, Ash, and Tess love me. That's all I need."

Moira's mouth turned down in a frown, but she changed the subject to less emotional things as I finished cooking.

Soon enough, everyone was gathered around the table, dishing out dinner. I thought it might be strange to have the Shifter Lord there. He'd never spent this much time in the presence of my friends, but I should have known he'd be able to fit in anywhere. Caelan even managed to get a laugh out of Tess, which surprised all of us.

Charming, handsome, powerful...whoever landed the Lord would be a lucky woman.

Our eyes met across the table. Silence fell inside my head, all the negative thoughts falling right out when I saw how he looked at me.

If only things were different. If only I was the woman I used to be. Even after my divorce, I was wounded but still me. I would have found my way back to myself if I hadn't gone—

Stop, I told myself. No good ever came from revisiting something I could never have again. This version of Evie was angrier, rawer, and much more powerful. She was willing to make the necessary sacrifices to protect those she loved.

And she'd never give her power to a man who wanted to cage her.

Caelan's brow furrowed, but he remained silent, accepting the second round of Brussels sprouts Ash passed him.

When dinner was finished, Ash was the first to rise. "Should we clean up first?"

"No. I'll take care of it later. Let's do the spell first. The dishes will hold."

Ash held his hand out for me. Our fingers slid against each other, our inherent power melding together. Ash wasn't one for grand gestures of affection, but he and I had always had an easy way with each other. I loved him like a brother, and our magic was similar, so I always felt deeply comfortable in his presence.

He leaned closer. "Are you sure about this?"

I knew he wasn't talking about the spell.

"Yes. Every little bit will boost the warding's power."

Ash nodded. "I care about you and want only the best. This spell will tie us all together in a way. Since I can't find any examples of spells like this done in the past, it's possible there might be complications."

"I'm right here, you know," Caelan said.

"I know," Ash said, his eyes flashing emerald. His fingers tightened around mine.

I frowned up at him. "Are you okay?"

The dryad's jaw tightened. "I only wanted to ensure you did not decide under duress."

"When does Evie do anything under duress?" Moira drawled. She flopped onto the couch and kicked her sandals off.

Tess floated over and sank to the floor. "She's very stubborn. I'm surprised you haven't noticed." She frowned up at Ash and patted the spot beside her.

His temper vanished in an instant, a smile tugging at his

mouth. "I noticed." He dragged me in for a hug, dropping a kiss on top of my head. "Sorry," he whispered.

"All good." I patted him on the arm and stepped away, reaching down for the small canvas bag I left by the recliner.

The coffee table was already cleared, the center taken up by a large, green pillar beeswax candle. Ash marked each spot with a small, beaded mat. Mine was a mix of green and browns. Tess's was silver and white. Ash had chosen burgundy and navy blue for Moira, which I thought was interesting—not the crimson and black I expected. Caelan's was an odd mix of colors, greens, golds, browns, and a deep, brilliant orange.

On top of the mats, he placed a small tea light. Next to those, a small cone of incense in matching colors. I watched him intently, curious about his method. Spell work had never been my strong suit. I was competent, but I'd never be a master at rituals and spells.

Ash took his time, ensuring everything was in its place, and none of us spoke as he worked. Caelan stood beside me, heat pulsing from his body.

"Lord," Ash said. "Do you have the jewelry?"

"Caelan, please." He pulled a small leather pouch from his pocket and handed it to Ash.

The dryad's brows went up. He let out a low whistle and tipped the contents of the pouch into his palm. "Where did this come from?"

Ash held up the pendant. Warm gold sparked in the light. At the bottom hung a small, elegant pendant made of gold woven in an intricate pattern. A gleaming black obsidian stone hung suspended in the center. Soft magic pulsed from the stone, a gentle, calming power.

"It belonged to one of our shifter queens and was given to her by a powerful mage." Caelan shrugged. "Some say it possesses extraordinary protective powers."

"How did you come to possess it?" Moira asked, an odd look on her face.

Caelan's eyes glinted. "With stealth and cunning."

Tess stared at Caelan. "You stole it?"

"I wouldn't say that."

When I opened my mouth to protest, Caelan shook his head. "You said no diamonds or anything ridiculous. It's small and neutral, so it will match anything you wear."

"But a priceless shifter artifact?" I pinched the space between my brows. "What if someone outside of your Pack recognizes what it is?"

"It belongs to the Pack now." Caelan's smile chilled me.

"You're impossible," I said softly.

"It's perfect for this purpose. Small, protective, and elegant." To Ash he gestured with his hand. "Shall we get on with it?"

Ash's lips twitched. "The Lord—"

"Caelan."

"Caelan is correct. The pendant is strong enough to hold the spell. I sense magic woven into its deepest layers. Protective magic. He chose well, Evie."

"And now I have to worry about losing it," I muttered.

"We hope you'd worry about that anyway since we're about to stuff it full of a world-ending seed," Moira said.

"The seed will find its way back to you," Tess said. "Or at least that's what your father said."

Silence fell like an anvil.

"Sonofabitch," I swore.

"Woah," Moira said.

I sank down onto the couch, suddenly boneless.

"Tess." Ash's voice was sharp. "How in the world would you know that?"

Tess waved a delicate hand. "The threads that bind them. Any of my kind would recognize they're kin."

"And you just thought to tell her now?" Moira said.

"Why would I tell her? If Evie looked hard enough, she would have seen the threads too."

Awesome. I rubbed my eyes.

Caelan sat down beside me. His posture bristled with tension. "You're a goddess," he said quietly. "A full one."

"I need a moment." Suspicion kept rearing its ugly head over the last few months. Why was Cernunnos so interested in me? Why was he helping me?

Moira pressed a glass of wine into my hand. "Drink."

Ash held up a finger. "I'm not sure drinking—"

"Shut up, Ash," Tess and Moira said at the same time.

The banshee floated over. "I'm sorry, Evie."

I tried to give her a reassuring smile but wasn't sure I was successful. "Don't be sorry. My paternity isn't your fault."

Tess wrung her hands together. "For not telling you." Her voice shook. "I don't always understand the right thing to do to be a good friend."

I sat up and reached out to her, taking her cool hand in mine. "Tess. You *are* a good friend. Being like everyone else is overrated anyway."

She ducked her head. "Are you okay?"

"I will be." I think. Holy shit. I wasn't just a goddess. I was a…

The world swirled around me. My heartbeat picked up.

"Evie?" A warm hand on my knee.

The world turned to a pinpoint, blackness creeping at the edge of my vision.

I wasn't just a goddess.

I was a freaking fae princess.

Twenty~Four

It took a good twenty minutes and another glass of wine for me to stop having an internal freak out. Caelan sat by me the entire time telling me stories of growing up in another Pack. Ash, Moira, and Tess crowded around as he spoke.

I didn't tell anyone about my realization. They were smart enough to figure it out on their own eventually.

"I'm ready," I said.

Moira shook her head. "This can wait. Your property is a safe place for one more night."

"No." I stood, shrugging off my cardigan. "We should do it now. The news is a shock, but what hasn't been these last few months?"

Caelan rose beside me. For once, I found his presence comforting, soothing in a way I hadn't before. But I wondered if he'd ramp up his efforts to pursue me now that he knew I wasn't an ordinary Floromancer.

I'd never be one again.

Something else nagged at me. If I was the fae king's daughter, how much more could I stretch my powers? What else could I do?

On the other hand, how much power was too much power?

And what would my mother do once she discovered I knew the truth?

"We can't tell Cliona," I said quietly.

"We don't tell your mother shit," Moira said. "Never have. Never will."

Four pairs of eyes turned to the Shifter Lord.

He put his hand to his mouth and mimed a zipper motion.

"Caelan." I took a step forward. "You don't know my mother. If she finds out what I am…" My voice trailed off before it broke.

Caelan's expression sobered. He laid a hand against his heart. "She will not find out from me. I swear it."

"Evie can kick your ass now," Ash said softly.

A crack of laughter escaped Moira. "Huh. I guess I hadn't thought of all the cool shit she should be able to do now."

My eyes twitched. "Can we please do this spell so I can sink into a coma?"

Ash searched my face. "Are you sure? Everyone's emotions need to be calm and collected when the spell begins."

"I'm a professional." Unless Caelan pissed me off, then I was a crazy person. But tonight, he was being awfully agreeable, and wasn't that suspicious? "Start the spell, Ash."

Ash picked up the lighter and began.

A dryad's power is unexplainable. I felt like Mother Earth wrapped me in a loving cocoon. The room was surrounded by warmth and the scent of green things. All the day's stress fell away as Ash's power swirled around us.

Caelan sucked in a sharp breath before releasing it in a slow shudder.

I couldn't help myself. "Good stuff, isn't it?"

Moira snickered.

"I've never felt a dryad's power," Caelan said in a hushed voice. "It's like yours but softer in a way."

"Evie's power is soft, too," Moira said quietly. "If she likes you."

Ash sighed. "Can everyone please stop talking?"

"I wasn't," Tess said.

"You are now," Moira whispered.

The pillar candle flared, soaking the room in a soft golden light.

"Everyone gather hands," Ash said in a hushed voice.

Caelan's calloused palm slid over mine, his fingers interlacing mine. My heartbeat kicked up a few notches, and from the slight tilt of his lips, I knew he noticed.

Moira took my other hand, hers cooler and smoother than Caelan's. As soon as Ash's hands closed the circle, every tea light ignited.

"Do you have the seed?" Ash asked.

I carefully extricated the small bead. Ash held up the pendant.

"It opens from the top," Caelan said. "There's a small catch at the bottom of the pendant."

Ash frowned and turned the pendant upside down. "Clever," he murmured after a moment. A tiny opening appeared at the top of the obsidian. "Drop the seed in, Evie."

I was disturbed by the fact that the seed fit perfectly, dropping into the small opening like it was meant to be there. Ash clicked the lid shut and placed the pendant around the beeswax candle, careful not to get any wax on the gold.

"Everyone except Caelan should concentrate on the pendant and touch it with your magic. Only a touch and retreat. This spell is …" His voice trailed off. "Greedy."

Caelan's hand tightened in mine.

"Why not him?" I asked. Ash was never rude, so I gave him the benefit of the doubt.

Ash's eyes glowed with emerald colored magic. "Because he will serve as the anchor. The pendant belongs to him, and its magic belongs to the shifters. When we're finished using the necklace, I will clear the spell and return it to him. Until then, Caelan should be able to retrieve the pendant if it's lost."

I frowned. "You're putting a tracking spell on the pendant?"

Ash let out a soft chuckle. "Yes, but not in the way you think.

If the pendant gets farther than six feet away from you for more than three minutes, the location spell will trigger and alert Caelan."

The distance from my shower to the sink was about four feet away, so that would work. I didn't love it, but I understood his logic. "But not when I'm wearing it?"

"What's the matter, flower girl? You don't want me to know where you are twenty-four hours a day?"

"I don't want *anyone* knowing where I'm at for the entire day."

"Take it off for showers and when you're sleeping if you want to," Ash continued. "But keep it on your nightstand, not your dresser."

"I don't sleep with jewelry on." The only thing I'd ever worn while sleeping was my wedding ring. Now I wore very little jewelry at all due to my job duties. With my hands constantly in the dirt, I didn't want to risk losing a piece I loved in one of my floral arrangements.

Losing Caelan's precious heirloom would be even worse.

The Shifter Lord was being too quiet. Too cooperative over the last few days.

And that made me suspicious.

"Any thoughts, Caelan?" I asked.

"You'll be wearing a piece of our history around your neck. Shower with it, don't shower with it. Sleep with it or don't." He shrugged. "I'm ready when you are, Ash."

One of Ash's eyebrows rose. He cleared his throat. "Of course. Tess. Are you ready to begin?"

Tess inhaled and closed her eyes. A soft silver outline formed around her body, ethereal and glittering. But instead of reaching for the pendant, Tess pursed her lips and blew out a thin thread of power.

"Cool," Moira whispered.

Ash reached for Tess's magic, guiding it toward the pendant. The spell caught her power and sucked it inside the obsidian, there and gone in an instant.

"Moira."

At Ash's urging, Moira smiled and let her eyes drift shut. The room temperature dropped by several degrees, and a swirl of crimson power flowed from Moira's fingertip. He once again guided Moira's power until it soaked into the obsidian.

For his turn, Ash merely touched the pendant. Emerald magic coated the pendant in a bright green glitter before sinking in and disappearing.

"Evie."

Six months ago, I wouldn't bat an eye at his request. Now, with my power going a little wonky, I was afraid I'd break the pendant. Caelan gave my hand a comforting squeeze.

I closed my eyes and calmed my breathing. When I was settled, I sent out a seeking tendril of watermelon tourmaline colored magic, tinged with a hint of crimson. At my touch against the pendant, my skin heated, the soft brush of fur against my mind, gentle yet inquisitive.

I sucked in a breath and opened my eyes. The pendant lifted in the air, swirling in a counterclockwise circle. My magic encased the necklace, glowing the green and pink of watermelon tourmaline.

"Ash?" My heartbeat picked up.

"Just wait," he assured me. "There's nothing wrong. Your magic is curious about what's happening."

"Tonight is not the night for curiosity," I mumbled.

A whoosh of wind and a pop of sound and my magic soaked into the pendant. Seconds later, it fell to the earth.

Ash's hand reached out and caught it a second before it crashed against the table.

Caelan's breath of relief sounded in the silence.

"That would have been bad," Moira said.

"Round two," Tess said.

"Let's not joke about breaking the priceless artifact," Ash murmured. "Alright. Caelan, come closer and pick up the pendant."

Caelan stepped forward and took the pendant in his hands. Ash leaned forward and murmured something in his ear.

At Caelan's nod, Ash rested his hand on the Lord's shoulder.

Power grew in the room, a heady sensation prickling the back of my neck. Caelan's eyes turned from a stormy gray with flecks of gold into warm pyrite, casting light over us all.

Within his palms, the pendant hummed, Caelan's power flowing into the pendant, Ash's power keeping the link between himself and the Lord.

All the candles blew out, the smell of sulfur rising from the table.

Ash whispered something I couldn't make out. Caelan nodded and opened his palms.

The dryad reached for the pendant and held it to his lips. A soft breath of emerald power and the pendant exploded in multicolored light. Green for Ash. Silver for Tess. Watermelon tourmaline tinged with blood red for me, pure crimson for Moira, and a mix of forest green and gold for Caelan.

"It's beautiful," I whispered.

Ash smiled as the light faded away, leaving the pendant inert in his palm.

"It worked." He motioned for me to come over.

I turned and was about to brush my hair away from my neck when Caelan spoke.

"I'll do it." A soft growling note in his voice made goosebumps rise on my skin.

Warm calloused fingers brushed against the side of my neck, gently moving my hair aside.

I swallowed hard as Caelan reached around and laid the pendant against the hollow of my throat. His breath was warm against my shoulder, fingers brushing against my skin as he fastened the clasp. An innocent touch that sparked the end of my nerves into flame.

"There." Caelan's hand wound through my hair as he moved it off my shoulder.

I turned, my fingers already playing with the pendant.

"How does it feel?" Ash asked, unable to mask the amusement in his eyes over my reaction to Caelan.

"Friendly." That wasn't quite the right word, but it fit. Warmth and joy spread from the obsidian, enclosing my heart in a warm cocoon of light. I smiled and placed my hand over my chest. "I sense all of you within."

"Good." Ash gathered the spell materials and put them inside the canvas bag he'd brought. Fine lines of weariness had gathered at his eyes. "I'm going to head out."

Tess yawned. "Me too. I'm wiped."

Moira sank onto the couch and groaned. "What did you do to us?"

Ash helped Tess up. The banshee swayed against him. He put a gentle arm around her shoulders. "Spell work is always hard on the body. We'll all be fine in the morning, after a good night's sleep."

Caelan stretched and yawned. "Thank the gods. I have a Council meeting tomorrow and need to be clear headed."

"I'll see you guys in the morning. We have a lot of work to catch up on."

All three of my friends groaned. "Now go on, get out of here," I said with a laugh.

They piled out the door, waving as they went. Caelan followed but turned before he stepped out.

"Let me know if there are any issues with the pendant."

"All seems well, but I'll call if things get weird."

He nodded and was poised to leave when I reached out and touched his arm.

"Caelan?" A question had been bothering me for the last few days.

"Hmm?"

"Why are you acting so...?" My voice trailed off as I tried to think of the right word. "Normal."

His eyebrows flicked up. "Normal? Isn't that what everyone wants?"

"Not necessarily. You've been extremely calm. Too calm."

Amusement glittered in his eyes. "You don't like me calm, flower girl?"

"You haven't been calm from the second I met you, so it's weirding me out a little, that's all."

"Maybe things are different now." He turned and walked down the steps.

"Are they?" I called.

"Perhaps I'm different."

We stared at each other.

"I'm not sure I like it," I blurted.

Caelan's grin was a flash of white in the darkness. "Good night, Evangeline."

A moment later he was gone.

This really felt like one of those shoe moments, and I wondered when the other one would drop.

That night I dreamed of running through a golden forest, a beast's glorious howl bursting from my throat. A full moon hung white and bloated in the sky, cool wind blowing against my fur as my paws pounded against the damp earth.

I awoke with a start, my heart thumping against my chest. The smell of fresh pine and cold wind surrounded the room. Unsettled, I lay there for a long time, unable to go to sleep, my fingers playing with the warm pendant around my neck.

Twenty-Five

CAELAN

I jerked awake after the strangest dream I'd ever had. The scent of fresh roses and jasmine flooded my bedroom. Odd dreams weren't out of the ordinary for me, but this one felt all too real.

My skin was sweat-soaked and cool, my legs tangled in damp sheets. A memory of feminine laughter and vines wrapping around my wrists tangled in my mind, sending my heartbeat racing.

I felt like I was going mad. Laying back against my pillow, I kicked the blankets off and swung my legs over the side of the bed. My hands gripped the edge of the mattress. I stared blankly at the wall, allowing remnants of the dream to sift through my thoughts before shaking my head. Dreams rarely rattled me, but this one felt like Evie.

"Fuck," I growled, scratching my jaw as I brushed the thought away. One odd dream did not mean the Floromancer was suddenly invading my mind.

"Get a grip," I muttered. Shaking my head, I rose and stretched. The clock blinked to 4 a.m.

Guess my day was getting started early.

I arrived at the meeting spot three hours early, calling ahead to let Rowan know. The other Lord had chosen the local botanical gardens. No surprise there. He was the most like Evie and skilled in natural magic.

Rowan waited for me at the front, his back pressed against the stone wall, one leg hitched up. A casual wave when he saw me, and he sauntered down the steps.

"Trouble sleeping?" Rowan quipped when he got closer.

"Shut it," I snarled.

Rowan's soft laughter made my shoulders slump. "Come inside. They have great coffee here."

ALL THE LORDS gathered a couple of hours later, but my mood hadn't improved much. When Ben walked in, I damn near bit his head off. The Healer merely laughed and slapped me on the back.

"Evie still giving you fits, Caelan?"

I sent the new Lord a dark look. Ben was one of my closest friends, but I knew in my heart, if Evie would have given anyone a chance, it'd be him. So I'd acted like a huge asshole and made him a Lord. In everyone else's eyes, this was a huge promotion. In Ben and Evie's it was a betrayal.

"Evie is fine," I said, the words a harsh growl.

"I didn't ask about her," Ben said, giving me an amused look.

"But you wanted to."

Ben sighed. "You got what you wanted. No need to rub it in my face."

A bark of laughter escaped me. "I'd be in a much better mood if I got what I wanted."

Shaking my head, I took my seat. "Let's get this over with."

HOURS LATER, I had the beginning of a pounding headache, and we were no closer to agreeing on anything.

Border incursions continued despite the best efforts of all the

Lords. Pockets of rogue magic continued to appear in random spots. Divine magic grew in wild areas.

Even with everything going on, all the Lords were more curious about Evie than anything else.

"You haven't landed her yet?" Soren asked, amusement making his lips twitch.

"She's not a fish, asshole," I snarled.

Donovan had said little today, but in this, he spoke up. "It's a shame Cernunnos outlawed forced marriage. Evie would be a prime candidate."

Claws slid from my fingertips.

A strong hand gripped the top of my shoulder, warning me not to react. "No need to be a dick, Donovan. We all know you like your women short, pretty, and unable to vote."

Surprised by Thorvin's words, my breathing settled. The Northeast Lord spoke very little, but when he opened his mouth, people listened. Thorvin was highly intelligent and highly logical and seemed more in tune with magic resonance than most of us.

Donovan's jaw tightened. "She's still a problem and will be until we bring her under our control."

"The Floromancer has brought no trouble to our doors," Rowan interjected.

"Said by a man just as enamored with her as Caelan," Ethan, Lord of the Rocky Mountains, drawled.

I knew Ethan the least, but he'd made no move against me.

Rowan turned on the charm. "How can I not be enamored with a woman whose magic is similar to mine? Someone who loves the earth and all its gifts as much as I do?" He shrugged and glanced at me, dark amusement in his eyes. "Evie is easy on the eyes, too. She's intelligent, magically gifted, and has a rack—"

My claws scraped down the table making deep gouges in the wood, the sound of pine cracking overriding his words.

Rowan laughed out loud. "You're merely proving their point."

"Be that as it may," Ethan said, "the Floromancer still has autonomy in your lands, Caelan."

I bit down the urge to tear him apart. "What's your point?"

"My point," Ethan said, leaning forward, "is the proof of divine magic saturating your territory. Your Floromancer must be linked."

Boy was she. For the first time in my life, when it came to the Council, I danced around the truth. "Evangeline Quinn is a Floromancer. She has never admitted to being divine, nor has anything in her file revealed any heritage other than mundane parentage."

All true. Evie's file wasn't remarkable, though there wasn't much on her until she was a teenager. She was raised in Seattle by two human parents, graduated toward the top of her class, went to college and did the same, married, divorced, and disappeared off the map until she set foot in Joy Springs seven years later. My intel was top notch. There was no way the other Lords had anything on her I didn't.

They had no reason to dig as deeply as I had on her.

"She doesn't need to be related to be in league with them," Donovan said.

"What does she stand to gain?" Rowan asked.

Donovan snorted. "Everything." His tone dripped with disdain. "She's dealing with the gods. They have the capability to give her everything she's ever wanted."

"Evie wants to run her flower shop and be left in peace." I rose and paced back and forth, the urge to shed my skin and run overwhelming. "She has nothing to do with this."

Rowan's eyes narrowed.

Shit. He knew me better than everyone and must scent the lie.

I backtracked. "The gods have always been interested in Joy Springs. There's been no indication Evie has ever met with any divine being other than a single guest at her shop who left without buying anything."

Donovan's attention sharpened. "So she has been in contact with the divine." His eyes gleamed with satisfaction.

"Let it go, Donovan," Soren snapped. "The girl has done

nothing to any of us. As far as I'm concerned, if Caelan wants to have the risk in his territory, let the chips fall where they may."

Rowan nodded. "I'm inclined to agree."

Ethan studied me, his dark, flat eyes missing nothing. "And if she becomes a risk to us all?"

"She already is a risk," Donovan said. "A Chimera breached our defenses and overtook one of our Lords. One far too interested in your Floromancer."

I stifled my rage and turned on the cold mask of a Lord. "Just like you are?"

Thorvin cleared his throat. "I'm all for allowing a Lord to run his own territory and believe in allowing one to fail, if need be, but there are too many incidents swirling around your Floromancer." He lifted his eyes to me. "I know a shifter in the first throes of a mating when I see one, Caelan."

Dammit. Power crackled along my palms.

Thorvin smiled, looking good natured.

My hackles rose.

"On this one, I fall with Donovan. Bring the Floromancer in line in whatever manner you wish. If the Lords have to get involved, your precious Evie will suffer." He laid a hand over his heart. "I don't agree she is evil or out for power, but no one who consorts with the gods is up to any good."

The situation was laughable. If they had an inkling of what Evie's potential was, they'd know she could wipe us all off the map with merely a thought. She wasn't a Floromancer or a demigod or anything of the sort.

She was a full-blown goddess, the daughter of the fae freaking king. If they thought anyone could bring her in line… Well, I had a bridge to Hawaii to sell them.

"Agreed," was all I said.

Rowan's attention was rapt on my face. He gave a slow nod.

"You have sixty days," Donovan said. "Get her under your Pack or neutralize her."

"Agreed," added Thorvin.

Ethan merely nodded.

"Soren?" I said.

The bastard grinned. "I like the idea of seeing Caelan attempt to get his Floromancer in line in sixty days. Agreed."

Outnumbered and overruled.

Ethan struck the gavel. "Meeting adjourned." He nodded. "Good luck, Caelan."

"Fuck off," I snarled.

I'd been irrationally pissed off all day and had no idea why. Besides the weird dream last night, the day had gone well. Customers came in and out. We sold a bunch of arrangements, booked two additional weddings, and had zero god sightings.

By my standards, that'd be cause for a party.

Except I couldn't enjoy any of it because I'd been in a rage since eight this morning.

"It's the way you like it," Moira said, gently pushing a steaming cup of coffee over.

"I want milk and sugar, and we don't have either."

"I forgot to go to the store, but I'll get some in the morning."

I clicked my tongue. "That doesn't help me today."

Moira's lips twitched. "Evie." She lay a hand over mine. "You know I never ask this, but are you about to start your cycle?"

I gasped in horror. "Moira!"

She cackled. "You are a raging bitch today. What is going on?"

I rubbed the space between my brows. "I don't know." My shoulders ached, and my jaw hurt like I'd been clenching it all day. "I feel weird. Angry and scared and hot and cold."

Moira glanced at Ash. "Is she okay?"

The dryad came over, Tess floating beside him. "You're linked to the Lord through the pendant."

Ash sent her an annoyed look; one I'd rarely seen on his face. "*Tess*. We may need to talk about your…gifts."

Tess's pale brow furrowed. "What. I'm right, aren't I?"

I held up a hand. "Wait. I'm linked to all of you, right? Technically."

Ash sat down. "Let me see the pendant."

I unclasped it and dropped it into his palm. Ash studied it, his eyes flashing emerald for a moment. When he was done, his lips twitched. "Tess is right. You have a deeper bond with the Shifter Lord than any of us. Our magic is on the pendant, but the necklace belonged to the shifters. Once Caelan's magic sank in, he laid claim to it. By wearing his necklace, your emotional resonances have attuned to each other."

"English, please," I snapped.

Moira laughed.

"I suspect Caelan is having a trying day and his emotions are bleeding over."

I stared at him for a beat. "I'm sorry. Are you saying I'm pissed off because Caelan is influencing me?"

Ash's nod made my heart drop to my stomach.

"I'd rather have PMS," I snarled.

Moira refastened the necklace around my neck, even as my fingers itched to rip it away and stomp it to pieces. "How do I stop it?"

Ash's expression softened. "I don't think you can."

"Great. Can he feel what I feel?" This was not good. Not only was it a major invasion of privacy, it had the potential to reveal my secrets.

"I believe it's a channel. You'll broadcast to him just as he will to you."

I sat back. "Shit," I breathed. "Then we have to find another way to hide the seed."

Ash's lips thinned. "There is no other way."

"What about the property? It's large and soaked in my power."

"Cliona will break your wards." Tess floated to sit by Ash. "She is my queen. I have seen evidence of her unfathomable power." The banshee's hands trembled. "Keep the pendant on, Evie. Don't risk her wrath. Emotional resonance with the Lord is a small price to pay." Her eyes filled with tears. "It will not be forever. The wheel of time spins quickly around you, and I see... much change in the future."

What had she gone through to make her so fearful of Cliona? "She's my mother, Tess. I'm well aware of her depravity."

But was I? She'd been cruel to me, but my mother had never harmed me. Not physically. She'd threatened me. A lot. She'd played mind games, disappeared for years at a time, and had even all but forgotten about me sometimes.

"And if Caelan discovers my secrets?"

"I'd say he's discovered enough to make life difficult already," Moira mused. "He knows you aren't only a Floromancer, and he knows who your father is. The other Lords would love to have that kind of dirt on you, and I haven't seen a single one come knocking."

"True," I grumbled. "But being a Chimera means instant death."

"And yet he hasn't killed you," Ash said. He rubbed his face. "Keep wearing the pendant for now while we research other means of hiding a world-ending object."

"I don't appreciate the sarcasm." A groan escaped me. "I need to shift soon." The itch had begun as a tingling at the back of my neck and intensified over the last several days. So far, I could go a full two weeks without using the Chimera magic until the power buildup became unbearable. "What if he senses the change?"

"Then we deal with it," Moira said. "Caelan has not been unreasonable in his dealings with you. In fact, he's been more than cooperative."

I bared my teeth at her.

Moira held both hands up. "Whoa. Listen. You have your reasons for not getting emotionally involved. And we all get it and do not blame you."

My brows drew together. "Why does this sound like you're about to, though?"

Moira took both my hands and held them. "Maybe it's time to trust someone else. You've had only us to rely on. Caelan is powerful."

"And he wants you," Ash added. "Men that head over heels are willing to overlook many things."

I stared at my friends. "Do you honestly believe Caelan won't turn me over to the Council or worse once he finds out?"

"I do," Moira said. "Things might be rocky for a while, but they have a way of working out."

Fear had driven all my decisions for so long. I knew they were right. Maybe it was time to take a leap of fate.

"And…" Moira hedged. "You've been kind of a baby about this for a while now. It's time to take a chance."

Ash winced. "Moira. There's a better way to say what needs to be said."

She let go of my hands and held them up. "Sometimes you gotta rip off the bandage even if it takes some skin off."

My gaze bounced between them. "You both think I'm acting like a brat?"

"No one said brat," Ash responded.

"That's because everyone is too nice," Tess said before floating away to the back.

"Tess," Ash breathed. He rubbed a hand over his face. "Your mother's presence has rattled her. She'll be better in a few days."

"I'm not mad at her," I assured him. "I'd rather hear it straight, and I agree with you. Maybe I have dragged this on long enough."

"You'll tell him?"

"I doubt it."

Groans all around. I laughed. "Not until it comes up naturally. He's bound to have tons of questions about Cernunnos. That's a large enough realization. Having a god in his territory is questionable at best."

Moira let out a breath. "A god. Spoken aloud that makes it seem real." She squinted her eyes at me. "You seem exactly the same."

"Which is good?" I didn't feel any different. Not that I would. My DNA had always been this way. Even being aware wouldn't have changed my magic. Would it?

I needed to track my errant father down and have some words with him. "Back to this pendant and resonance. I'll tackle research on my end, but you all have different ways of finding out information I may not be able to access. Can we reconvene tomorrow and discuss any info we might uncover?"

Ash and Moira nodded, and the conversation turned to work issues.

Before I knew it, the day was over, and everyone had gone home. I stayed behind to finish up a few things and work on the centerpieces for Caelan's fall event. When I was ready to go, I rose, wincing as stiff muscles in my back pulled. Sitting for so long wasn't good for anyone, not even a god.

I shuddered at the thought. Now that I knew, would Cernunnos begin to demand things from me? After cashing out the register and taking care of the closing tasks, the sun had set, leaving Joy Springs in full dusk. I stepped out, locked the door behind me, and headed to the car.

"Hello, Evie."

A voice from behind stopped me in my tracks. My grip tightened on my bag as I slowly turned to face Rhona.

"What do you want?"

The Chimera smiled. "So touchy. Did I frighten you?"

Everything about Chimeras frightened me. Rhona was dressed

in high-waisted cream-colored pants, brown boots, and a thin burgundy sweater. Her hair hung loose around her shoulders. In the dark, the red color looked like congealed blood.

"No. I need to get home, so if you need something, let's skip the small talk."

"You hold something of great importance to me."

I stared. "Last time we spoke, you said I was of no importance to you and suddenly I have something you want?"

Her eyes glittered. "Things change."

"Not usually," I said. "Paranormals like things to stay the same. Change is a nuisance for most."

"Chimeras are not most."

"What do I have that you need so much?" I sent a soft pulse of magic through my body to keep my heart rate from spiking. There was only one thing I'd recently gained that might ping on her radar. But the question was, how did she know I supposedly had it?

The most probable answer sent fear rolling down my spine. She'd admitted knowing my mother. Was it possible they were working together? If that were the case, I was well and truly fucked.

Rhona's gaze flicked to the new pendant. "Pretty," she remarked. "Is it new?"

I fingered the gold cage of the obsidian. "A gift from a few years ago. No idea where they got it. But it is pretty, isn't it?"

"Mmm."

"I need to go. Since I'm not sure what you're looking for, I can't help you."

"You know what it is, and I know you have it," Rhona said softly. "It's in your best interest to hand it over now. Otherwise things might get ugly."

I adjusted my bag to free my hands. "I'm sorry you feel that way. I hope you find whatever it is you seek."

"Don't worry, Evie." Her smile was cold. "I always do."

Rhona turned and walked away, her hair blowing like a sheet of blood behind her back.

I waited until I was in the car and a mile down the road before I let myself shiver.

I DREAMED of Griffin for the first time in months.

The front door was unlocked, unusual, but Griffin was absentminded sometimes. His work as an academic went in ebbs and flows.

Must be a flow, I thought as I came inside, quietly clicking the door shut. I'd gotten off early today and stopped by the bakery to get his favorite cookies—brown sugar oatmeal.

Once the box was set on the counter, and I'd kicked my shoes off, I grabbed a plate and a couple of cookies, then padded upstairs to his office. That's where he was ninety percent of the time, working on research or grading papers or…all of the other things he did I had yet to understand.

I smiled and reached to push open his door when a soft sound from our bedroom had me turning toward the master. Griffin never napped, but maybe he didn't feel well.

Not thinking anything of it, I turned and went to the bedroom, pausing at the entrance as soft laughter came through the cracked door.

My blood froze. That was not Griffin's laughter, nor was it the sound of his phone or the television. I squared my shoulders and told myself this was not what it sounded like, and Griffin would have a good reason for having a woman in our bedroom.

He'd always been a little awkward socially, but he made up for it with the care he took with my heart. I pasted a smile on my face and pushed open the door.

Love is a funny emotion. It's found in the smallest of gestures, a smile, a touch, a cup of coffee by the bedside you didn't make. But what no one tells you is sometimes that feeling can die with no notice and no preparation.

Some betrayals are too great for love to survive.

And while many love stories died by a thousand cuts, mine died with a soft, feminine laugh and the play of muscles as my husband rose above a woman who wasn't me.

I woke with a pained sob, feeling that same crack in my heart that I felt when I realized what Griffin had done, was doing. My palm pressed over that spot, healed but still a little tender.

I survived his betrayal and the fallout, and I knew I would make it through the worst of things. What came after almost broke me.

Twenty-Seven

CAELAN

shouldn't be here, I thought, even as I crept along the underbrush in wolf form. The night was chillier than usual, a precursor to a longer winter than normal. Dew clung to the underside of my fur as I breached Evie's territory lines.

The wards slid over my skin, allowing me entrance, and I paused, debating whether to turn back and return to the Keep.

Evie's breaking heart had woken me from a sound sleep, the sound of her anguished cry something that would live forever in my nightmares. I couldn't help myself as I slipped out of the Keep, knowing I had to go to her, to see if she was okay.

Once I saw her, I'd return home.

To my surprise, she sat on the back deck, wrapped in a duster sweater and a lap blanket. She held a steaming mug.

I lifted my nose.

Coffee. Dark roast.

Evie had no plans to return to sleep.

"Caelan," she said, her voice raw.

I jogged to the porch, staying in wolf form.

My animal form was so large, our faces were at the same level. I dug my cold nose into the crook of her neck, making her squawk.

"You're freezing!"

But she laughed and that made the man and the beast happy. I licked her cheek and sat beside her, nudging her with my head.

Evie snorted. "You're incorrigible." She dug her fingers into the ruff of my neck and scratched.

I let out a happy growl and stretched to allow her the most access before I braved the consequences and lay my head in her lap.

Evie sighed. "I'll allow it. Only tonight," she warned.

I'd take it. She rubbed her hand down my face, smoothing the damp fur, sliding down my neck and back. Few people touched me, and I allowed no one the liberties Evie was taking with me now.

But damned if I wasn't starved for touch.

Or maybe hers. But as Evie stroked me, I felt her heartbeat slow, and her sadness diminish.

"I know about the link," she said a few minutes later.

I whined.

"Yep. We're both smart enough to figure it out. I can't take the pendant off, but we're looking for an alternative."

A growl escaped me.

Evie laughed, though the sound was touched with sadness. "I know why you're here. I'm sorry those dreams touched you. It's been a while since I dreamed of him."

I wanted to shift into human form, but I knew Evie would clam up. So I lay perfectly still, allowing her to touch me in whatever way she wanted. The stroke of her fingers and soft words mesmerized me, allowing her to weave whatever spell she was casting over me as she spoke.

"I never wanted to get married, but I didn't realize it until later. Maybe it was Griffin, or maybe it was the first feeling I had of ever being truly loved. When everything was over, I realized all I wanted was love. Griffin wanted the whole package, the quintessential American life. But it was my fault as much as his."

I turned my head and nipped at her arm for that last part. It was not her fault, and if it wouldn't break Evie's heart, I'd find this Griffin and tear him into tiny chunks to help the vultures devour him faster.

"I was so busy with work and trying to get my master's that I neglected him, I suppose."

I had no idea she'd done that much schooling, but I nipped her again for her thought process.

"Stop that," she admonished, tugging on my neck fur. Regret spilled through me when she didn't speak for a while. I nudged her belly.

"I couldn't look at him the same afterward. He begged me for another chance, but all the love I felt for him…it dried up in that moment. How does that happen? One day your heart is so full, and you can see a beautiful life in the horizon, but in the next, all your dreams lay shattered and that person, your person—"

Her voice shuddered and broke on the last word.

"They become someone you never knew. Someone you never wanted to know. And suddenly a stranger you've given everything to stands before you and you don't know what to do. Life becomes unsure and the steady path you just stood on gets washed away in the storm that comes after."

And then she went to Scotland where something happened. My intel never clarified what, but Evie's movements after that were erratic until she landed in Joy Springs.

"Just when I was picking up the pieces, I took that trip." She stopped talking. "Well. Things changed after that, and I drifted for a long time until I found Moira and Ash and Tess."

She toyed with my ear, and I let out a happy little growl. Evie's soft chuckle emboldened me, and I turned my head to let my tongue loll out.

"You charmer," she said softly. "And now I'm here on a porch pouring my heart out to a Shifter Lord."

Evie sighed and took a sip of her coffee. "You must think me maudlin tonight."

I nudged her belly again and then her hand because she'd

stopped petting me. This is the most she'd ever told me about herself, and the longest we'd probably gone in a conversation without being awkward or getting into a fight.

She dug her fingers into the fur on my spine and scratched.

I died and went to heaven.

"I'm going into work early today, I guess."

A whine escaped me. She needed more rest.

"I can't sleep. The memories are too fresh."

I whined again and lifted my head to stare at her.

She snorted and pushed my face away. "Quit. I'm tired but I can't sleep."

I went and padded to her door, pawing at the handle. I could open it, but she was being awfully sweet tonight, and I didn't want to do anything to make her snappy. My instincts kicked in. I knew what she needed, even if Evie didn't.

She sighed. "Is this your idea of trying to get into my bed?"

Yes, but not in the way she was thinking.

Evie frowned. "Your paws are all dirty."

I wiped them on her rug and stared at her.

Sighing, she rose. "Fine. But one wrong move, and I'll let the plants eat you. Got it?"

I sat down like a good doggie and let my tongue hang out.

"I'm going to regret this," she muttered to herself.

I'd make sure she did not.

When Evie rose and opened the door, I sent up a mental fist pump. She set her coffee down on the counter and watched me.

Padding over, I got behind her and nudged her hip toward her bedroom.

"Caelan!"

I yipped and nudged her until she finally headed toward her bedroom. She kicked off her shoes and slid her duster off.

It was hard not to notice how soft Evie was in all the right places, but this was not the right time. Careful not to use my teeth, I nudged her blankets aside and waited for her to crawl underneath them. When she was settled in, the blankets pulled over her shoulder, I hopped onto her bed. She watched me with wary eyes, but when I settled at the foot of her bed, my head resting on her calves, Evie let out a shaky sigh.

She reached over and flicked her lamp off, plunging the room into moonlight-tinged darkness.

"Don't make me regret this."

I huffed an indignant breath. I'd do nothing of the sort. Her showing this much trust meant we'd crossed a bridge. I had no intention of damaging this tentative truce, even as it came about because of her broken heart.

CHAPTER
Twenty~Eight

I awoke to the smell of waffles and bacon. My eyes adjusted to the light, squinting against the sunlight through the partially opened blinds. Last night's events came back in a flurry of memories, and a furious blush hit my cheeks.

But there was no warmth on my calves and no Lord in my bed. Letting out a sigh of relief, I got out of bed and pulled my duster cardigan on.

The kitchen and living room proved empty, but there was a sticky note on the oven that said, *Look Inside* in Caelan's heavy scrawl.

I grabbed a pair of potholders and pulled the tray out. A stack of still steaming waffles, fresh bacon, and warm maple syrup looked up at me.

My heart went mushy.

I set the tray on the countertop and found another note.

Breakfast is in the oven, and the coffee is fresh.

Thank you for trusting me.

I swallowed to get rid of the lump in my throat. My friends knew what had happened to me, all the things I could bear to say aloud, but Caelan was the first person I'd told outside of them. I felt raw this morning, a little unsteady on my feet.

A sense of freedom settled inside me, slipping past the battered permanent bruise currently acting as my heart. If I could get through everything that had happened to me and still thrive… maybe it was time to trust someone else with the biggest secret I had.

With that thought in mind, I ate every single thing Caelan had made me, failing to notice all the extra bacon he'd included as I inhaled the food.

A FEW HOURS LATER, I was putting the final touches on a bridal bouquet, discussing Rhona's visit with everyone.

"She looked at the necklace. It should be impossible, but I had a feeling she suspects what's inside." I trimmed a woody stem from a white rose and carefully inserted it into the foam.

Ash's lips tightened. "I'm not familiar with a Chimera's magic. Cliona would have already been here if the seed was still traceable. But it's possible Rhona might be able to sense its power even with the safeguards we put into place."

"Any tips on dealing with her if she shows up again?" Moira asked, handing me a pristine piece of baby's breath.

"I don't even know what a Chimera can do," I said dryly. "Finn was a master at glamour, as most Chimeras are. I know I can shift into anything, but I haven't tried plant life yet."

I tried to remember everything I'd seen him do. "They can break and pass through wards. Rhona was in my greenhouse. Cliona hasn't tried to break the wards, though I suspect she could if she tried hard enough. She's played nice lately."

"Maybe that's it. The pendant isn't glamoured. Not exactly. It's disguised by our magic and an old spell. Rhona might be able to see through it." Ash reached over and pulled the pendant away from my neck to study it. "I'm not sure what else we can do to prevent her from sensing it."

"Should we move the seed to a safer location?" Moira asked.

She slapped my hand away when I was about to slide a piece

of greenery next to the white roses and handed me a burgundy piece of foliage. I put it up to the bouquet and nodded.

"Good call." I wiggled my fingers for a few more pieces.

We brainstormed for a while before I realized Tess was missing. She must have floated away sometime during our conversation. "Where'd Tess go?"

Ash pointed to the back. "She has a test in Calculus she has to study for."

"School already started?" I groaned. Time was flying these days.

"A week ago," Ash confirmed. "She has two semesters left before she's done."

"Oh," I breathed. "Does she know what she's going to do when she finishes?"

Ash shook his head. "She's mulling over a lot of things these days."

"Well I hope she mulls staying with us. I'm happy to offer a pay raise once she graduates."

Ash gave me a grateful smile that didn't reach his eyes. "Thanks. She's going through some things, but I'll talk to her."

I reached out and touched his hand. "Are you guys okay?"

"I hope so," Ash said. When he said nothing else, I nodded.

"Okay. I'm here if you ever want to talk."

"Thanks, Evie."

I put the final touches on the bouquet, activated the preservation spell, and passed it to Moira to tuck in the fridge to hold for the bride.

Ash headed over to his alcove to work on his next bonsai project. The bell over the door jingled, announcing the arrival of a group of older women.

"Evie!" Marnie, half owner of the Thistle and Thread Cafe, entered, holding a basket that I hoped was full of goodies.

Twila, her sister, came in behind her, followed by Sirena, the owner of my favorite gelato food truck.

Marnie and Twila were hedgewitches, who made the best soup

on the planet. Marnie was the smaller and more boisterous of the pair.

She made a beeline for my worktable. "We brought you some things!"

"I'm already drooling," I assured her.

Twila waved shyly, and Sirena winked. Out of the three, I was most wary of Sirena. She was a Siren, and like all Sirens, she had a way with men and women. But in addition, she was somewhat of a foreseer.

I didn't like anyone diving into my future because the future revealed secrets, and I liked mine untold.

Marnie's pale blue eyes twinkled. "Can I use your table?"

"Of course." I moved the clippers and supplies out of the way.

She unpacked a small, still steaming pot pie, four containers of soup, and a large portion of sliced bread.

"Oh my goodness," I breathed. "Marnie!" The bounty before me smelled like heaven. "How much do I owe you for all of this?"

Marnie scoffed and waved a hand. "Since you asked for none of it, you don't owe me a dime."

She jerked her head at Sirena. "This one said you might be busy for the next few days and could use some fortification. I brought enough to last you a few days. Twila made the soup."

"It's country potato," the quieter sister said, her light brown eyes kind and happy.

"And the pot pie is beef and mushroom." Marnie frowned. "Sirena said to add a lot of extra beef. I hope that's okay."

I swallowed, carefully not meeting the Siren's eyes. "Umm. Yes. That's perfect. Thank you."

Did she know about me?

"I'm a little anemic these days," I said quietly. "A little extra red meat is just what I need."

Marnie clicked her tongue. "It's hard being a woman, especially when you hit your thirties. Everything goes wild down there."

Ash couldn't cover his snort in time.

She grinned and turned. "I brought you something too, you handsome man."

Ash blushed and ducked his head.

"Marnie," Twila groaned.

The hedgewitch scoffed. "Please. If we talk about it, we don't get surprised by it. And our mothers weren't talkers, we all know that, don't we?"

Sirena shrugged. "You're right. Though some of us don't experience those changes like others may." Her eyes lingered on me.

She had to know something.

"We have a couple of weddings coming up, so I will be busy, but hopefully not enough to be cooped up inside eating all this pot pie!" I smiled at Marnie. "Thank you so much for thinking of me."

She patted my hand and closed her basket. "It's nothing, dear. We noticed you haven't been visiting any of the shops and we wanted to make sure you were okay more than anything."

My cheeks colored. "I've had some personal things going on," I confessed. "But I'll do better."

"No worries. Just try not to be a stranger. There's an entire magical community out there you have yet to meet." Her eyes softened. "You've been here for a long time, my dear. Don't you think it's about time you got to know the rest of us?"

Guilt flooded me. "You're right," I said softly. "I've gotten way too comfortable at the shop and at my house and rarely venture out these days."

"Or date," Moira muttered as she came out from the back.

"I sense things will change on that front," said Sirena. Her eyes glittered with amusement. "Whether you want them to or not."

Sirena was gorgeous but really annoying sometimes.

Twila reached over and touched my arm. "We have a new dish coming next week made especially for autumn, not to mention the apple pie. Stop by and have a slice on the house."

I smiled and rose. "I have a new variety of pothos I created. Would you like a cutting?"

Twila gasped. "Yes! I would love one."

"Marnie? Sirena?"

Marnie nodded with enthusiasm. Sirena dipped her head. "I'd be honored to have such a gift."

And then she said things like that and made me feel guilty. I thought she was annoying.

Once I'd given everyone a pothos cutting and pushed a bag of peony bulbs on Marnie, they loaded Ash up with food and left with a cheery wave.

"She's right," Moira said.

"Ugh. Is it beat up on Evie week again? I know she's right. I've had things going on and needed some time to get my shit together." I rubbed my temples. "If you haven't forgotten, my magic was a little weird there for a while, too."

Ever since the greenhouse incident, things had settled down, but I felt that insistent pricking at the back of my mind telling me I needed to siphon more magic than I ever had before. Taking care of it at the shop would no longer cut it.

"We know," Ash said. "But it doesn't mean you should close yourself off from everyone who cares about you. Doing so is bad for people like us. Mages and paranormals need groups. They keep checks and balances on our power."

I never thought about it that way, but it explained how they were always able to bring me back to normalcy when my power wanted to rage. "Alright. I hear you. I'll do better. I promise."

I'd run over to Marnie's for lunch next week and actually sit and eat at the table instead of hoarding my food back in my office like Gollum.

After repacking the bounty Marnie brought, I carried the basket toward the back. "I'll be in the office for a little while."

"Hogging all the pot pie?" Ash called.

"Don't be jealous, she loves you more than me!" I grinned and waved before disappearing through the door.

• • •

A BELLY FULL of delicious comfort food was not conducive to staying awake during work hours. I stretched out on the couch for just a minute to get ready for the second half of the day and nodded off within seconds.

I stood in a dark and twisted garden, black vines and an enormous burned-out tree in the center. The land pulsed with malevolence, all of it coming from that tree. I turned to see Caelan walking up behind me.

"You couldn't stay awake either?" he quipped.

"Pot pie. How about you?"

Our eyes met. "Worry."

My heart banged against my ribcage. "Oh? Everything okay?"

"It will be," he promised. Whatever that meant.

Caelan jerked his head toward the tree. "Any idea what we're looking at?"

I had a terrible idea I did but slowly shook my head. "I've never seen anything like it. I'm more worried about you being in my dream."

"Until we figure out that seed, I don't think either of us will stay out of the other's dreams." He glanced over. "And how are you so sure it's your dream and not mine?"

Because my mother was here. I could *feel* her. No wind blew, the air unnaturally stale. I bent and touched my palm to the ground, sending a seeking pulse of power into the earth to try to find any semblance of life.

Nothing lived in this place. No buried seeds or earthworms or grubs. The land was devoid of anything living except for us.

Cliona's presence loomed like a cancer. I turned, my gaze sweeping the desolate plains to find her. There wasn't anywhere physical to hide. She managed it, nonetheless.

You will never be enough, Evangeline, a mocking voice whispered in my mind.

There you are, I sent back. On the winning track for Mother of the Year once again.

Rage brushed over my skin.

What is this place? Not expecting an answer, I walked closer to the tree.

What will be if you don't relinquish the seed.

This is Yggdrasil?

Our tree. The bridge between the worlds.

I know you better than you think, Mother. You won't use the seed for everyone.

You know nothing about me.

Daughters always know their mothers.

Her mocking laughter surrounded me.

Caelan was staring at me, a quizzical look on his face. He couldn't hear her.

You aren't strong enough to hold its power. Give it to me.

I don't have what you seek.

Your human body will burn alive.

I stilled. Was it possible she didn't know Cernunnos had fathered me?

"Evie?"

I held my finger up to my lips.

I'm far more powerful than you think I am.

It doesn't matter. A demigod is not meant to wield such power.

Oh man. Cernunnos and I were going to discuss some things next time he showed his face.

Give it to me, Evangeline. Walk away to tend your little flower shop.

And that was exactly the reason why I wouldn't.

I may not be powerful enough to wield the seed, but you are not worthy of such power.

She hissed in rage.

I awoke with a start, burning pain between my breasts. Hissing, I rolled over, the necklace falling away from my chest.

I picked the pendant up by the chain and stared.

The obsidian was smoking.

CHAPTER

Twenty~Nine

My phone rang.

"What the hell was that?" Caelan barked.

"My mother. She sends her regards."

The Shifter Lord snorted. "I'm sure she did. Want to tell me what she said?"

"How about I come over tonight?"

A thump and a muffled curse, then static.

I grinned. "Did you just drop the phone?"

"Hell just froze over, so yes, I did. When?" His voice was deeper than usual, a growl just under the surface.

"Right after sunset." I was going to tell him. I had to tell him. "I want to see Fee and Poe, and there are some things we should discuss. Don't make it weird."

"I'll feed you."

"Please do."

Caelan laughed. "Steak?"

"Whatever you want. I'm not picky."

"Done. See you tonight."

I hung up without saying goodbye.

Ash and Moira stared at me open-mouthed.

"That was the hottest thing I've ever heard in my life," Moira said, fanning herself with junk mail.

My cheeks colored. "Shut up. I'm going to tell him."

"You should," Ash agreed.

"And if he kicks me out?" I asked.

"Then you'll know." Moira tapped her chin. "What are you going to wear?"

I stared down at my jeans and sweater. "Um. This?"

Moira gasped in horror and clutched her necklace. "Absolutely not."

"This is not a date. I'm going to ask if I can use his property to help siphon magic. Mine isn't large enough." Eight acres was a ton of land, but my magic needed more. I could easily maintain mine and Caelan's lands with zero issues.

If he let me.

"And tell him what you are," Ash added.

"The rest of it, yes," I agreed.

If I didn't tell him, he'd figure it out. He was close already.

Tess floated in. "Are you going to wear that?"

Moira laughed.

"Dammit," I muttered. What was wrong with what I had on? "I am not wearing a dress tonight. We'll be outside, so it has to be a sweater."

"I'll follow you home and go through your closet," Moira offered.

"Fine." Giving in was the only way to get them off my back. "This is *not* a date."

"Of course it isn't," Moira said with wide, innocent eyes.

A FEW HOURS LATER, Moira was throwing most of my clothing into donation bags. "When's the last time you went shopping?" She held up a holey t-shirt with the Thundercats logo. "1986?"

I snatched it away from her. "That is not going in the donation bag. To answer your question, I bought that dress for Caelan's wedding not too long ago."

Moira stared. "Excluding special occasion wear."

I thought about it. "Umm. Seattle, I think?"

Moira sank down onto the carpet. "Evie. That was over seven years ago."

I rolled my eyes and flopped onto the bed. "I'm a Floromancer. We're the exact opposite of an over-consumer. And I try not to buy anything that's not made of natural materials. My clothing is old but still in great shape. I wash only in cold water, and I hang dry most of my items."

Moira huffed a breath. "It's annoying when you flaunt your environmental superiority over my head."

"You should try it. Classic pieces that feel good against your skin and last for much longer than anything fast fashion puts out."

Moira pulled her geometric printed top away from her chest. "You don't like this polyester and rayon couture piece?"

I inhaled deeply. "I can feel the microplastics invading me as we speak."

She tossed a t-shirt at my head. "Ass."

"I have a sixty-year-old cashmere sweater in there somewhere."

"Stop," Moira begged. "I might cry."

"We can go shopping soon." I toyed with the pendant at my throat. "Once we figure out what to do with this seed."

"You have to get one trendy piece." Moira eyed me from behind a pile of old t-shirts.

"Absolutely not. Classics or die."

"Jewelry then. One trendy jewelry piece."

"Silver only. *Sterling*," I emphasized.

Moira threw up her hands. "Fine! But you're going to pay for it. Nothing is cheap these days."

"If you agree to buy classic pieces only."

Moira's eyes narrowed. "This is the only time I've ever wanted to bite you."

"Once you have quality cashmere and silk against your skin, you'll never go back."

"Fine," she grumbled. "Now hold on and let me see if I can find anything more current than the year 2000 in this closet."

I LEFT THE HOUSE WEARING, much to Moira's chagrin, a gorgeous vintage cashmere sweater, butter soft and comfortable, and a pair of sharp dark wash blue jeans. I drew the line at Moira choosing my shoes because I could not stand uncomfortable things on my body. This was one of the main reasons I rarely wore t-shirts. I had some great vintage ones with super soft cotton and stretched necks, but those were far and few between.

She'd gone through my jewelry and got mad at me that she hadn't done it before now. I was the same with my clothing as I was my jewelry. All sterling or gold classic pieces, though I was a little more adventurous with jewelry than clothing. She'd borrowed three pairs of earrings and left with a stunning enameled necklace I'd loved in the window but hadn't been brave enough to wear yet.

I'd probably gift her the piece later on.

No one stopped me at the gate, and I drove right up to Caelan's front door.

When no one came out to take my keys, I smiled to myself and dropped them in my purse. He was finally getting to know me. Before I could ring the doorbell, the doors opened.

To my surprise, Caelan stood there wearing a pair of jeans and a pullover sweater.

My eyes widened. "Is that cashmere?"

Caelan grinned. "It is."

"May I?" I reached my hand out.

Caelan's eyes darkened. "You never have to ask to touch me, flower girl."

I swallowed hard and stroked my fingers over his pec. "Nicely made." I touched the buttons at the top of the sweater. "Bone?" I asked.

"Yes," he gritted out, golden flecks glowing in his irises.

I jerked my hand back. "Sorry. I'm somewhat of a cashmere connoisseur. I buy most of my pieces secondhand because it can be cost prohibitive, especially with the brands I like."

I stepped inside, Caelan's wild scent teasing my nose.

"I'll buy you all the cashmere you want."

I shook my head at him, trying not to smile.

The doors shut behind us. "Where is everyone?"

"Off tonight." He walked by my side. "I made dinner."

I stopped in my tracks. "You cooked? For me?"

"My kitchen staff almost had a mutiny over it, but yes. I enjoy cooking. This morning's breakfast made me remember how much. I hope to start cooking for myself again every once in a while."

I stared at him, a little flabbergasted. "That's um, amazing. Really."

Amusement quirked his lips up. "You seem surprised."

I waved a hand around to encompass the house. "You live in a mansion. Usually people who live in places like this do not cook or dress themselves."

His eyes glittered. "In the morning I can show you who dresses me, Evangeline."

Heat clawed at me. "I'm here to discuss something with you," I said primly. "I won't be here in the morning."

He grinned. "We'll see."

Shaking my head, I followed Caelan down the hall and was about to turn into the formal dining room, when he grabbed me by the elbow. "Not there."

Surprised, I let him lead me along, farther into the main house of the Keep than I'd been before. Caelan stopped at two large mahogany doors and pressed a button. The doors swung inward, revealing a cozy room lined with enormous bookshelves.

I stepped inside and gasped. Two massive windows at the

back had a perfect view of the moon and trees at the back of his property. A stone wood-burning fireplace crackled merrily, warming the room enough to chase autumn's chill away. There was a small table on the other side of the room set with two place settings and a bottle of red wine. Two plates covered with antique silver lids sat close to each other.

"Come, before it gets cold," Caelan said.

Dinner passed by quickly. For once, there was no pressure of anything. Just me and a handsome man having a nice dinner and getting to know each other. It made what I was about to tell him so much worse because even though Moira and Ash thought it would eventually be fine, I didn't.

He was a Lord. His rule was total and all-encompassing. Having a Chimera within his territory, even one he liked, could destabilize his rule. With the gods sniffing around, there was no way I could keep my secret any longer.

Sadness threatened to choke me. I forced myself to eat his delicious dinner and drink his wine, laugh at his jokes, but inside I mourned what could be if only we'd met under different circumstances.

When I'd finished the last bite of an incredible apple crumble, I folded my napkin.

"Uh oh," Caelan said, his eyes sparkling with amusement. "Down to business so soon?"

I stilled the rapid pounding of my heart. "It's time sensitive."

He set his wineglass down. "Let's walk the property. Fee and Poe are itching to see you."

We walked in silence for a while until we reached the back. "Are you fine with walking or do you want to take a cart and walk the rest of the way?"

The moon was almost full, and I was curious about Caelan's property. "Let's walk the entirety. Where are the birds?"

"They're on my private lands," was all he said.

We started on a moonlit path and walked for several minutes

until the path dropped off and we were plunged into the woods. Pine and fresh autumn air tickled my senses.

I held up a glowing palm. "May I?"

He swept his hand out. "Please. I'm interested to know what a Floromancer thinks of my lands."

I crouched and sank my fingers into the dirt.

Life cried out, joyful and free. Tears sprang to my eyes. This place was saturated with happiness and memories, but as I sank deeper, I realized it had its fair share of pain, too. I sank to the ground and sat cross legged, closing my eyes as I sank the other hand into the ground. Threads of life everywhere. Every root, every vine, every creepy crawly thing blipped against my senses. Caelan's soil was well cared for but mostly left alone, the perfect way to allow nature to thrive.

Someone had done the work to nurse the soil back to health and then let it be. I smiled.

Magic poured from my body into the ground, saturating a good acre of Caelan's property with extra nutrients. Flowers burst from the ground, trees straightened, seeds sprouted. My senses touched the back of the house—a kitchen garden.

"Your basil is struggling," I rasped. "It doesn't have enough light, and it's too close to your cucumbers."

I sensed Caelan sitting down beside me. "Evie. Do whatever you think is right."

I uprooted the basil with barely a thought and moved it next to the oregano, where full sunlight would reach both. A couple additional tweaks and the garden would flourish. "You might want to warn whoever planted it, so they won't be freaked out tomorrow."

I could almost feel his grin. "He already knows and is a little embarrassed."

Startled, I cracked an eye open. "You planted everything?"

Caelan nodded. "I try to do a small kitchen garden every year, and no one ever corrects me." He rolled his eyes. "It's annoying being a Lord sometimes."

"I bet Simone would."

He laughed. "She gets her hands dirty all the time dealing with my affairs. The last thing she wants is to dig in literal dirt."

I closed my eyes again, doing one final check on his garden. "You planted your cilantro too deep." Almost missed it the first time. A quick tweak and…"There. It should sprout soon. Don't worry if you don't see anything for a while. Cilantro is a slow grower."

Another quick scan and I pulled my fingers from the dirt and rose, dusting off the seat of my pants. "Your land is healthy and happy."

"Shifters tend to care for their lands well, flower girl." He looked to the distance. "Shall we?"

We walked on, and even though I stopped periodically to investigate, Caelan never grew annoyed. We'd just turned a corner when something orange and blue streaked past my face. I gasped and spun to follow it.

A shriek of pure happiness exploded in the clearing.

"Fee!" Tears sprang to my eyes.

The phoenix soared high in the air and dive bombed straight for me. Caelan tensed, but I held out my arms. Fee screeched to a halt, inches from my face, and I grabbed her, bringing her in for a gentle hug.

Ancient magic hummed from her body. I stroked a gentle hand down her silky, glowing feathers. "You look stunning."

Fee rubbed her head against my cheek and made an odd chirping noise. I lifted my head and locked eyes with Caelan.

He'd done this for me and didn't have to, done it for no other reason than me asking. "Thank you," I breathed.

A small nod.

A dark, sleek bomb with vivid purple eyes headed right for me, the raven's cry piercing the quiet. He flew over me, circled back, and landed on my shoulder, his feathers brushing my hair as he nuzzled me.

"Hello Poe."

"Evie. Hello."

I reached up and stroked his cheek. "Fee is flying."

The raven dipped his head. "Fee. Fly. Happy."

"I'm glad. Are you coming home any time soon?"

Poe said nothing for a moment. "Fee. Home."

My brows lifted. "You want to stay with Fee?"

Another dip of his head. "Oh Poe. Forever?"

"Fee is home."

He reached for Fee, and she reached for him, Poe stroking her head with his. My heart warmed even as it cracked. If I wanted to visit Poe, I'd have to come here. Fee couldn't leave.

"Are you sure?"

"Poe sure. Poe stay."

I blinked away tears. Everything was changing. "Okay. You're happy?"

Poe ruffled his feathers. "Wolves give meat. Hunt with wolves."

I glanced at the Lord who shrugged. "Poe has excellent eyesight and a bird's eye view."

I chuckled. "Isn't that cheating?"

"Acquiring dinner is never cheating."

Poe flapped over and landed on Caelan's shoulder, nuzzling the Shifter Lord's cheek. "Caelan. Friend."

Well. Shit. Even the raven was charmed.

"Yes, Poe," I whispered as our eyes met once again. "Caelan friend."

Poe lifted off and soared through the air. Fee nuzzled me one more time and followed, spreading her wings wide, a cry of joy shattering the night.

I sniffed away the tears. "They're both happy."

"I'm not the dastardly villain you think I am."

I rubbed my face. "I never said you were a villain. Things are complicated."

He took a step forward. "They don't have to be."

A half sob escaped me. "Says the Shifter Lord. Not everyone

has your power, Caelan." I held my hand up and stepped away. "But that's not why I'm here."

He came closer. "Why are you here, flower girl?"

"For two things. One you may agree to. The other will…" I sighed.

"Evie?" Concern brimmed in his eyes.

"The other may sunder us."

He gripped me by the upper arms. "Have you paid attention to nothing?" His nostrils flared, and anger flashed bright over his handsome face. "Nothing will break this."

I reached up and touched his face. "Promise me you will care for Poe and Fee no matter what happens."

"Evie."

"Swear to me, Caelan. And please don't take anything out on Moira, Ash, or Tessa."

His jaw tightened, irises expanding until there was no silvery gray left. "You think me a monster."

I shook my head. "No. I'm the monster."

The pendant, lying warm and serene between my breasts, flared with heat. I hissed and pulled it away, and as I did, an awareness came over me. Caelan's attention snapped to the edge of the clearing.

I pulled my cellphone out and shot off a text to the others.
Caelan's Keep. Now.

"Moira and the others will be here soon," I murmured.

Rhona and Cliona stepped out of the woods, Finn was behind him. Someone else stood in the shadows to the right. He looked familiar, but he was too far away for me to identify.

Caelan swore viciously. "Donovan."

The other Lord stepped forward. "I told you things weren't right here."

Vicious glee swam over his face. "Do you know what you have in your territory, *Lord*?" The last word was a sneer, an insult to Caelan's position.

Donovan's gaze flicked to me, satisfaction lighting his eyes. I reached over and touched Caelan's arm.

"I'm sorry," I whispered. "I was going to tell you."

Caelan's attention snapped to me.

To my surprise, my mother didn't say a word and allowed Donovan to take the lead. Caelan's pendant heated, the temperature so high I winced.

I touched it, the obsidian pulsing under my fingers.

Rhona smiled. "It wants to grow and yet, you stifle it."

"I have no idea what you're talking about."

"Donovan," Caelan snapped. "Get out of my territory. You're here without permission." His eyes narrowed. "How did you get onto my land?"

A wolf padded out from the woods. Caelan sucked in a breath.

"Pack defectors," Donovan said, his voice dripping with derision. "Gods, rogue magic, betrayal by your Pack." He made a tsking noise. "And even worse, you have—"

A boom of sound, something slamming into the earth. A man —no, a god rose from his crouch, crimson runes sparking against his dark armor.

"You cannot interfere in the affairs of the paranormals," Neit said, his gaze on my mother.

Cliona smirked. "Evangeline has something that belongs to me. She refuses to hand it over. Am I to allow theft now, Neit?"

Neit turned to me. Dark hair, dark eyes glowing with vivid violet magic, his face a mask of anger. "Is this true?"

I shook my head. "It doesn't belong to her."

"She admits she has it!" Cliona barked.

Neit's jaw tightened. "Silence!"

He strode over, his armor silent as he moved. His eyes burned with anger, but I didn't feel like it was directed at me. Caelan stiffened at Neit's proximity, and a soft growl escaped him when Neit leaned so close he could kiss me.

"Do you have it?" he whispered so low only Caelan and I could hear him.

"What's going to happen if I say yes?" I whispered back.

Neit closed his eyes for a brief moment. "Whatever you do, do not let your mother take it from you. Everything depends on this, Evie. Do you understand?"

I froze. "Yes," I said after a long moment.

"Good."

He turned to face my mother. "She says she doesn't have it."

I could almost hear my mother's teeth crack when her jaw tightened. "The seed is in the pendant she wears."

"Evie, do you have something that belongs to your mother inside the pendant you wear?"

I noticed his careful wording. "Nope."

"Getting involved is a direct violation of our law, Cliona. Walk away now or tangle with me."

Rage flashed over my mother's face, there and gone in an instant. A second later, her eyes softened and went limpid.

A soft laugh escaped Neit as Cliona floated toward him, her dress flowing away from her body like a fae queen. Commotion from behind and the scent of fresh greenery told me Ash and the others were here. I shifted closer to Caelan and turned.

Ash and Moira walked toward us, Tess nowhere to be seen, but I knew she was here. I could feel her.

"Where is she?" I whispered in Moira's ear.

"Close, but she won't engage unless it's the last resort."

It made sense. Tess had terrible magic and spent years getting it under control. "Thank you for coming."

Moira nudged me with her shoulder. "We're besties. I love family drama."

Neit didn't let Cliona get too close. He met her in the middle. She reached out a pale hand and traced an elegant finger down his armor. "Neit. Don't let my daughter stand in the way of this. She's nothing, a demigod. The seed will reject her once it realizes how little power she possesses."

Moira leaned over. "What the fuck is she talking about?"

"I think Mom has some baby daddy paternity confusion," I whispered. "She thinks I'm still half human."

Moira's eyes widened. "Holy shit." A grin spread across her face. "This is going to be epic."

Dozens of birds appeared in the sky behind my mother, floating behind her like a dark, feathered cloud.

Oh. Fuck. I sent a desperate look to Caelan.

"Fee," I whispered.

Caelan stiffened. He snatched his cell phone from his back pocket and fired off a quick text. "Simone will handle it."

I hoped so. If my mother was pissed off now, wait until she saw the phoenix. Not to mention the complications if Fee revealed herself. The seed might not belong to her, but Fee…under fae law, she belonged to my mother.

Once he put his cell back in his pocket, Caelan moved.

One moment he stood right next to me. The next, Caelan held his rogue shifter by the neck with one hand. A savage howl tore from the Lord's throat seconds before he used his other hand to tear the shifter's head off. The sound of snapping tendons and breaking bones would live forever in my nightmares.

Blood sprayed in an arc, covering Caelan's face in a crimson truth. A Shifter Lord never allowed a traitor to live.

Caelan tossed the body aside like trash and stalked toward the other Lord. Donovan paled and took a step back, his hands held out. "I have information you need," he blurted.

My magic tugged from my stomach, a sickening lurch of power. I swayed on my feet. Cliona was no longer staring at Neit. A small smile curved her lips as our eyes met.

"Evangeline. Are you okay?" False concern made my mother's voice an octave higher.

A ripping pain tore through my chest. Blood bubbled from my lips.

The earth responded. Trees ripped from the ground, shooting toward the sky. Vines slithered across the ground. Sleeping bulbs sprouted, sending fully grown stalks up, blooms unfurling to send an intoxicating aroma through the air.

I went to my knees. Moira went down beside me, her hands stroking over me with urgency, searching for a wound that wasn't there.

Ash crouched beside me, his eyes pained. Emerald light glowed in his palms. He touched my back and closed his eyes. Earth magic poured into me, but Ash's magic was no use against such power.

"Cliona!" Neit barked. "Release her!"

"I'm not doing a thing," my mother said. She floated over and bent at the waist, a cool hand reaching out to brush my hair from my brow. "Poor thing." Her tongue clicked. "You don't look so good."

"Rhona," I breathed through the blood pouring from my mouth. The Chimera stood off to the side, eyes crimson red as she poured magic into me.

Hundreds of wolves streamed through the Keep grounds, their coordinated howls piercing the air.

Cliona reached for the necklace, poised to tear it from my throat. I lurched back, remembering Neit's words. With trembling fingers, I opened the catch, tipping the seed into my hand.

It pulsed with warmth, with life, and called to me more than any magic I'd ever known.

"I'm glad you came to your senses," my mother said. She bent down and flicked her hand. "Give it to me."

Power cracked through the air, the skies splitting open. An enormous stag flew from the tear, shifting into the fae king an instant before he hit the ground.

Cliona's face whitened. She turned to me. "Give me the seed," she hissed.

When I didn't react, she lunged, fast as a snake.

I panicked. Not my finest moment.

And popped the world seed into my mouth like it was a Tic Tac and swallowed the world ending magic down.

Thirty

Moira choked. "Oh Evie," she breathed. "*No.*"

Ash gasped in horror.

My mother went chalk white, her fury erased by her surprise. She reared back and fell flat on her ass. "You *stupid* child."

Cernunnos' eyebrows lifted. "That's one way to do it, I suppose."

For a moment, nothing happened, and all I could feel was relief. Maybe I could treat myself like a puppy and wait to shit it out, then pretend none of this ever happened.

But, alas, my luck was not to hold.

A flash of intense white light set the world aflame. Every single neuron in my body was set ablaze. My muscles ached as my DNA rewrote itself, all the channels of power inside my veins expanding, magic flooding my veins. Floromancer, goddess, Chimera, bits and pieces of my mother and father, and I knew the truth in my blood.

Cernunnos *was* my father, and the forest lived in my cells.

Something long blocked dislodged, sending a fiery blaze of staggering power through me, and my muscles began to stretch and elongate.

A scream tore from my throat, my body bending in impossible ways as the seed changed my very essence. I tried to open my eyes, but I was blind, everything cast in deep gray shadow.

When the shift came, all I knew was power and horrified screams for a long moment until I locked on the two people I wanted dead more than anything.

A red haze over my vision disoriented me. Everything living glowed a soft white, but there—two people glowing white and red.

I stumbled, not used to my cloven feet, but it didn't take me long to figure things out. A horrified Rhona gaped before she turned and hauled ass toward the forest. Unrelenting burning in my chest screamed for release, and I answered the call, sending a streaming blaze of angry crimson fire at her back.

Rhona's pained scream echoed through Caelan's land for the seconds it took for her body to catch fire and disappear in a hail of ash. My eyes swept the property.

Moira and Ash stood there, staring upward, an identical expression on their faces I couldn't decipher. Caelan was locked in battle with the other Lord but holding his own.

I would not interfere. Donovan was not mine to kill.

But the other Chimera… Where was he?

My roar shook the buildings. I tested the membranous wings on my back, flapping once, twice, until I crookedly lifted off.

"The left!" Moira shouted.

I veered left, my night vision so much better than it ever had been, sweeping my gaze across the forest to acquire my second target.

There.

A hint of white and red speeding through the woods. I dipped low, edging the tips of the trees, and realized the bastard had fled through the heaviest cover to evade me. Amusement tinged my lips.

Fire from…another head—somewhere on my body? I didn't

know, but I took advantage of my new powers and scorched the trees, to uncover Finn.

Guilt speared me at the damage, but I'd heal them later. Right now, I had to take care of this threat, this thing that had brought so much trauma into my life.

Finn veered right. I lowered my bulk closer, tearing through trees and brush in my pursuit. A primal scream ripped from Finn's throat when he made the mistake of looking back. Whatever he saw scared the shit out of him, but I didn't care. I'd worry about it later and hope it wasn't permanent.

He shifted into a sleek panther, dark as night with jade green eyes, and attempted to slip away.

But I could still see him. I could see everything.

I could feel everything. Power roared through me, but all I felt was the urge to kill, kill, kill the threat.

Finn. I had to kill Finn.

I toyed with him, keeping my speed steady enough to keep up with him but not overtake him, even though I easily could. When he attempted to veer away, I'd send a blaze of fire out and make him head the other way. I pursued him for what felt like hours until the edges of his ribs heaved, his tongue hung out, and his speed slowed. Eventually, he stopped and collapsed, rolling onto his stomach.

Finn shifted into human form; fear etched into the very bones of his face.

"Evie," he croaked, his chest heaving and nostrils flaring as he sucked in oxygen. "Please. It was never anything personal."

Not personal to him. That was the difference. Everything he'd done to me was personal. It affected every single thing in my life. His actions kept me from living, kept me hidden away, afraid of myself and my power, afraid of love.

Simply afraid.

I loomed above him, staring at him dispassionately.

"You—" His throat worked. "You are stunning. I've never seen the Chimera's true form. None of us have ever been able to shift into it."

A sliver of calculation brimmed in his eyes. "I can help you become what you were meant to be. I can show you what you can do."

I roared, the sound shaking the tops of the trees.

Finn snapped his mouth shut and stared at me. A wet spot soaked the front of his jeans.

I felt no sympathy or empathy. I was past the point of such human emotions. This thing had ruined me and deserved to pay.

"Evangeline," a voice said quietly.

I shuddered. Caelan came into the clearing, proudly nude and bloody. Scratches grazed his face and chest, but nothing serious. His gaze traveled over my form, his lips pressed tight. Golden and green magic shimmered around him, and his eyes blazed with power.

He exhaled and nodded to himself as if he'd come to a long overdue conclusion. "First rule of shifting, Evie. We don't play with our food."

I huffed, a puff of fire burning the leaves off the tree to my left. My back feet had hooves, but my front were tipped with retractable lethal claws. I lifted one up and sent my claws out with a powerful snick.

Caelan's lips edged upward. "Yes, pretty kitty. I see how beautiful you are. How lethal."

I was a cat? Cool. But no. I had wings and hooves and…paws. What in the actual fuck?

He jerked his head toward Finn. "Would you like me to finish him?"

Another roar that blew Caelan's hair back. The Lord held his hands up and took a step back, a huff of laughter escaping him. "Fair enough."

He turned his head. "Others are coming. As much as I'd love to help you bring this asshole to justice, you might want to make a decision on whether he lives or dies."

"Not living," I bit out. My voice sounded like I was garbling rocks, deep and rough and ancient.

Caelan blinked. "And you talk. Holy fucking hell. Okay. Right." He shoved a hand through his hair. "Then kill him, flower girl. Don't let them hold you back with legalities."

My teeth pulled back in a smile. Caelan swore and shook his head.

"Goddamn. You are hot and fucking terrifying and if you hurry up and kill him, we can make a detour, if you get what I'm saying."

Another huff of laughter.

Finn whimpered and flipped onto his stomach, belly crawling away. I lifted my paw and put it on his back, holding him there.

The Chimera began to cry.

I dipped my massive head low, right next to his ear, and snarled. Saliva dripped onto his hair.

Caelan laughed.

I lifted my paw again and smashed it into his spine. His bones broke like toothpicks, snap, snap, snap. Tiny pieces of popcorn in a microwave.

Finn's scream of pain made me smile.

I used a claw to flip him over. His arms and legs were useless, but he was still alive.

He needed to see my face, to see what he'd done to me.

Finn needed to see his retribution coming right for him.

Fire blasted through the clearing. I tipped my head up and screamed, a bone-shaking primal cry of defiance and rage, the sound a deep, resonant bellow announcing I was the apex predator tonight. The trees and ground shook, Finn's crying softened to whimpers, his eyes round with terror.

I reached for him, split the Chimera wide open with a wicked, black tipped claw and dug my muzzle into his chest, searching for his energy source. I found the still beating meaty piece controlling his life and tore it from his ribcage, tossing it into the air before I swallowed it down.

Then I turned that sonofabitch into ash.

An eerie quiet settled around Caelan's land. Energy slammed into me from Finn's heart. I took a deep breath, reveling in my new power and focused on returning to myself.

A few moments passed until the familiar magic shimmered around me. My bones and muscles shrank until I was me again or…maybe not the me I once was.

The new me.

Caelan stood a few feet away watching me. Our eyes met.

"You are so fucking beautiful," he whispered.

Cernunnos stepped into the clearing.

"Go away," Caelan and I snarled at the same time.

The fae king's surprised bark of laughter faded a second later, but he left us a gift.

An impenetrable, opaque bubble rose above us, at least a hundred feet around, ensuring we wouldn't be disturbed.

Caelan and I both took a hesitant step forward.

A second later, we crashed into each other, a whirlwind of lips and teeth and hands.

I wrapped my bare legs around him; my breasts crushed against his chest. My hands cupped his face as our lips met, hot and hungry. Need roared through my veins, blazing hot.

Caelan's length jutted against my stomach, and for once, I didn't care that I was Chimera and he was a Lord, or that we were both naked and covered in blood.

He was a man, and I was a woman, and I wanted him, and he wanted me.

Tonight it was all that mattered.

His lips trailed hot and hungry down my neck as he walked me back to one of the few trees I hadn't destroyed. Teeth edged the hollow of my throat, my collarbone, a soft claiming bite proclaiming I belonged to him.

And tonight I did. His hand cupped my breast, teasing the nipple. Caelan hauled me higher, dipping his head to claim the place his hand had been. I moaned and arched my back, giving him everything, all I was.

"Evie," he growled.

I ran my hands through his hair, marveling at the silky texture, trailing down his neck and powerful back. We glowed with magic, red and gold and green and watermelon tourmaline.

This was not sex. This was a claiming, and I let it happen. I *wanted* it to happen.

His teeth gently clamped down, but it would leave a mark. I surged forward, snarling at him. "Harder."

He adjusted me, his fingers finding the slick heat between my legs.

"Caelan," I breathed.

Our lips met again, our equal power casting a metallic glow across the bubble we were in.

Caelan slid home, his thick length filling me.

A primal scream, half me, half cat ripped from my lungs. Caelan threw back his head, a howl splitting the night. His hands gripped my hips as he took me, each slide a wicked, delicious torture.

My nails scraped his back, and I leaned forward, licking his neck down his shoulder to his collarbone before sinking my teeth into the hollow of his shoulder. Caelan barked, his movements turning jerky.

"Again." Caelan snarled as he moved. "Make me yours."

A delicious heat built in my core. I bit him again, tasting the salt of his skin, the copper of his blood, licking the wound closed.

His hands tightened on my hips, his movements brutal and claiming. Rough bark cut into my back as we moved, but I didn't care about anything other than Caelan.

"You are *mine*. No one else's."

I lay my palm against his heart. "Yours," I promised.

His movements slowed, became languorous, each slide bringing me to the edge.

"Don't stop," I begged.

He flicked my nipple, sliding his hand down my body to find the small place in my slick heat. A gentle press, and withdrawal.

My throat worked, a hoarse cry escaping. *"Caelan."*

His wicked chuckle slid over my skin. "Come for me, Evangeline."

Our eyes met as he moved, and when his hand slid against me, small motions tearing screams from my throat, stars exploded behind my eyes, and magic boomed in the skies above us, ancient stars not seen in millennia lighting up the skies of Joy Springs.

Caelan followed me over the edge, and together, we claimed the land for our own.

Thirty-One

CAELAN

We walked out of the forest nude and bloody, Evangeline's arm wrapped around my waist, her touch proprietary, claiming. The wolf inside me preened at her possessiveness.

Her dark hair flowed down her back, azure eyes glowing with mixed power, a goddess in her own right.

One who belonged to me.

Finally.

I'd known what she was for a while or suspected at least. There were too many coincidences for her not to be Chimera, not with Finn's presence and Rhona's arrival.

At first, I'd cared and wondered what it might do to my rule, my grip on power in this place. But Evie proved difficult to resist.

We still had secrets between us. Big ones. The fallout of this night would echo for years to come, and Evangeline would have to come to terms with what she'd become, what she might yet become when the ramifications of the seed came home to roost.

And I had no doubt they would.

Cernunnos was her father, the fucking fae king. I still couldn't wrap my head around that one.

And her mother was a raging bitch who'd disappeared as soon

as Evie sent Rhona up in flames, though I was satisfied to see Cliona's bone white, horrified expression when Evie had risen from the ground in legendary Chimera form.

I'd be a fool to believe the battle between them was over. There was a long way to go before their war was resolved.

Evie didn't hesitate at the edge of the forest. She walked by my side, up to the place where she'd revealed her heritage. Hundreds of wolves sat on their haunches, silently waiting.

They'd all felt the claiming, by both of us. And another curious claiming I'd need to investigate later. My territory boundaries had expanded, and I knew the Lords would lose their shit over it when they realized.

Well, everyone but Donovan. He lay quite dead at the edge of the forest. One useless fucker down, and no one would mourn his loss.

As much as I wanted to take Evie to my bed and claim her again, we had one more important thing to face.

My shifters sat quietly, expectant, their glowing eyes trained on Evie.

We might not be officially mated, *yet*, but she was their Lady now, and as such, her word was their law.

Moira sucked in a breath and shrugged her cardigan off, hurrying over to Evie. She wrapped it around her friend's shoulders, frowning as Evie let it slip and fall. "There's probably something to wear in the house if you want me to find it," Moira whispered.

Evie shook her head and gripped Moira's hand tightly. The vampire swallowed hard, knowing things had changed forever tonight. Tears swam in her eyes as she stepped back and bowed her head.

Ash came forward and went to his knees. He gripped both of Evie's hands in his.

"I knew you'd claim your heritage." Not caring about her blood-soaked hands, he kissed the back of her palms.

Evie touched the top of his head. "Let's never talk about the fact that you've seen me naked, okay?"

Ash let out a broken laugh. "Glad to see you haven't lost yourself." He rose and dragged her in for a hug.

My jaw tightened and jealousy reared its ugly head as Ash put his hands on her, and I had to take a deep, steadying breath before I swiped the dryad with a claw-tipped paw. I'd be an angry, jealous wreck for the next few weeks until the claiming settled.

And Evie would be, too.

Tess floated over. She reached a pale hand up and touched Evie's face. "Don't forget about those two weddings we booked. We're going to be busy as hell."

A laugh bubbled from Evie's chest. "I won't."

Tess offered a faint smile and floated over to Ash's side.

Cernunnos leaned against a tree, not interfering. Yet.

I swept my gaze across my people. "We were betrayed tonight," I began

A few wolves shifted. I made a mental note of who they were.

"If you don't want to be in this Pack, drop a request to Simone within the next twelve hours. I will make arrangements for your release or transfer. If you choose not to transfer and prefer to act as a lone shifter, you must be out of the Keep and out of the boundaries of my territory within twenty-four hours."

Evie's hand tightened around my waist.

"I know none of you missed what happened a little while ago." Cool hands pressed a large towel into my hands.

Evie's attention snapped to Simone, eyes flashing bright red. A snarl curled her upper lip as her gaze locked on the woman who'd given it to me.

Pride at Evie's possessiveness burst in my chest as Simone held her hands up and slowly backed away. "A towel, Evie. That's all."

Evie hadn't bothered putting on the cardigan, so I didn't bother with the towel. Having her stand with me, regal and covered in her enemies' blood, hair streaming down her back and eyes shimmering with power, I'd never felt so raw, so real.

So *alive.*

The Floromancer watched my Omega until she disappeared into the crowd, her teeth pulling away from her lips in a silent snarl.

Creepy, violent, and possessive, just how I liked my Lady.

"Some of you have met Evangeline Quinn. Many of you have talked about her. She is a Floromancer and a Chimera." I left out the goddess part. It was neither here nor there, and my wolves had seen quite enough tonight. "And she is mine."

My eyes swept the crowd. "If anyone would like to challenge me for her, you are more than welcome."

Evie shifted and glanced at me. "Do I have to kill them?" She stretched her neck. "I'm a little tired but I could be persuaded."

She was going to be so embarrassed when she came down off her blood high. "No," I murmured. "I get to this time."

"Ah. Cool." Evie gave an unnerving smile to the other wolves. "But I get to watch?"

I laughed. "All you want, flower girl."

Evie closed her eyes and inhaled. "We did something to this land tonight," she murmured in a voice for my ears only. "Should I be worried about it?"

"No. You did what you were born to do."

A screech high in the air sounded, a flash of orange and purple streaking above, and Fee circled around, landing on Evie's shoulder. Poe followed behind, landing on mine.

A few more wolves shifted uncomfortably. A small part of me understood. We were shifters, born under a full moon, and born to run. Freedom ran in our blood, but Evie was different. She claimed land and healed wherever she went. Home was wherever Evie chose to put down roots, literal and metaphorical.

But tonight, we'd all seen another side of her. A violent predator lived within her, one who thirsted for the blood of those who wronged her. Rhona and Finn were dead. Cliona would think twice before she tangled with Evie again, but Cernunnos still stood there, arms crossed over his chest. He hadn't once taken his eyes off Evie.

And that was beginning to make my blood stir. He wanted something from her.

Donovan was dead, slain by my hands. I hadn't violated the law, but I was one of the few Lords who kept to his territory and rarely caused issues. I wasn't known for being a hothead.

The other Lord's death would cause a firestorm of political upheaval.

His land was directly above mine. I stilled. Had Evie and I claimed it during our tryst in the woods after his death?

Satisfaction roared through my blood. It would serve him right if we had. Evie would know, but now wasn't the time to ask.

When no one challenged me, I sent out a small pulse of power letting the wolves know I still reigned supreme over this land. I was still their Alpha, but there was someone new who commanded their loyalty as much as I.

Evie tilted her head back and inhaled, her breasts tilted toward the sky, her throat bare. She was the picture of earth, of life.

Mine.

As we watched, flowers sprouted under her feet, the destroyed trees healed and rose higher in the sky, forming a thick canopy above us, allowing only a sliver of moonlight to peek through. Vines stretched around those trees, blooming with purple and white flowers, the heady scent of tropical blossoms sweeping across the property.

Roots sprang from her fingertips, and she crouched to sink her fingers into the earth. When she looked at the wolves, a small, serene smile tilted her lips, and flowers bloomed in her hair.

"Run," she said quietly, her eyes flashing with crimson light. "I require the attention of your Lord."

As if pulled by a string, every wolf under my command rose and streaked past us, headed for the glorious, healed forest Evie had created.

Exultant howls pierced the night, excited yips and howls as wolves tumbled over each other, tangling playfully, their paws tearing clods from the soil.

Cernunnos disappeared, but not without a mental warning.

I will return, he whispered through our minds.

Fee and Poe lifted into the air, soaring above us with a show of brilliant color.

And when Evie laughed, I pulled her to me and claimed her mouth in a kiss.

Thirty-Two

I spent over a week in Caelan's bed, drunk on his love. Moira and the others tended to the shop while I shirked my duties in an epic way.

But it was Monday, and real life could wait no longer. Caelan's strong arm was locked on my waist, keeping me pressed against him. I shoved at his arm.

"I have to go to work."

A hot, possessive kiss against my shoulder blade. "No."

I laughed. "You have to go to work, too. Don't think I missed all the calls you're getting from the other Lords. Donovan's death needs to be reported."

"It already has been. His people felt his demise." He nipped my neck.

I shivered and arched against him. "What are you going to do?" My voice was a little breathless, but Caelan kept me that way.

"You tell me, Evangeline."

I stilled. "What?" Shifting, I rolled to face him.

"Did you claim his land when you claimed me?" His eyes were warm and languid, a hint of glow in his irises. Ever since that night, the glow hadn't faded.

I thought about it. "Umm. I don't know." Honestly, I hadn't given it another thought because I'd been tangled up in Caelan.

"Check." He pressed a kiss to my lips, one warm hand wandering south until it found gold.

I arched and moaned against his mouth. "If you keep doing that, neither of us will be checking anything."

He slithered down my body. "Good."

Possessive little nips all over my breasts and stomach until he ventured farther—

A scream ripped from me. "*Caelan!*"

He smiled against my thighs. One rough lick later, and I was lost in the Shifter Lord once again.

I was three hours late for my shift.

Little Shop of Florals was so full I had trouble pushing through to get to the register. When Moira spotted me, a slow smile curved her lips.

"You look like you've been fucking for days."

I gasped and slapped her arm. "Moira!" Heat burned my cheeks.

Her wicked laugh made me grin. "It's about damn time. We called the Keep multiple times. All Simone would say is 'she's busy. Send hard liquor. And maybe a marching band. I can't take it anymore.' We figured you and Caelan were occupied, so we left it alone." She grimaced. "You should probably send Simone a basket of whiskey and chocolates, though. The poor woman is traumatized."

Ash came up to the desk, grinning from ear to ear. "You're the talk of the town, Evie," he whispered before dropping a kiss on my cheek. "Business has never been better."

I blanched. "They're all here because of…"

"You two horny kids lit the skies of Joy Springs up like the fourth of July," Moira said gleefully. "Anyone with a lick of blood felt the power you stirred up that night."

"What about…" My voice trailed off.

"Your secret is safe," Ash whispered. "But there are a few hundred wolves who know what you are, so you can't expect it to stay that way. Caelan already had one defector. There are bound to be more uncomfortable with someone of your bloodline in charge."

I snorted. "I'm not in charge."

Moira and Ash both rolled their eyes. "You told the wolves to run like they were errant puppies and every single one of them did." Her face softened. "You and Caelan are bonded in a way greater than blood now, Evie. It's too late to take it back."

I didn't want to take it back. Every time I thought about what we'd done in those woods, my veins boiled with desire. I wasn't quite myself that night, but I'd seen Caelan there, staring at me, heaving with power, his eyes drinking me up, and my reservations fell away.

I'd seen him.

I wanted him.

I took him.

And Caelan had gleefully gone along with it, claiming me in a way that a week later still got me hot and bothered under the collar.

All I wanted was to return to the Keep and slide back under the covers with him, but real life didn't work like that. We both had responsibilities, his greater than mine right now, though I suspected that would end soon.

Cernunnos hadn't shown back up. Maybe he was giving me time to adjust. Maybe he knew I needed this time to take a piece of myself back.

Maybe he was waiting for the right time to bitch at me for swallowing the world seed.

Hell, I don't know. Whatever it was, I knew it was waiting right around the corner to pounce when I least expected.

If I could take Caelan by the hand and lead us both into a peaceful life with no people to care for and no responsibilities, I would. But life didn't work like that, and we'd be at each other's throat without some outlet.

Tess handled customers with ease, and I counted no less than ten people who came in and bought something.

When the rush finally died down, all three of my friends gathered around the register and stared.

"You look different," Tess said, tilting her head to study me. "On the inside."

I bet I did. "I feel different on the inside," I agreed.

Moira leaned forward, resting her chin on her hands. "So... how was it?"

Ash snickered.

Tess blinked owlishly. "You didn't hear all the screaming in the woods that night?"

Three pairs of eyes turned to her.

"Um. What? You heard us?" I asked, horror unfurling in my stomach.

"There is no barrier a banshee can't pierce," she said with a shrug. "People slated to die do all kinds of tricky things to escape their fate."

"Awesome," I said and sighed. "Sorry about that."

She leaned against Ash. "That's okay. I hope I scream like that when Ash and I—"

"Tess!" Ash barked, his cheeks turning crimson.

Moira's mouth opened in a shocked o.

A laugh bubbled from me. "Tess, I'm sure that will happen for you both. It's important to be one hundred percent sure when it's your first time."

Tess nodded. "Ash hasn't pressured me."

The dryad pinched the space between his brows. "For the love of the gods," he muttered.

Moira punched him in the shoulder. "Aww. Ash. We always knew you were a gentleman. Glad to see we weren't wrong."

"We do other stuff," Tess volunteered.

I pressed my lips together to keep from laughing.

Moira fluttered her eyelashes. "Oh? Do tell."

"Moira!" Ash closed his eyes, a pained expression on his face. "Tess—"

But Tess wasn't known for understanding nuance. "Is it normal for it to be so large?" She made a motion with her hands that had Moira slapping her hands over her mouth. "You know like so…"

Ash took Tess by the elbow and marched her away. "We will never speak of this again!" he called back to us.

"The hell we won't," Moira said, her eyes twinkling with mirth.

I'd missed them. I missed this.

I missed the normalcy we once had, and I knew this small reprieve wouldn't last.

Not with the supernova of power I had burning in my veins.

Thirty-Three

The fae king appeared in my living room just as I put the final touches on dinner. I'd made enough for two this time, fully expecting him to show up now that I was home and Caelan was nowhere to be seen.

He wore casual clothes this time. No antlers. No crown. No Wild Hunt.

Just a male burning with the power of a thousand suns.

I pushed a glass of red wine and a plate of spaghetti carbonara over. "Should I call you Dad now, or are we sticking with Cernunnos?"

One side of his mouth tugged into a smile. "When did you realize?"

I fixed my plate. "Technically, I didn't, though I suspected. The banshee told me."

Cernunnos nodded and picked up his fork. He jerked his head. "Living room?"

"I'll be there in a minute."

He walked over and settled in my reading chair, balancing his plate on his knee.

"I knew for sure when I shifted at Caelan's."

"Thought you might have." He twirled pasta around his fork

and took a bite. His eyes closed and a look of bliss crossed his face. "You are an excellent cook."

He poked at the pasta. "What is this?"

"Carbonara. It's a simple dish. Comfort food for me."

He tilted his head and studied me. "Are you in need of comfort?"

He was so human sometimes and so *other* in moments like this —a king born to rule the natural world and so far removed from humanity, it burned being in his presence. "I'm preparing myself for what you might tell me."

"Ah. Let's break bread together first. As father and daughter."

I brought my plate over and sat down to eat.

For a while, everything was normal. Ish. As normal as things could be when your father was the king of the fae, and you were a magical mutt. We talked about inane things and got to know each other a little more.

Cernunnos hadn't spent much time on Earth until he figured out who I was.

As far as the reason Mom didn't realize he was my father, Cernunnos had a hand in that and had basically whammied Cliona. When she got curious about my powers, a clever spell turned her attention to other things.

Cernunnos had known since I was eighteen months that I belonged to him. My heart broke at the reveal, but he said he couldn't risk Cliona realizing who I was.

By staying away, Cernunnos had saved my life.

"Why did you come to me if that was a possibility?"

He smiled. "Because you are a survivor and would have figured out a way to survive."

"Like swallowing the world tree?" I asked dryly.

Cernunnos set his plate down.

Here we go…

"Evie, I'm here because I want to make sure you aren't blind-sided by this."

"That's a first."

At his dark look, I waved my fork. "Fine. Sorry. What bomb are you about to drop on me?"

My father drained his wine, set his glass down, and leaned forward, crossing his fingers together. A crown of oak leaves appeared on his head, and moss dripped from his hair.

"You are my only progeny, Evangeline."

A horrible feeling burned in my stomach, a sense that a train was barreling right toward me and I was too slow to dodge.

"You are a princess of the fae, the second in command of all our people."

I snorted. "They've never been my people."

"For your own safety," he agreed. "But things have changed. You hold my power in your veins and that of the world seed." A grim smile. "Your power now exceeds mine."

A shocked laugh escaped me. "Impossible."

But Cernunnos' eyes were serious, his handsome face grave. "I know you feel it burning through your body. You're eating more, burning more magic, restless under your skin, aren't you? Food and sex stave it off for a little while, but you crave more, don't you, Evangeline?"

I stared at him, sick to my stomach.

"What are you trying to tell me?" I whispered.

A faint smile tugged at his mouth. "I'm tired, daughter."

My brow furrowed. "I have a guest room. We can finish this conversation later, though I'd rather hash this out now."

He chuckled. "Not that kind of tired. I am ancient, daughter. The first winds that swept across this world cradled me when I was a babe. I wish to hang up my crown."

"You want to *retire*?" I blurted. "Are you allowed to do that?"

Cernunnos smiled. "Now that I have an heir, I can do whatever I want."

I blinked. "What."

"You are my successor, Evangeline Quinn. We must prepare for you to take my crown and rule over your people."

I stared at him for a long moment and burst out laughing.

"Good one. It's weird being a princess and all, but you can't actually believe I'd want to take over for you."

Cernunnos rose. "It is your bloodline," he said quietly.

Horror roiled through me. "You're serious," I whispered.

Antlers rose above his head, whispering against the ceiling. "I will return one week each month to prepare you for your role."

I swallowed hard. "How long," I croaked.

The fae king shrugged. "Time is a construct. We are immortal. You have as much time as it takes to be ready."

Tears swam in my eyes. "Cernunnos. You can't do this to me."

Sorrow filled his face. "Heavy is the head that wears the crown, my child."

I licked my lips. "Everyone gets that quote wrong," I whispered. "It's *'uneasy lies the head that wears the crown.'*"

"Even more appropriate," he said with a thoughtful nod. A soft whisper of green, verdant magic swept my way. My hair blew back and something cool rested atop my head.

He dipped his head. "Princess Evangeline. I will see you in one month's time."

In a whisper of pine scented air, he was gone.

I sat there on the couch for a long moment, my entire body trembling. When I could stand without falling, I walked over to the mirror.

A delicate silver crown of oak leaves, ivy, and holly berries rested atop my head.

Also by S.E. Babin

Shifter Lords

Shift of Heart

Shift of Morals

Power Shift

Shifting Winds

Shifting Resolve

Shift of Rule

Shift of the Wild

OTHER SERIES

A Shelf Indulgence Cozy Mystery Series

Book of the Virago

Trailer Park Transylvania

Psychic Cleaner

The Magical Soapmaker Mysteries

The Goddess Chronicles

Cocktails in Hell

About the Author

Sheryl likes cake too much and can be found hoarding it while hiding from her children in the pantry closet.

Follow her on Amazon at: https://www.amazon.com/S-E-Babin/e/B00J1J236A

f